Glass Slipper Press

Embrace the Darkness

By

Lilly Gayle

The Darkness Series, Book Two

Publishing History: **First Edition** publication 2013 by The Wild Rose Press

Originally edited by Lillian Farrell

Second Edition Glass Slipper Press, 2025

Cover Art by AGW Visual Alchemy using cover model generated by Copilot

https://agwvisual.myportfolio.com/

Published in the United States of America

Print ISBN 978-1-7323904-5-4

Digital ISBN 978-1-7323904-4-7

Dedication:

For Johnny: Miss you always. Love you still.

And to my family: Thank you for being there when my world fell apart. Love you all.

Prologue

March 2018

Goosebumps pebbled her skin. She jerked, glancing over her shoulder, hand hovering above the light switch. The lab was blessedly empty—but there'd been a sound to her left. A whisper as faint as silk sliding over satin—barely audible.

"Is someone there?"

Silence answered. She was alone, yet fear held her immobile. She tasted it in her mouth, hot and metallic—felt it in the sudden rush of blood pounding in her ears.

"I'm being ridiculous," she said aloud, trying to believe it.

Security at Lifeblood of America was state-of-the-art. No one could break in. No one human, anyway. But could any system keep out something darker and more sinister?

Acid rose in her throat. She swallowed bitter bile and switched off the lights. Then drawing a steading breath, she pushed open the door and stepped into the quiet corridor.

At this late hour, the facility was nearly deserted. The other labs were dark and empty. Yet it felt as if unseen eyes tracked her.

She glanced down the hall, willing Axle to step off the elevator. Seconds ticked by like hours, but the door didn't open.

Where was he?

Axle, one of the night guards, always made his rounds at five a.m., escorting her and Dr. Megan Harper to the lobby. But Megan hadn't worked tonight, and Axle was a no-show. Had Grant's wife gone into labor? Maybe Axle was covering for him. But wouldn't he have called? Or stopped by? Then again, maybe he was just late.

That thought offered a sliver of comfort. Most likely, Axle would arrive just as she reached the elevator.

Forcing herself to relax, she released the handle and let the lab door close behind her. The LED on the control panel blinked red as it clicked softly shut. She took a deep breath and straightened her shoulders before walking the fifteen feet to the elevator.

It felt like fifteen miles.

By the time she reached the polished doors and pushed the down arrow, she'd broken out in a cold sweat. Her blouse clung to her back, her heart hammering so hard against her ribs it took everything she had to step into the empty four-by-six box.

She was alone. Nothing crouched above the ceiling, waiting to pounce. Yet, it seemed as if something far less innocuous than the cold, inanimate eye of the camera watched her.

Fear prickled her skin. She wiped her palms on her lab coat and pressed the button for the lobby. The moment the elevator doors slid open on the ground floor, she ran toward the reception area.

"Axle? Grant? Richard?"

During the day, a receptionist manned the curved mahogany desk in front of the mountain mural. At night, Axle and Grant alternated patrols while Richard monitored the cameras from the office behind the desk. But Axle hadn't made it to the third floor, and neither he nor Grant was at the desk.

"Hello?" The hairs on her neck rose as she stepped around the corner and opened the door marked Security.

"Richard?"

Flickering images cast eerie shadows on the walls as the security monitors switched to different cameras and angles. Nothing moved on the screens and no one watched. It was as if she were the only living soul on earth.

Where were the guards? They wouldn't abandon their posts. Not without an emergency. But why hadn't they called? Or triggered an alarm?

She rushed back to the desk and picked up the phone. Dead. She tried another line. Then another. No dial tone. All four lines were dead.

Dread settled in her gut like a stone. Her mouth went dry. Pulse pounding, she ran toward the employee lounge to get her cell phone and keys. Something was coming. Something dangerous.

As she rounded the corner, she reached for the ID tag clipped to the collar of her lab coat. When she reached the door, she swiped her badge. The digital lock blinked yellow. She punched in her personal security code and placed her palm over the scanner. The lock blinked green. She exhaled, unaware she'd been holding her breath.

At her locker, her fingers fumbled the combination, getting it wrong twice before finally getting it right. Hands still shaking, she pulled off the lock and dropped it to the floor. Metal thunked against tile—loud as a gunshot. She jumped, stifling a scream as she jerked open her locker and grabbed her purse.

As she ran back toward the lobby, she pulled out her cellphone and dialed 911. She hit send. Nothing.

"Shit. No signal." She dropped her phone back into her bag.

Shaking with terror, she stood before the plate glass door, fumbling through her purse, trying to find her keys. Air stirred behind her. Warm breath touched the back of her neck. Her heart nearly stopped.

Slowly, she raised her chin and stared at her reflection in the dark glass. No one stood behind her. But she wasn't alone.

Chapter 1

A smoky haze shrouded the blue-gray mountains surrounding Asheville, North Carolina as Detective Amber Buckley slid from the passenger seat and met her partner at the hood of the car. She had more investigative experience, but she'd let him take lead in the Lifeblood slayings. Reid Sheridan had an ego, and this was the south. She could play along. Up to a point. But she was about ready to call it a day, and her patience was growing short.

The late afternoon sun cast long shadows over the parking lot, and the sweet fragrance of honeysuckle tinged the humid air. The crime scene tape had been taken down months ago, and the employees had returned to work as usual. Birds sang above the distant sound of traffic and nothing disturbed the peaceful tranquility of the day. And yet, something about the tissue bank turned research facility raised the fine hairs on the back of Amber's neck.

Without warning, her pulse jumped as a wave of dizziness washed over her. She took a deep breath and then another, trying to slow her spinning head.

Was she having another episode—a precursor to a full-blown anxiety attack?

Struggling to keep up with Reid, her gaze swept the parking lot, hoping to find a cause for her anxiety—hoping her partner wouldn't turn around and notice her shaking limbs or the sweat on her brow. This wasn't Iraq. Or—

Deep breaths. Imagine the ocean. Hear the gently rolling waves of calm surf. Release the fear. Relax. The relaxation technique slowed her heart rate. She drew in a slow, even breath, forcing her shoulders down and away from her ears.

"I hate that we have to do these follow up interviews," Reid said as they approached the front entrance to Lifeblood of America. "Makes me feel like a flunky."

"I prefer doing the follow up interviews," she said, forcing herself to remain calm. "In the initial investigation there isn't much to go on but instinct and that first visceral reaction to the crime scene. Now, we have a trail of evidence and prior statements."

And no dead bodies...or blood. Memories of Iraq weren't the only nightmares haunting her. A shiver snaked down her spine as she reached for the door. Reid got to it first.

"It's a shame the murders didn't occur in our district," he grumbled. "I don't like getting Daniels' and Tanner's sloppy seconds."

Amber slapped her palm flat against the glass before Reid could pull open the door. "How can you be so callous? Two people are dead and another is missing."

"Yeah, well, you got your experience in Iraq. I need this. You don't. And it's not like I can bring the vics back to life." He curled his fingers around her wrist and peeled her hand from the door.

Biting back a sharp retort, she balled her fingers into fists and followed him inside.

Okay, so maybe Reid was just overly ambitious. She got that. He wanted more homicide experience before applying to the NYPD, but he wouldn't get it in Asheville. The city only had about eight homicides a year, and the detectives with the department's Criminal Investigation Unit were assigned to geographic patrol areas. Amber and Reid worked the Adam District, which covered the northwest area of the city. The Lifeblood Slayings occurred northeast of the city in the Baker District. After five months and no additional leads, Captain Stratford had asked Reid and Amber to look at the evidence and conduct follow up interviews before he called in the North Carolina State Bureau of Investigation. Daniels and Tanner didn't like sharing their case, but nobody wanted the captain bringing in the SBI.

Inside Lifeblood of America's lobby, black and white Terrazzo floors gleamed like polished glass. Back in March, those same floors had been spattered with blood. The thought sent Amber's pulse skyrocketing. Mental images of crime scene photos overlapped her vision like a holographic Polaroid. She could almost see research assistant Tina Gallagher slumped next to the door in a pool of blood, her mouth opened in a silent scream.

Had Miss Gallagher known she was going to die? Had she felt the paralyzing grip of fear before her throat had been cut? Amber understood terror—the inability to move, rendering a person incapable of action or speech—of rational thought.

Memories tapped at her brain—painful, bloody memories.

Don't go there.

Taking a deep, steadying breath, she visualized the ocean again as she followed her colleague to a mahogany reception desk in front of a peaceful mountain mural. The Blue Ridge in spring. Waterfall and mountain laurel—calming, peaceful—the antithesis of what had occurred in the lobby last March.

"May I help you?" a petite brunette asked in a somber voice.

Both Amber and Reid flipped open their badges. Reid spoke in a deep authoritative voice. "I'm Detective Reid Sheridan. This is my partner, Amber Buckley."

Amber tensed. Once again, he'd failed to identify her as a detective. But she let it slide. No sense calling public attention to his lack of respect.

She smiled and put away her badge. The receptionist's gaze slid across the lobby to where Tina Gallagher's body had been found. Her cheeks paled. "What can I do for you?" she stammered.

"Delaroche's office. Where is it?" Reid said, clearly enjoying the receptionist's anxiety. Amber wanted to whack him on the back of the head.

The name Julia Jackson was stenciled on a brass nameplate on the desk, but Reid ignored it. Amber pasted a smile on her face and softened her voice. "Ms. Jackson?"

The young woman nodded. Amber held her gaze, trying to put her at ease. "We're here to conduct a follow up interview with Mr. Delaroche and Mr. Maxwell. We were asked to meet them in the second floor conference room at four. Could you have someone show us up please?"

"Of course." Ms. Jackson pressed the side of her earpiece and turned her head, speaking in hushed tones for privacy. Then she looked up and offered a wobbly smile.

"Jimmy's in the security office," she said, her voice dropping to a whisper as she tilted her head toward the door behind her desk. "Since the murders, he's not allowed to step away from the monitors, and Grant switched to days. He should be here momentarily to show you up."

"We don't have all day." Reid opened his suit jacket wide enough to show his shoulder harness. Amber suppressed a groan. He'd obviously watched one too many Bruce Willis movies.

"Thank you," she said to Ms. Jackson before turning to glare at her partner.

He rolled his eyes. "Fine. We'll wait." Patience was not his middle name.

While Reid paced, Amber turned her attention to Ms. Jackson. "How well did you know Miss Gallagher?"

Blank stare. "I didn't."

"You didn't know her at all? Or you didn't know her well?"

"We never met."

Amber tried not to scowl, but she'd yet to master a poker face, and her appearance would never inspire female solidarity. She kept her dark hair pulled back in a tight French braid with the end clipped underneath so a perp couldn't grab it in a scuffle. She also dressed in bland business attire in an attempt to blend-into a male dominant career. Lip gloss, a light coating of mascara, a tiny sterling silver cross necklace, and dainty hoop earrings, were the only visible feminine touches she allowed herself on the job. But underneath her clothes, she wore sexy lingerie—a personal reminder that she was still a desirable woman, despite her lack of any recognizable form of a love life for the past two years.

She smoothed out the frown lines and tried holding a smile. "Miss Gallagher was Dr. Harper's research assistant. How could you not have met her?"

Ms. Jackson nervously twisted her fingers together. "They worked nights. I work days."

During the initial interviews, Dr. Harper, Vincent Maxwell, Dr. Harper's husband, and Gerard Delaroche, claimed Miss Gallagher was working the night she was killed. No one mentioned it was hers and Dr. Harper's usual shift or why Dr. Harper skipped work that night to visit a friend of her husband's in the middle of the night—a friend named Sonia with no known last name, no phone number, and no address.

So, how the hell did Dr. Harper visit Sonia if she didn't know her last name or where she lived? Did Sonia know something Maxwell and Harper didn't want divulged? Was she an employee?

"Do you know a woman named Sonia?" Amber asked Ms. Jackson.

Another blank stare. "No."

Aside from serial killers and the infrequent, random acts of violence, most murder victims were killed for money, vengeance, or sex, and the killer wasn't normally a stranger. So, who had a motive to kill Tina Gallagher?

The initial investigators believed Delaroche and Harper were having an affair and that Miss Gallagher found out and threatened to tell Dr. Harper's husband, Vincent Maxwell. Delaroche didn't want to lose his business partner or his lover so he killed the research assistant to shut her up.

It was a reasonable hypothesis. Richard Baxter, the young security guard also killed that night, could have seen Delaroche lurking outside the lab. That would explain why his body was found stuffed in a janitor's closet two doors down. It didn't explain why his throat had been cut—after his body was drained of blood. According to the autopsy report, there wasn't enough blood left in his tissues to cause liver mortis, and Axle Travers, who'd also been working that night, was still missing.

Was Travers involved in the murders? Or had he seen something so terrifying he'd gone into hiding?

Fighting her own lingering fears, Amber held Ms. Jackson's gaze. "What about Axle Travers? How well did you know him?"

A muscle jumped in Ms. Jackson's jaw. "I don't work nights. Ever. I met Axle once when he came in to fill out a hiring package."

Maybe Reid was on to something with the tough cop routine. Amber leaned over the counter and glared. "You do know your bosses. Don't you?"

Ms. Jackson twisted her fingers together on top of her desk. A flush stained her cheeks, but she showed no overt signs of deceit when she said, "Of course, I've met them. They hired me, and I've seen them on the rare occasions when I work late, but I don't really see much of them either."

Lifeblood of America was a multi-million dollar business. So, why wasn't it run like one? Why did the owners and two highly-paid researchers work nights when most everyone else was home sleeping?

Amber pulled a thick pad from her purse and flipped through her notes. Delaroche was the after-hours procurement agent, but Maxwell was CEO. He had no reason to work nights. The research division of the company was a nine to five operation—nine in the morning to five in the evening. Yet Dr. Harper and Ms. Gallagher worked from nine at night to five in the morning.

Why the odd hours? What were they researching? Did it have something to do with Ms. Gallagher's death?

"Was Ms. Gallagher working on a special project?" Amber asked.

Ms. Jackson tapped a red-lacquered nail on the counter. "I wouldn't know."

No. Probably not. Ms. Jackson was a receptionist, not an executive assistant. "Did Ms. Gallagher always work so late? Or had her hours recently changed?"

Ms. Jackson raised her brows. "Miss Gallagher is—was—Dr. Harper's lab assistant, and Dr. Harper is married to Mr. Maxwell."

"And what does that have to do with either of their work schedules?"

Ms. Jackson's jaw dropped; her brows rose. "You're kidding. Right? That's like common knowledge around here. Everyone gossips about it, and you guys haven't figured it out yet?"

Unease skittered down Amber's spine. She had a bad feeling. Someone on her team had missed something. But she wasn't about to admit ignorance or criticize a fellow officer in front of a civilian. Holding Ms. Jackson's gaze, she said, "We have boxes of evidence and interview notes. Which piece of information do your co-workers gossip about that you feel is pertinent to Miss Gallagher's schedule?"

Ms. Jackson rolled her eyes. "Dr. Harper and Miss Gallagher work nights so Dr. Harper can spend time with her husband. Both Mr. Maxwell and Mr. Delaroche have XP."

"XP?" Amber flipped through her notes again, trying to find the initials, knowing it had nothing to do with older computers' operating systems.

"Xeroderma Pigmentosum," Ms. Jackson said, as if the answer was obvious. "It's one of the medical conditions we research here at Lifeblood of America. It's a rare genetic light sensitivity disorder. People with the condition have to avoid sunlight or risk disfiguring sunburns and fatal skin cancers. You should have known that already."

That explained Mr. Maxwell and Mr. Delaroche's insistence that all interviews be conducted before 0700 hours or after 1600 hours—that much, at least, was in the initial interview notes. But there was no mention of XP—or anything else that might explain Ms. Gallagher's late hours. Screw Reid's bad cop tactics. When Amber tried it, she came across as a bitch.

Forcing a smile, she opted for a conciliatory tone, hoping to regain some of the ground she'd lost. "Like I said, we have a lot of information. But I appreciate you bringing me up to speed." She'd rather take the blame for not preparing for the interview than hint at departmental incompetence.

Ms. Jackson pursed her lips in an expression of disapproval. "Well, you should have gone over your notes before coming here."

The secretary's attitude tried Amber's patience. Her smile faltered. "I have a lot of catching up to do. But again, thank you for your assistance."

"Sure." Ms. Jackson shrugged and then leaned forward on her elbows, lowering her voice to a conspiratorial whisper. "I hear a lot of rumors down here. So, if you ever want to know something off the record, just ask. I'm not trying to get involved, but... I hear things. You know?"

Amber mirrored her posture; chin nestled in her palm, voice dropping to match. "Really? What kind of things?"

"Personal stuff, you know?" Ms. Jackson's eyes flicked nervously around the lobby. Her voice dropped to a whisper. "Like how Grant's got PTSD from that night—even though he wasn't even here. That's why he works days now. Or how Miss Gallagher and Mr. Delaroche were involved, but you knew that part, right?"

She didn't. Everyone on the force assumed Delaroche was having an affair with Dr. Harper. Amber kept her tone neutral. "That's the kind of detail that could help the investigation," she said just as the elevator doors slid open and a tall, man in his late thirties stepped into the lobby. She handed Ms. Jackson her card. "If you hear anything else, please call."

Reid strode forward, introducing himself to the security guard. "Detective Sheridan," he said. "And this is my partner, Amber Buckley."

Amber smiled, trying not to bristle at her partner's continued lack of respect for her rank.

The security guard shook Reid's hand. "Grant Simmons, Chief of Security." He turned to Amber, extending his hand. "Detective?"

"Yes." A ghost of a smile flashed across his broad face before he turned toward a security panel beside the elevator. He swiped his badge. A red LED blinked yellow. Then he entered a numeric code and placed his palm on a sensor. The light flashed green, and the elevator doors slid open. "You need a badge and code to go up, but not to come back down." He stepped inside, holding the door.

"So, we need a babysitter while we're up there?" Reid asked as the doors closed.

"I trust you not to wander," Simmons replied. "Not that you could. You don't have a badge, a code, and your palm isn't in the system."

"So, you're saying these murders were an inside job?" Reid's tone implied he hadn't already considered the possibility. Amber knew better. From the beginning, they'd both thought it likely.

Simmons paled. "I'm not accusing anybody, but Axle had nothing to do with the murders."

Reid folded his arms. "Who said anything about Axle Travers?"

Simmons turned a sickly shade of green, staring at the control panel in silence.

Reid's approach was blunt, his people skills lacking. But he was right—whoever killed Tina Gallagher and Richard Baxter had security clearance at Lifeblood of America.

"So, where were you the night Richard and Tina died," Reid asked.

Simmons' face drained of color. "At the hospital. My wife was giving birth."

That alibi had already been confirmed by Daniels and Tanner. Judging by Simmons' expression and his defense of Axle, he was likely grappling with survivor's guilt—something Amber understood all too well.

She softened. Simmons had never been a suspect. "Boy or girl."

"Boy. We named him Richard Axle."

"Congratulations," she said. Reid nodded, silent.

When the elevator opened on the second floor, Simmons stepped out but kept his hand on the hold button, preventing the doors from sliding shut. Staring straight ahead, he said, "Conference room is the third door on your right. It's unlocked, so you won't need a code to get in."

Amber and Reid exited. Simmons nodded and pressed the button. The silver doors slid shut, leaving them in a sterile corridor lined with metal doors, electronic locks, and palm pads. The air smelled faintly of ozone, bleach, and formaldehyde.

Reid wrinkled his nose. "Think anyone ever gets used to that stench?"

"I've smelled worse." The remembered scents evoked memories best forgotten, memories of a flash of light followed by a hissing boom.

Eight years hadn't dulled the sensory onslaught. Sulfur, melted plastic, chard flesh. Private Piner thrown to the ground, clutching a bloody stump with mangled fingers, his screams echoing through the deserted streets of an Iraqi village as the remains of his leg landed fifteen feet away in a pulpy heap.

Amber swallowed bile and refocused. "Lifeblood isn't just a blood and tissue bank anymore. They've expanded into research. That explains the smell. I guess Maxwell and Delaroche decided to use their resources for themselves."

Sympathy tugged at the armor she wore, tightening her raw throat even more. She couldn't imagine never going into the sunlight without layers of protective clothing, dark glasses, and massive amounts of sunblock.

Were Vincent Maxwell and Gerard Delaroche deathly pale? Did lesions mar their skin?

Reid gave her a sideways look. "What are you talking about?"

She blinked, grounding herself. "They have a rare genetic condition. XP."

She repeated what Ms. Jackson had said about xeroderma pigmentosum but withheld the detail about Delaroche and Tina Gallagher. Reid didn't need another reason to jump to conclusions. He needed an open mind to analyze the evidence.

He grimaced. "So they're like vampires? Only come out after dark?"

"No," she said with disgust as an unexpected shiver crawled down her spine, but Baxter's autopsy had raised disturbing questions. Complete exsanguination. Two puncture marks in the carotid artery beneath the knife wound. The medical examiner believed the killer used a trocar to drain Baxter's blood before slashing his throat. But what had the killer done with the blood? And why hadn't Tina Gallagher been killed in a like manner?

Two assailants—or something worse?

Images of blood clouded her vision. She blinked it away. "It's a medical condition, Reid."

"Maybe they just think they're vampires. It would explain the security guard's death. If they actually drink blood..."

"There's no proof either of them were involved. And Miss Gallagher's blood was all over the lobby." Still, Amber couldn't shake the image of cloaked figures with fangs lurking in the dark. The vision clung to her until they reached the only door with a blinking green LED.

Reid turned the handle and pushed it open without knocking. Amber would've apologized for his rudeness—if her mouth hadn't gone dry.

"The cops, I presume?" A tall, dark-haired man with a trim beard and faint accent said. His shoulder-length hair was tied back, and his coffee-colored eyes seemed to pierce her soul. His complexion was only slightly pale, and it did nothing to diminish his striking features.

The man beside him was pure eye candy. Shorter, broader, built like a bodybuilder but without the exaggerated bone structure. His neck was proportional, his cheekbones chiseled, jaw square. No Neanderthal here—just devastatingly handsome.

Silver streaks threaded his brown hair, and when he turned those baby blues on her, Amber felt like she'd been tasered in the gut—minus the pain. But damn if her brain didn't react in the same confused fashion. After the first electric jolt, her brain misfired, signals scrambled. She couldn't think. Couldn't move. She just stared into Gerard Delaroche's eyes while a slow sensual heat bathed her body, turning her knees to mush.

Chapter 2

Sergeant Reid Sheridan tried to appear intimidating, but he didn't look all that tough. Average height. Lean. Business-short dark hair and dark sunglasses in a not so brightly lit room. Gerard gave him a cursory inspection and came to a swift conclusion. Sheridan was ambitious but lacked the experience to climb above his current rank. He wasn't a threat, although, he could prove as irritating as a gnat. The woman, on the other hand...

Gerard's gaze slid to Sheridan's partner, an attractive brunette in a shapeless brown suit and cream-colored blouse. A thin chain with a silver cross drew his attention, not that he or any vampire had an aversion to crosses. It was the silver. Vampires had a deadly allergy to silver and a respiratory reaction to garlic. Funny the way mortals developed entire myths around the tiniest bit of information.

Amber Buckley wore her hair scraped back in a severe style that made her high cheekbones stand out, giving her an air of superiority. She carried herself with quiet confidence and barely flinched when her partner failed to introduce her by rank. Gerard attributed it to class and sophistication. Then he met her direct gray gaze.

Bon Dieu! Such fire and intelligence in those beautiful eyes. His body tightened as if an electric current passed between them. Tina was barely cold in her grave.

Pain as sharp as the blade that took his life over two hundred years ago twisted his gut. Tina was dead because of him—viciously murdered because she'd wanted to help bring him out of the dark world he inhabited.

Inhaling sharply, he fisted his hands at his sides and tried to calm his raging anger. His gaze shifted from Buckley to Sheridan. Perhaps the sensation he'd felt when looking at Buckley was nothing more than a warning. Between her and her partner, Buckley was the more dangerous of the two. She was open-minded and intelligent enough to discover things best left undiscovered. It didn't take glamour to see that.

Even with the "deer caught in the headlights" expression she wore when he glanced at her, he could see the wheels in her mind spinning. Then her spine stiffened and those shapely brows snapped down over deep-set eyes—as if she were trying to read his thoughts.

Now, that was a truly frightening concept.

Sheridan removed his sunglasses, drawing Gerard's attention once more. "Where were you on the night of March 5, between four and five a.m.?"

Vincent bristled. "Hasn't he answered those questions already?"

Sheridan ignored him, keeping his gaze on Gerard. Gerard didn't want mortals investigating the murders, but if he wanted to live among them, he couldn't manipulate them—much. He folded his arms over his chest. His eyes narrowed. "Like I told those other two detectives, I was in Alexandria."

La beauté's lips twitched in a smile that looked more like a sneer. Had he thought her a class act? Class A bitch was a role she played well too, and he didn't mean that in a bad way. She was cool. Sophisticated. And she carried authority like a man.

"Can anyone verify that?" she asked.

His expression never changed. He'd invented cool before her great-great-great-great-great grandfather was even born. "Yes."

This time, Sheridan bristled. "What were you doing in Alexandria, Virginia at four in the morning? You weren't sleeping. We didn't find any record of a hotel reservation in your name for that night."

Gerard looked at Vincent who was now leaning casually against the conference table, his cool demeanor restored. Their minds briefly connected. Sonia, Vincent's creator and master manipulator of mortal technology, had done her magic and covered Gerard's ass. Gerard suppressed a smile.

"Of course you didn't. I used a corporate credit card to pay for a two-night stay at the Morgan Suites. As the major shareholder in Lifeblood of America, Vincent's name is on the account."

Detective Buckley jolted as if caught off guard. Of course, she couldn't have been prepared for his answer. He hadn't given this information to the original detectives. Sonia had needed time to manipulate credit card records and flight logs. He'd needed time to manipulate Lifeblood's pilot and the hotel night clerk's memories.

Anger twisted his gut. Safeguarding vampires hampered his efforts to investigate the murders himself.

"Why haven't you cooperated before now?" Detective Buckley asked.

There was no practical excuse for an innocent man keeping such vital information to himself. An objective analysis of possible responses made him look guilty—or like an uncooperative ass.

He adjusted his tie, hating the modern fashion accessory. The detectives watched his movements with suspicion, most likely interpreting his actions as the nervous gesture of a guilty man. Stifling a groan, he lowered his hands and shoved them into his suit pockets. "I answered the other detective's questions. I just didn't elaborate. I wanted to confer with our attorney first. Axle Travers is his son."

With Axel still missing, Brit wouldn't remember if he'd discussed the case with Gerard or not. Concern for his son took precedence over everything else.

"We haven't forgotten Mr. Travers' son," the beautiful detective responded, her voice losing its sharp edge.

Sheridan glared, his jaw set at a rigid angle. "Can you produce receipts to prove you were in Alexandria?"

Vincent responded in an authoritative tone that inspired obedience without the use of glamour. "Our accountant can. If you'll stop by the reception desk on your way out, Miss Jackson can give you whatever you need, including the name of our company pilot who can confirm Gerard's flight to Alexandria that night."

His veiled dismissal went unheeded. If the situation weren't so dire, Gerard would have laughed. Vincent didn't like being ignored. Fortunately for the detectives, he didn't like manipulating mortal thoughts either. Otherwise, he would have mentally compelled them to leave without their knowledge or understanding.

"Did you order room service while you were there? Make any long distance calls?" Detective Buckley's voice remained cool. Undeterred.

Gerard smiled. "I ordered a meal before checking out on the evening of the sixth."

Buckley wasn't a fool. Even if Gerard could verify having checked into the hotel, she wanted proof of his whereabouts during the time of the murders. Claiming to have flown to Alexandria didn't preclude his renting a car and driving back to Asheville in time to kill Tina and Richard—except he was supposed to have XP. The timing of the murders would have prevented him—or anyone who actually had XP—from making it back to Alexandria before sunrise.

Ironically, those afflicted with xeroderma pigmentosum were almost as vulnerable to the killing rays of the sun as vampires.

While Sheridan drilled Vincent about Gerard's credit card usage and room service order, Gerard stared into Detective Buckley's eyes, searching her thoughts. He hated the necessity, but he had to find out what she knew of Tina's killer. It wasn't just about revenge. It was about protection. When mortals knew vampires existed, it put everyone in danger. And he didn't want the authorities focusing on him while Tina's killer went free.

He reached for the table behind him. Reading mortal minds made him dizzy. Getting past Detective Buckley's defenses challenged his abilities. Her mind rebuffed him like a brick wall. He persisted, breaking through her mental barriers until distorted images and random thoughts from the detective's brain filled his head, confirming what he already suspected. Despite careful planning, he was still a person of interest.

The police believed he had the means, opportunity, and motive to commit murder. He was Lifeblood's after-hours acquisition consultant. He worked with the transplant teams and procurement groups, coordinating the transfer of organs and unallocated body parts. The initial detectives believed this gave him access to morgues—and a trocar—the weapon supposedly used to kill Richard Baxter.

A rogue vampire drained Richard of blood, and a knife was used to cover up the fang marks. But a mortal killed Tina—a mortal who knew about the vampire vaccine, and there was only one mortal who knew so much about vampires and had the ability to capture them. But how had Dr. Steve Weldon gained a vampire's cooperation?

Gerard looked deeper into the detective's mind. The Asheville PD suspected him of having an affair with Megan and believed Tina threatened to tell Vincent. They believed the murders were the result of a love triangle gone wrong.

Quelle idée idiote. The idea was ridiculous. Nothing could be further from the truth, but at least the Asheville PD didn't suspect vampires. He should be grateful for small favors.

As he pushed at Detective Buckley's uncooperative mind, trying to delve deeper, random flashes of unrelated events diverted her thoughts—horrific images of blood and war. Gerard intensified his efforts, trying to understand the discordant memories that flashed through her mind without rhyme or reason until a wave of dizziness broke his concentration. Gripping the table to keep his balance, he backed out of her head, taking several deep breaths to regain his equilibrium. Detective Buckley blinked back into focus. Her face was pale, her big gray eyes wide and frightened.

"Gerard!" Vincent snapped, gaining his attention. "You did sign your own name to the credit card slips. Didn't you? It's company policy."

His name was added later, and the night clerk—whom he'd not met until several days after the murders—would swear in a court of law he remembered Gerard checking in because of the discrepancy between the name on his credit card and the name used when he signed the bill. It was so much easier to manipulate the mind than read it. But mental manipulation wasn't always reliable and implanted memories were often forgotten.

"Oui. Don't I always? Besides, I'd never do anything to make Megan jealous. And I was on company business," he said, implying Vincent's sharp tone was about the credit card usage. The mortal detectives would never guess the real cause of Vincent's irritation was Gerard's intrusion into the detective's mind.

"What sort of company business?" Detective Buckley asked.

Sheridan sneered. "Did you do something to make Maxwell jealous?"

A flash of anger heated his skin. Grinding his back teeth, he ignored Sheridan and answered Detective Buckley. "I had an appointment with Dr. Geniis. We met in the hotel lobby that night. He's done extensive research on protein therapy lotions. We're trying to acquire his services."

The lie slipped smoothly from his tongue. Years of practice, he supposed. He hated the necessity, but it had become a matter of survival when he first began the practice as a mortal fighting with General Marquis de Lafayette against the radical Jacobins during the French Revolution.

Detective Buckley's eyes softened. "What's the lotion for?"

She knew. Or suspected. Gerard could smell her pity like a noxious perfume. His lip curled. He didn't need her sympathy. If she couldn't find Tina's killer, he needed nothing from her. "It's a sunblock."

"For people like yourself and Mr. Maxwell who suffer from XP?" She leaned in. Sheridan's sneer turned nasty. His bad cop to her sympathetic cop. Vincent was thinking the same thing.

Gerard almost laughed. The protein therapy lotion helped vampires taking the anti-vampiric vaccine tolerate minimal exposure to sunlight without bursting into flames. It allowed them to venture out before sunset and pass more easily as human, but its major benefit was to patients with XP.

"The lotion is protein specific. It enables those of us with XP to better tolerate brief periods of sunlight without risking serious burns or cancer," he said by rote.

"It's my wife's pet project," Vincent added. "Megan's sister died from complications of XP. That's how we met."

What he didn't say was that he'd sought out Megan because she once worked for Dr. Weldon, the researcher who'd tried cloning vampires for the military. Megan had inadvertently created the sedative that enabled him to capture Gerard for his experiments. Weldon's attempt at cloning had failed, and the colonel who hired him for the black ops project had been court-martialed, but Dr. Weldon remained at large, and he now had samples of the vampire vaccine.

Had promises of a cure convinced an unsuspecting vampire to assist Weldon with his latest project? It's the ruse Weldon had used two years ago to lure Gerard. Anger flared once more at the reminder of his own naivety.

Sheridan's mouth curved upward, his smile contemptuous. "Is that how you met Dr. Harper? Did she show you as much sympathy as she showed her husband? Did the two of you get close? Maybe a little too close?"

Gerard narrowed his eyes but said nothing. Bâtard. Vincent, hotheaded as ever even after two-hundred years, moved at vampiric speed reaching the arrogant detective before the last word left his mouth. He glared down at the shorter man, fury radiating from every pore. Somehow, he managed to resist snatching Sheridan up by his lapels.

"My wife has nothing to do with this. She's not to be questioned," Vincent ground out between clinched teeth. It was more than a hypnotic suggestion. It was a command the detective wouldn't disobey.

"Stand down, Maxwell." Detective Buckley slipped her hand inside her brown jacket. Her voice was sharp, her movements militarily precise.

Vincent's gaze remained fixed. Intense. Had Buckley been able to see his eyes from where she stood, she would have seen the glowing red gaze of a nocturnal predator.

"I said, stand down!" She withdrew her weapon.

Gerard eased away from the conference table. She swung her aim toward him. He held up his hands and smiled. "Easy now. There's no need for violence. My partner was just defending his wife. He's made no threats, and he's calm now. See?"

She glanced at Vincent. He'd stepped away from Sheridan. His face was as expressionless as marble and just as cold. Sheridan nodded.

"No need to question his wife," he parroted. "She's not involved. Our focus belongs on his partner, Mr. Delaroche."

Gerard raised a brow and looked at Vincent. Thanks, mon ami. Put the focus back on me, he said, telepathically.

Even speaking without words, Vincent somehow managed to sneer. You can handle it. Megan can't.

Gerard got his meaning loud and clear, but Vincent was wrong. Megan was tougher than he gave her credit for, but his partner loved his wife beyond reason, and he'd die to protect her. Gerard envied them that. He'd hoped to find that kind of love with Tina, but now he was destined to spend his life alone, and that hurt almost as much as losing her.

#

Amber holstered her Glock and eased her hand away, her fingers missing the security of the checkered-textured grip. "You going to give me trouble, Maxwell?"

"Of course not." He sounded calm. Reasonable. But he'd seemed that way milliseconds before he snapped, moving faster than humanly possible to stand menacingly close to Reid. One minute he'd been calmly leaning against the conference table. Then he wasn't. And she never even saw him move.

Just like that time in Germany. A chill crawled over her skin. She shook it off. This wasn't Germany. She wasn't newly arrived from a fifteen month deployment in Iraq, and she wasn't suffering from combat fatigue or post-traumatic stress. She knew what she'd seen. Or hadn't seen. And she hadn't seen Vincent Maxwell move.

So how the hell had he gotten from Point A to Point B?

She looked at Reid. He was glaring at Delaroche instead of Maxwell. "You okay?" she asked.

"Why wouldn't I be?" He glanced at her from over his shoulder and then returned his attention to Delaroche. "I want to see your receipts. And don't think for a minute we won't go to Alexandria. We're not only going to request a copy from the Morgan Suites, we're going to show the clerk some photographs and ask him to identify you. You got a problem with supplying a copy of your employment photo?"

Delaroche looked at Maxwell. Both smiled the oddest little smile. "Not at all," Delaroche said. "Miss Jackson can get that for you too."

"Fine." Reid turned sharply and headed for the door.

Amber stood for a moment, looking from Delaroche to Maxwell. What the hell just happened? They'd lost total control of the interview. Somehow, the suspects had taken charge. Not that she'd gone in thinking Delaroche or Maxwell was a cold-blooded killer, but now, she suspected both men of a cover-up. They may not be directly involved, but they knew something, and they weren't talking.

Her chest tightened. So did her fists. She raised her chin and met Delaroche's gaze. His penetrating blue eyes jolted her. She wouldn't call it attraction, but there was definitely chemistry, and she didn't like it. She would, however, use it to her advantage.

"Where's Axle Travers?" she asked, her voice as compassionate as she could make it.

Mr. Cool shrugged those massive shoulders, showing no emotion except in the depths of his blue gaze. He wasn't the iceberg he pretended to be. There was a crack in his frozen armor, and that crack shone in his eyes. Grandma always said the eyes were the windows to the soul—God rest hers.

"He's obviously involved, but is he a conspirator or a victim?" she asked.

Maxwell snarled. "If we knew that, we'd find him."

Delaroche said nothing, but there was now a tick at the corner of his left eye. Her questions were getting to him. She hid a smile and turned her focus on Maxwell while keeping Delaroche in her peripheral vision. "So, you admit you're not helping."

"I didn't say that," he ground out.

Maxwell was the hothead. The one with the temper. She could push him—rile him until he made a mistake. If these two were involved in the killings, Maxwell was the one who'd get them caught.

"Well, you pretty much admitted you could find him if you knew whether he was a victim or not. Sounds like you just don't want to cooperate. Too much bother," she said with a shrug.

Fury colored Maxwell's face. His eyes flashed red. Amber jerked and met his gaze. His eyes were a dark, angry brown—not the glowing red of a predatory animal's.

Shaking off a momentary chill, she reached inside her jacket pocket and pulled out two cards. "If you change your mind and want to talk, give me a call."

She handed one card to Maxwell. He tossed it on the table without looking at it. She gave the other card to Delaroche. When he took it from her hand, their fingers touched. The resulting sensation was like grabbing hold of a live wire. Hot sparks rushed up her arm and pierced her chest. Her heart jumped.

Delaroche pulled his hand away as if burned. He'd felt it too.

She rubbed her fingers and met his gaze. Her mind went all fuzzy again.

"Are you coming?" Reid called from the door.

She shook her head to clear the sudden lethargy that seemed to steal her strength. Before she left the room, she turned one last time, meeting Gerard Delaroche's intense gaze. "We'll be back."

His smile stole the breath from her lungs. "I'm looking forward to it."

Chapter 3

"What the hell just happened in there?" Amber asked Reid once they were back in the car. He glanced at her from behind his sunglasses before returning his attention to the road. "We dragged information from Delaroche that Daniels and Tanner couldn't. We have the pilot's statement, credit card receipts, and a picture of Delaroche from his employment file. If there's a discrepancy in the flight plan or the night clerk at Morgan Suites can't identify him from his photograph, we'll drag his ass in for more extensive questioning. That's what happened in there."

"You didn't find the exchange with Maxwell odd? I mean, one minute he was lounging against that conference table and the next he was about to jack you up by your lapels. And I never saw him move."

Just like that time in Germany...

Anxiety quickened her pulse. She took a calming breath and wiped her sweat-slicked palms on her thighs.

"Maybe you should get your eyes checked," Reid said, keeping his on the road. "Of course, I saw him move. And why wouldn't he be pissed? I practically accused his wife of cheating. And she's not involved. I know it and he knows it. It was just an interview technique to get what we wanted from Delaroche."

Reid wasn't an easy man to manipulate. Yet Maxwell had only suggested Reid not question his wife and Reid obeyed. And he didn't seem to remember.

Maybe I'm just being paranoid. It had to be those damn crime scene photos. All that blood under Tina Gallagher's body. The weird way Richard Baxter had died—the awful, gaping wound with so little blood. Was it any wonder she'd dreamt of vampires last night?

She shivered. Germany was the past. So was Iraq. She needed to get a grip and get over it already. Or ask the doctor to up her meds.

She took another deep breath and let it out slowly. "Do you still think Delaroche is involved?"

"He definitely knows something about Travers."

Delaroche was hiding something. That deep blue gaze gave away more than he realized. She pulled her notebook from her purse and flipped through the pages. "So, maybe we need to take a closer look at Travers."

Reid slid another sideways glance in her direction. "What do we have on him?"

"Not much," she said, scanning her notes. "He's the son of Lifeblood's attorney Brit Travers from a previous marriage. His mother, Shannon Travers, is in the Henrico County jail awaiting trial on drug charges."

Glancing up from her notes, she added, "Maybe we should pay her a visit on our way back from Alexandria tomorrow. If Axle murdered his co-workers or let the killers in and witnessed the murders, he could have gone into hiding. Maybe his mother knows where."

Reid swung his gaze from the road. His eyes shone with excitement. "What if Axle is into drugs too?"

Amber's pulse quickened. "Then Daniels and Tanner got it all wrong."

"Damn right." Reid turned his attention back to the road. His fingers curled around the steering wheel in a white-knuckled grip. "These murders aren't about an affair. They're drug-related."

And Delaroche had nothing to do with drugs. A man with his medical condition wouldn't take such a risk. And it wasn't as if he needed money. He earned a sizeable and legitimate income from Lifeblood Labs. "You think Axle was dealing?" she asked.

"What better way to get equipment for a meth lab than to hook back up with Daddy? Axle knew his father could get him a job. And who'd suspect a lawyer's kid-turned-security guard of stealing?"

Her previous excitement waned. The evidence didn't add up. They had enough pieces to build a case for Reid's drug theory, but when they started putting those pieces together, she'd bet her pension some of them wouldn't fit. They were looking at two different puzzles.

"Nothing was reported missing, and Axle Travers has no prior history of violence. He wouldn't commit two murders and then walk away without taking the equipment he needed."

"He didn't commit the murders," Reid said. "He witnessed them. If his mama's suppliers knew he was going into business for himself, they'd try to stop him. Maybe they went to Lifeblood that night, intending to scare the shit out of him. Axle probably let them in so they could talk. Then Tina Gallagher showed up and they killed her. Now, Axle's running scared. Baxter's death was probably a warning of what would happen if he snitched or went into business for himself. The way he died was pretty gruesome."

Puncture wounds to the neck, his body drained of blood—gruesome wasn't the word for it. It was the stuff of nightmares. It was the stuff of her nightmares. The fear came rushing back. Her pulse quickened. Forcing herself to relax, she thought of gently rolling waves smoothing the shoreline as they carried her dark memories out to sea. The tension eased from her shoulders. She took a deep breath and let it out slowly.

"Gruesome or not, we don't have proof. We don't even have a shred of real evidence." And she wasn't about to run off half-cocked. But Reid was on a roll. She could see the excitement in his eyes—hear the exhilaration in his voice. He was vibrating with it. If she didn't say or do something to slow him down, he'd leap before seeing where the evidence led.

"Don't worry," he said. "I'm not going to espouse my theories to Captain Stratford or anyone else. I don't want this case going to the Feds or to narcotics. This is our baby, and we're going to rock it."

The knot in her stomach tightened. This case was going to end badly. She sensed it as surely as she'd sensed impending disaster in Iraq.

She swallowed the lump of fear that suddenly lodged in her throat. "I agree. It's possible this case has nothing to do with Delaroche or Maxwell and everything to do with Axle Travers. Maybe he split after witnessing the murders. Or maybe he's dead. A missing employee makes a damn good murder suspect, but we need evidence. Not theories."

Reid slowly turned. His face broke into a wide grin. "Oh, we'll get our evidence. We're not going to Alexandria tomorrow. First thing in the morning, we're going to Richmond."

#

Shannon Travers looked older than her forty-seven years. Haggard and worn, she raked a strand of stringy, bleached-blond hair behind her ear and stared at Reid with rheumy blue eyes. Her thin fingers shook. Her chin trembled. "I haven't seen my son in almost two years."

Her voice was soft and southern and more cultured than Amber expected. The woman sitting across from them in the interrogation room was awaiting trial for her third count of possession with intent to sell. Three strikes. She was possibly looking at hard time.

"He ever get strung out with you?" Reid asked in his "I'm such a bad-ass voice." He was playing bad cop to Amber's good cop. It wasn't a role for Reid. He thought threatening a suspect was the best way to get answers.

Nervously chewing a ragged nail, Shannon shook her head and spoke around her index finger. "Axle doesn't do drugs."

Reid leaned across the battered table, glaring. The suspect shrank back, her skin seeming to shrivel on her bony frame as Reid continued his verbal pounding. "He was eleven when you split with Brit Travers. Yet when given the choice, he chose to live with you instead of his father. Your husband was an attorney. He had a home and a job. You were unemployed and left him to live in a hotel. You were busted on drug charges before the ink was even dry on the divorce papers. How do you explain that?"

The finger slid from her mouth. "It was a misdemeanor possession charge."

Reid gave no quarter. "Axle stayed with you for fourteen years. Paid your rent when he was older. And you're telling me the two of you never got high together? That he never dealt?"

"Axle don't do drugs!" she snapped, her grammar slipping along with her cultured voice. "He ain't no dealer, and he ain't no gang-banger."

"Have you heard from him since he went to visit his father?" Amber said in a soft voice, trying to calm the agitated woman, hoping Reid would back off and let her handle the rest of the interrogation. "Has he called since he left Richmond?"

Shannon lowered her pointed chin, her eyes shifting from Reid to Amber, some of the hostility in her expression fading. "Yeah. A few times. At first. Before I run out of minutes on my cellphone. He called the night he arrived in Asheville to say he was safe. Then he called again to say he met his dad and that Brit didn't ask no questions, just welcomed him into the family. Axle has a brother, you know." She smiled briefly, revealing stained, decayed teeth and enflamed gums.

Meth mouth.

"I knew his dad remarried," she added softly, the lingering resentment fading from her eyes, "but I didn't know Brit had another kid."

Amber glanced sharply at Reid, warning him not to interrupt. Then she smiled at Shannon. "His name is Jerome. He's eleven. The same age Axle was when you left your husband, but you knew that already."

She shrugged. "Okay, so maybe I knew Brit had another kid, but I didn't know his name until Axle told me. He said he and his little brother got close real fast like."

That didn't sound like a man who'd walk away from a newly discovered family. Or a man who'd get involved in a drug deal or murder. Amber had a bad feeling they weren't going to find Axle Travers alive. "Can you think of any reason Axle would disappear? Why he'd walk away from a father and brother he only recently found? Or where he might have gone?"

"You know it has to do with drugs. Don't you, Shannon?" Reid said in the same sharp tone drill sergeants used on new recruits. "You're the reason your son is missing."

"No!"

Stifling a groan, Amber curled her fingers into fists. She'd never wanted to punch anyone as badly as she wanted to punch Reid. Now was not the time to play bad cop. Shannon had been about to open up, but she shut down fast in the face of Reid's anger. Her lips firmed, and her eyes hardened. And she didn't say another word.

#

"I still think we should have gone to Alexandria. We should at least question the night clerk at Morgan Suites to see if Delaroche was actually there that night."

"We have the credit card receipts," Amber said as Reid turned onto her road. She'd barely spoken to him on the ride back from Richmond. She was still angry he'd let his arrogance overrule his common sense.

"How long you gonna give me the cold shoulder?" He slammed on the brakes and threw the car into park outside of her house.

Amber jerked forward, the seatbelt pulling against her shoulder and scraping her neck. She waited until the rocking motion of the car subsided before turning to glare. "You blew it."

"Don't you think I know that?" He raked a hand threw his short dark hair and slammed his fists on the steering wheel. "She looked scared and weak. I thought I could break her."

"It was the wrong time and in the wrong way. She already feels helpless and you not only hinted that her son was in danger, you blamed her. How did you expect her to react?"

"I said I was sorry. Now how do we fix it? We have to talk to her again. She's our only link to Travers."

"She's not our only link. We can talk to Brit Travers tomorrow."

"Fine." He leaned back against the seat with an irritated huff. His hands still clung to the steering wheel. "I'll let you take lead this time."

Not that he'd like it. But at least he was trying to tone down the testosterone and treat her as an equal. She'd give him an "A" for effort. Or maybe a "B."

"This isn't a power struggle," she said with a sigh.

"It feels like one. Worse, it feels like I'm losing." He turned his head, his mouth stretching into a lopsided grin. "We both know you're better trained. You were in the military. You drove Humvees and tanks. And you have a hell of a lot more experience with weapons than I do. And now I'm finding out you're a better detective. I don't like it. Sorry, but I can't fight my nature. I'm a bit sexist. I admit it. And we're both going to have to deal with that."

"A bit sexist?" She choked on a laugh. Reid could be such an ass at times, but he was a genuinely nice guy. And a good partner—when he wasn't being sexist and arrogant. But she trusted him with her life.

He chuckled. "Okay. A lot. But I'm trying. Okay? Give me a break."

"I will. But give yourself some credit. I'm not a better detective. I just have more patience. You can't force the evidence. You have to follow where it leads."

"I'll try to remember that. Now get out of my car and get some sleep. You're picking me up tomorrow."

Warmth settled in the pit of Amber's stomach. She liked her job when she and Reid got along. And things seemed to click when they weren't butting heads. Like earlier today when they agreed on a drug connection.

Hand on the door, she paused before opening it. "Gerard Delaroche isn't involved in the killings. Agreed?"

But he damn sure knew something about the case—not that he'd talk with Reid around. The two of them mixed about as well as gunpowder and a match. Reid's gaze narrowed, but he didn't disagree. Stubborn man.

"Can we at least agree he's not involved with drugs, and this case most likely involves drugs?" she asked.

"I'll agree with that," he said, carefully weighing his words.

"Can we also agree that you and Delaroche don't get along?"

"No shit, Sherlock. The man's hiding something. That's obvious. Even to me."

It was obvious, but Amber wasn't sure if it had something to do with the murders, Axle Travers' disappearance, or both. "Well, Watson, then may I suggest the next time we interview Delaroche, you let me go alone?"

"No! Absolutely not." The vehemence of his reply startled her.

"Why not?"

"Because I don't trust him. He's dangerous."

She was more concerned about Maxwell. He was the hothead and the more dangerous of the two. Fear crawled down her spine, pebbling her skin with gooseflesh. "What about Maxwell?"

A blank look came over Reid. Total and utter confusion. "What about him?"

"Do you trust him? Do you think he's dangerous?"

Had Reid been "brainwashed" with a look? Or was she slipping back into a dark world of nightmares and paranoia?

Did fearing paranoia make her paranoid?

Reid shrugged. "I haven't given him much thought. Now go on and get out. I'll watch until you get inside."

Amber sighed and opened the door. "I'm a big girl, Reid. And I carry a gun. I don't need a baby sitter."

"Fine. Suit yourself."

He peeled out as soon as she shut the door. She knew he'd regret his childish outburst in the morning, but whether he apologized or not was another matter. She hadn't expected the apology she got tonight. Shaking her head, Amber dug her keys from her over-sized handbag. Reid wasn't a bad partner. He was just sexist, arrogant, and impatient.

"It's almost like being in the army again," she said aloud as she walked up the sidewalk toward the modest Cape Cod on the corner lot.

The porch light was on and the shrubs were neatly trimmed. Her car was parked inside the garage with the inside door closed and locked. Everything looked safe. Secure. And yet the hairs on the nape of her neck stood on end.

She pushed the edge of her jacket aside and touched the grip of her Glock. An instant feeling of calm came over her. Armed, she felt prepared to defend herself against any intruder. She unsnapped the thumb break on the strap of her nylon shoulder holster. Damn. I shouldn't have let Reid drive away. I'll never hear the end of it if I have to disarm a suspect on my own property.

Senses on high alert, she walked slowly toward the steps leading to her front door, her hand sliding deliberately over the gun's checkered grip, her finger slipping into place between the trigger and trigger guard.

"You shouldn't have let him drive away," an accented voice said from the shadows.

Amber turned—gun in hand, body crouched and ready to fire. "Give me a reason not to shoot."

Gerard Delaroche stepped into the circle of light beneath a streetlamp. "I'm unarmed."

In a well-lit room dressed in a suit, the man was handsome. On a shadowy street corner wearing dark jeans and a dark tee shirt that clung irresistibly to his wide chest, he was downright sexy. Shadows concealed his face, but his eyes sparkled. Like a nocturnal animal's in the dark.

A chill traveled the length of Amber's spine and settled in her stomach. Her muscles tensed. Her aim steadied. "You may be unarmed, but I'm not foolish enough to consider you harmless."

"Merci beaucoup."

"It wasn't a compliment." His smile was disarming. She gripped the Glock tighter.

"Truly. I'm quite harmless." His voice was smooth. Enchanting.

A buzzing sounded in her ears. Tension eased from her shoulders. She lowered the gun but didn't holster it. Her mind began to fog. Resisting the temptation to relax her guard, she forced herself to look away. Call it women's intuition or some inner awareness all soldiers develop after their first tour of duty, but she knew not to look into those eyes when he stared so intently.

"Aren't you going to invite me in?" he continued in a coaxing tone, stepping closer. "We need to talk."

"No." She raised her eyes and quickly lowered them again. She could almost feel him compelling her to look at him, but her will was stronger than his. She refused to look.

"I know you have questions."

"Then I'll ask them tomorrow when I'm with my partner."

His attitude altered. Like the wind changing direction before a storm. His shoulders stiffened. His voice hardened. "I won't talk to you when he's around. He's an arrogant ass with a closed mind. He won't listen."

"And what makes you think I will?"

"Because you've already started to question what you've seen."

Another shiver snaked down her spine. This one left her skin as cold as ice. Her heart knocked against her ribs, stealing her breath.

How close am I to the house? How far from safety? Every instinct she possessed told her a gun would be useless against this man. But could she make it up the stairs, onto her porch, and inside her house before he stopped her? If she didn't invite him in, would she be safe inside her home?

Irrational fears clouded logical thinking. She took a deep breath, trying to calm her frazzled nerves and runaway imagination. In as steady a voice as she could muster, she said, "I don't know what you think I've seen or questioned, but it's late. And I'm tired."

"We need someone in law enforcement to help us find Tina's killer."

Fear turned to exasperation. "That's what we're trying to do. Find out who killed Miss Gallagher and Mr. Baxter. We're also looking for Axle Travers. Do you have any idea where he might be?"

"Maybe."

He tried meeting her gaze, but she looked away. She'd seen how quickly Reid changed his opinion when faced with the force of Vincent Maxwell's stare, and Gerard Delaroche had the same penetrating gaze—a hypnotic stare she'd encountered only once before.

Don't go there!

"If you know where Travers is, then you need to speak up. He could be in danger," she said as calmly as she could. Her voice shook almost as badly as her body.

"He is in danger. Haven't you been paying attention?"

Amber holstered her Glock and forced herself to meet Gerard's gaze. One on one. He wasn't a threat. He was just upset over the deaths of his employees, and she refused to have another breakdown some shrink could blame on post-traumatic stress. She'd like to keep her job, thank you very much.

"Go home, Delaroche. Let the police handle this. If you have information you'd like to share, Detective Sheridan and I will talk to you tomorrow."

"But I need to talk to you now. Alone. Tonight." He stepped forward. She slipped her hand back inside her jacket. Her fingers never touched her Glock. Fear—or something else—held her immobile.

"You know what's going on," Delaroche said, staring into her eyes. "You've encountered us before."

"Us?" She was off her meds. It wasn't real then, and it wasn't real now. Just an acute stress response. Post-traumatic Stress Disorder. She'd been diagnosed in Germany. Now, she was experiencing symptoms again. Or maybe it was just good old fashioned anxiety and depression. Either way, she was so going back on her meds—all of them.

Maybe I need a stronger damn prescription.

She closed her eyes and concentrated on breathing, trying to remember the doctor's advice. Imagine the ocean's tide washing everything clean. Try to de-stress. Relax. Breathe. Don't think about Andrew or the cemetery in Nuremberg.

"It was real, you know. What you saw in Germany."

A chill penetrated her chest, piercing her heart. Her eyes snapped open. Her fingers fumbled for the Glock. "How do you know about Germany?"

He'd been inside her head. Just like Nicolas. But Nicolas wasn't real. Gerard was, and he was a danger to her life and her sanity. He stepped closer—an imminent threat. Heart pounding, Amber pulled the gun from its holster and fired.

Chapter 4

Gerard Delaroche grabbed his chest. "Putain de merde! That hurts like hell."

He rubbed the oozing wound, smearing blood on his dark shirt. He didn't fall or stagger. He just stood there, glaring at Amber as if he couldn't believe she'd actually shot him. She couldn't believe it either. It was the first time she'd fired on anyone since Iraq, but Delaroche wasn't dead. He wasn't even mortally wounded, and she'd shot him in the chest at point-blank range. "What the hell?"

He wiped his hand on his pant leg—as if he'd just changed the oil in his car and had gotten grease on his fingers instead of blood. Then he snatched the gun from her trembling grasp. She didn't resist and hardly even noticed. She could only stare, paralyzed with fear as the blood flowing from his chest slowed—as if the wound were already healing.

Fear shook her. *It's Germany all over again.*

Gerard tucked her Glock in the waistband of his jeans and said, "Do you want to get yourself thrown off this case? Even if you don't have to explain a dead body on your lawn, do you want to explain firing your weapon?"

Blood drained from her cold cheeks. She shook her head. What the hell could she say? *I thought you were a vam—Oh hell to the hell no!* She would not say those words aloud ever again.

Gerard squeezed her arm. The warm, metallic scent of blood filled the air. "Invite me in," he said, "before I drip all over the sidewalk. Or, before someone sees me standing here bleeding from what should have been a fatal gunshot wound."

She opened her mouth, but no sound emerged. She shook her head, trying to clear it. There had to be a logical explanation. Her brain just couldn't grasp it.

Delaroche's scowl faded. His features softened. Then he raised a hand to her face, noticed the blood on his fingertips, and lowered his arm. "Please," he added in a softly pleading tone. "We need to talk. The situation is now urgent. I won't hurt you. I swear it on my very long life, but we have to get inside before someone decides to investigate that gunshot."

Had anyone heard? Would they bother to investigate if they had? Or would they assume it was a car backfiring?

Gerard propelled her across the sidewalk and up the steps to stand at the front door. "If I was going to harm you, I would have done so already."

He had a point. Whatever he was—and she wasn't about to think the word, much less say it—he wasn't an immediate threat. But was he really a...

Idiot. There's no such thing. But she was so upping her meds.

Hands shaking, she reached inside her purse. Gerard plucked the key from her grasp and unlocked the door to pull her inside. "Which way to the kitchen?"

"What?" Her thoughts were a jumbled mess—as if she'd just awakened from a nightmare. But this wasn't a dream. It was real.

"You're in shock. You need some water or something." He looked down at his shirt. The dark fabric camouflaged the bloodstain, but a tiny stream ran down his arm and dripped from his fingertips. He wiped his hand on his pants again, but it looked as if the bleeding had stopped, which wasn't possible.

Amber stared at the ruby droplets on her oak floor—tiny specks of blood spatter evidence in her foyer. At least forensics could get DNA if she turned up dead or missing. Her purse slipped from her shoulder and landed beside her left foot with a soft thump. If he attacked, no one would even hear her scream.

"Amber," he said softly, gently nudging her forward. "Which way to the kitchen?"

She blinked, trying to focus her fear-numbed mind. A shiver passed over her. She cleared her throat. "Through the foyer and to the right."

Gerard cupped her elbow and guided her through the dark house as if the rooms were brightly lit. She tried not to think about it, but her mind kept going back to that night in Germany and the St. Rochus Cemetery in Nuremberg. If only she'd had her gun. If only she had it now.

Once in the kitchen, Gerard released her arm and turned away from her, revealing the grip of her gun hanging over the waistband of his jeans. She tugged it free and held it to her chest like a security blanket. It might be useless against him, but it made her feel safer, and she would not go down without a fight.

Gerard looked at her with brows raised but said nothing. Then he turned to the refrigerator and opened the door. Light filled the darkened kitchen. He reached for a bottle of water. She brushed his hand aside and grabbed a beer instead.

"I think I'm going to need it," she said, placing the gun on the counter. She pulled a magnetic bottle opener from the side of the refrigerator and opened the beer. Turning up the cold brew, she chugged nearly half. Gerard watched, his eyes glowing with interest—or hunger. Her throat knotted. She forced herself to swallow before she strangled. Lowering the bottle with shaking hands, she suppressed a shiver. Would he attack now? Could she reach her gun in time if he did?

"Can you turn on the light? I don't like the dark." It reminded her of Germany and that terrifying night in the cemetery, but this time, she had a gun.

Nodding, he turned from the counter and walked to the wall to switch on the light. When he turned back around, she had the Glock drawn and aimed...this time at his head. "If I blow your brains out, will you recover as quickly?" Her voice was calm, her aim steady. This wasn't Germany, and she wasn't unarmed.

"Not unless the bullet lodges in my brain. The brain can't heal if there's a bullet inside. Or you could use silver bullets. Your aim doesn't have to be as precise then."

The gun shook. Her heart slammed against her ribs, stealing her breath. She wheezed.

"You could also set me ablaze. We don't like to burn. It's very painful, and I might not survive. A sterling silver stake through the heart would do it. Or a wooden stake in a pinch. Just make sure the body explodes into dust before removing the weapon or walking away. We're hard to kill."

"We?" As in more than one like him? Her heart pounded against her ribs. Her hands felt like ice. "It's not possible. It can't be."

Yet, she'd seen first-hand proof in Germany. She'd even reported it to her commander. He convinced her it was post-traumatic stress. After the incident in Iraq, it made sense. And the meds helped. Oh, how they'd helped. Take enough Trazadone and you slept like the dead. And woke up feeling real damn mellow, no matter how crazy your dreams.

"Yes, we. We need someone on the inside." His eyes narrowed to concentrated slits. She avoided his gaze.

"I saw your picture." And everyone knew vampires didn't photograph.

He smiled a patronizing smile that reminded her of First Sergeant Clifton's, an enlisted superior who treated female soldiers like half-wits.

"We can blur our image on regular film, but digital photos are instant and don't need developing, so it's easier to catch us unaware." His tone lacked even a hint of scorn, and the disparity between his attitude and his words was disconcerting. Not to mention the fact that he was bat-shit crazy.

Delaroche wasn't a vampire, and he wasn't a threat. She lowered the gun and met his gaze. "I'm sure dealing with Miss Gallagher's death has been stressful. But there are people you can talk to—professional people who can help. I can recommend someone if you'd like." At one time, she'd had her therapist on speed-dial.

He rolled his eyes and huffed. "Stop pretending ignorance. You know what I am."

"A vampire. Really?" She wanted to scoff, but a chill shivered over her skin. He wasn't dead, and she'd shot him—at point blank range.

Maybe he was wearing Kevlar. But wouldn't Kevlar show through that tight-fitting shirt? Perhaps not. But there had to be a logical explanation. Ignoring the warning bells clanging inside her skull, she shoved the Glock back in its holster and reached for the beer she'd deposited on the counter. She took another long, hard pull on the bottle, hoping to douse irrational thoughts.

Gerard inhaled sharply. His eyes devoured her. Despite renewed fear, she managed to set the bottle back on the counter without dropping it. He's not a vampire.

"I'd give anything to drink beer again," he said in a reverent voice.

Amber nearly laughed out loud. Her shoulders sagged. Gerard Delaroche wasn't a vampire, and he didn't want to drink her blood. He wanted a beer—like a normal guy—because he was normal. She was the one off her rocker.

"Want one?" She forced herself to meet his intense stare.

He smiled. "Can't. Vampire. Remember?"

Like that was something a girl could forget. It wasn't every day a hot guy claimed to be a vampire. Hell, maybe he was a vampire. The man could stop bullets with his chest.

He took a hesitant step closer. She stiffened and took another cautious swallow of beer. He stopped three feet away. Good. Sexy and crazy was a dangerous combination.

"Vampirism is a virus," he said, eyeing her beer like a man dying of thirst. "We lack the enzymes needed to digest solid foods and most liquids. Other than blood, the only thing vampires drink is wine. I guess it has something to do with the alcohol. I don't know." He smiled as if recalling a fond memory. "We can also eat sugar free popsicles. I found that out a couple of years ago before Megan—Dr. Harper—created the anti-virus. She fell in love with Vincent and risked her life to help him, but the vaccine works. It's not the cure we'd hoped for, but it alleviates some of our symptoms so we can live more human lives."

"A cure for vampirism?" Really? She was so not buying into this bullshit. But she'd humor him. For now. "I suppose the vaccine is the reason you can come out before sunset."

"Oui. It's also how I can now eat very rare stake and pork. But other foods still make me violently ill. So, I've been afraid to try beer. The malt and hops..."

He shook his head. "The last time I tried it, I thought I'd die. I didn't of course, but for several hours, I wanted to."

He didn't look crazy. He looked damn good—for a man suffering from psychotic delusions. She assumed a non-threatening posture, relaxing her shoulders and holding her hands loosely at her side. She didn't want him to snap and go all vampire on her. "Uh huh. And when was that?"

"1799," he said with a smile. "I died when I was forty-two."

He sounded serious—and perfectly sane. Shouldn't a man suffering from paranoid delusions look crazy? Delaroche's eyes weren't wild, and they weren't feverishly darting about. His gaze was steady, though he didn't stare in that intense way that made her paranoid. He didn't act as irrational as he sounded either. He wasn't sweating or ringing his hands. He didn't twitch or jump at shadows. In fact, he seemed perfectly calm.

She raked his hard body with a steady gaze, searching for some visible sign of mental illness. If he was sick, he didn't look it. His skin was a bit pale, but it wasn't an unhealthy pallor. He had streaks of silver in his brown hair and crow's feet at the corner of his deep blue eyes, but he looked pretty damn good for a man who claimed to be a middle-aged vampire.

"You could pass for a man in his mid-thirties." She reached for her beer and took another swallow.

"That's one benefit of being a vampire. It preserves the body and erases all environmental signs of aging."

"Uh huh. So, how old do you claim to be?" Not that she wanted to know. Not that she was sure she'd even believe him.

"Over two hundred. And it's not bullshit."

Anger fueled her blood. She drained her beer and slammed the empty bottle on the counter. "Reading my mind again?"

"No. Your face. Don't ever play poker." His lips quirked in one hell of a smile. She didn't know whether to apologize for her outburst or slap the smirk off his handsome face.

Ignoring him, she turned toward the refrigerator and reached inside for another beer. Before she could shut the door, he edged her out of the way and pushed his head inside.

"What are you looking for?"

"Wine."

"Not blood?" Did he really expect her to believe he was a vampire?

He pulled his head from the refrigerator and caught her gaze. "I drink blood because I have too to survive—cold blood by the way, from a supply we keep at Lifeblood. I drink wine because I can."

"Cut the bullshit. Tell me why you're here and then get the hell out of my house." She narrowed her gaze. "And if I'm not satisfied with your answers, I might still slap handcuffs on your sorry ass and place you under arrest."

"You could try that," he said, ducking back into the refrigerator. There was a bottle of Bordeaux on the bottom shelf. He captured his prize and straightened.

"You can't drink that. It was a gift from my father." He'd given it to her as a belated birthday present the last time she saw him. Two years ago. At Christmas—a Christmas he didn't spend with her because he was on a

Christmas cruise with his wife and her daughter. Amber had eaten Christmas dinner with Reid and his mother before returning to her empty house to spend the remainder of the holiday alone.

A frown marred Gerard's face. "He can give you another bottle. Can't he?"

"I was going to drink it with him." If they ever made up—if he'd swallow his damn stubborn pride and apologize for choosing his wife and step daughter over her—his own flesh and blood. She sure as hell wasn't going to Florida to apologize to him—or spend time with that woman and her bubble-headed teen.

She crossed the kitchen and sat at the table without telling him where she kept the glasses or corkscrew. He rummaged through cabinets and drawers until he found what he needed. After pouring a glass of the dark red wine, he sat across from her, eyeing her with suspicion. "Who's Nicolas?"

Fear zapped her like an electric current. The tingle set her heart and mind racing with disturbing thoughts and nightmarish memories that couldn't have been real. She swallowed, a terrible suspicion warring with dread. "How do you know about Nicolas?"

"Today at the office, you thought of him while you were questioning me."

She stared at his reflection in the kitchen table. Vampires weren't supposed to have reflections. Then again, mortal men didn't sip wine after being shot in the chest at point-blank range either. "Are you psychic?"

The corner of his mouth twitched. He didn't smile. "No. But I do have certain abilities. We all do."

There's that "we" again. Her subconscious had known for years, but acknowledging the truth didn't make it easier to accept. Vampires were real. But how many were there? A couple? A couple thousand?

My name is Legion: for we are many.

She forced irrational thoughts aside, refusing to listen to her subconscious mind spouting scripture from the Book of Mark. Armed with logic, she said, "You can't be a vampire. I see your reflection."

He shrugged. "It doesn't come naturally because most vampires believe the legends. It's all in the mind, really. We just have to ignore what we believe about our own nature."

A shiver snaked down her spine. She rubbed the back of her neck, loosening the pins that held her braid in place at the nape. Then she pulled the rubber band free and raked her fingers through her hair, fluffing it around her shoulders. It had been pinned to her scalp so long the roots ached. Hell, her whole head ached, but it had nothing to do with the rubber band. Her mind was in turmoil, searching for a logical explanation that didn't include vampires.

She took a long, hard swallow of beer and gently placed the bottle back on the table. Glass clinked against glass. If Vampires existed, they lived in a shadowy unseen world because their survival hinged on mortals believing they were nothing more than legends.

"Why are you telling me this?" she asked, already suspecting his motives.

"Because we're both in danger," Gerard said in a voice filled with compassion.

Amber bared her teeth. "I'm a big girl. And I carry a gun. Remember?"

"How useful was that gun when you shot me?" he said, leaning forward to rest his forearms on the table.

The smile slipped from her face. Shit! If vampires were real, then mortals were at the bottom of the food chain. "If you're invincible, I guess that puts me in danger."

"Not from me. Technically, I'm the one in danger."

"How?" Whether she wanted to openly admit it or not, she was afraid, but knowledge was power, and she needed all the information she could gather.

Gerard shrugged those wide shoulders. "I'm vulnerable during the day. Remember? Stake in the heart and all that. And if the government knew vampires existed, they'd wipe us out or release Colonel Timmons from prison and let him complete his project."

She might not believe in vampires, but she was a cop, and Timmons' name was in her files. "What project?"

"Timmons was working on a black ops military operation designed to improve a soldier's endurance in the field. Dr. Steve Weldon was lead scientist on the project. He extracted vampire DNA in a failed attempt to clone vampires. I was his guinea pig."

Despite Gerard's irrational claims and the offhand way he spoke, she saw the truth in his eyes. Or at least, the truth as he believed it to be.

Sympathy tugged at her heart. If vampires were real, they healed at an incredible rate. How much pain could they endure without dying? Was that part of Weldon's experiments—to test a vampire's tolerance? Had Gerard suffered intolerable pain?

She straightened, pretending she hadn't noticed the hurt in his eyes. Vampire or not, Delaroche had information about the case. "Was Tina Gallagher involved in the colonel's research?"

Tina Gallagher had worked at Baldwin Industries before going to Lifeblood, and Colonel Timmons had been arrested for misappropriation of government funds after an incident at the research facility in Alexandria, Virginia. Whether the incident involved vampires or not didn't change the facts. Timmons had lost a government contract worth millions.

"Tina was Megan's lab assistant at Baldwin, and they both worked with Weldon," Gerard said in a voice laced with sorrow. "They didn't know about vampires then. They thought Weldon was crazy."

Weldon probably was crazy and dangerous. If he blamed Tina for Timmons' arrest, he could have been the one to slit her throat. At least it was a logical motive—more logical than vampires.

"Do you have proof of Weldon's involvement in the Lifeblood murders?" She needed evidence—not conjecture based on wild tales of vampire experiments.

Gerard ground his teeth. "There's no mortal proof, at least nothing I can share without exposing my kind, but the facts remain. A vampire killed Richard and tried to cover it up by slicing his throat afterward, and Weldon killed Tina." Pain flashed across his face, deeper than before. "He threatened her when she left Baldwin, and he's still experimenting. We destroyed evidence of our existence before the government shut down Baldwin Industries, but Weldon escaped justice, and now he's working with a vampire."

"There was no mention of Weldon communicating threats to Ms. Gallagher in the case file. So, if there's no mortal proof, what's your immortal proof?" Had she really asked such an absurd question?

He averted his gaze. "Because samples of Megan's vampire vaccine are missing."

She crossed her arms and glared. "That wasn't in the report either."

His sexy snort did nothing to lessen her irritation. "We want to pass for human. Reporting a stolen vampire vaccine wouldn't accomplish that goal, and Tina wasn't the primary target. Megan was."

"What about Richard? And Axle? How do they fit into your scenario?" Even if he was right on all counts, she couldn't investigate. Who'd believe her?

Gerard shrugged. "Richard's death was a reward for Weldon's rogue vampire friend or a way to send the cops scurrying in a hundred different directions while Vincent and I sit around with our thumbs up our asses, too afraid to do anything for fear of discovery, but Axle's disappearance frightens me. I think Weldon took him—maybe to test the vaccine after turning him into a vampire." He shrugged again before his shoulders sagged on a defeated sigh. "It would explain why he hasn't resurfaced."

"So would a drug connection." She told him Reid's theory. Gerard didn't buy it.

"Axle had nothing to do with the murders. He's a victim."

"Until we find him, we can't be sure." As if she could be sure of anything. And since when were she and Gerard a team? Reid was her partner even if she couldn't share what she'd learned tonight without him thinking she was crazy. She just needed to approach the investigation without acknowledging the existence of vampires so she could keep him in the loop.

Vampires needed an invitation to enter a building. Didn't they? She'd more or less invited Gerard into her home. Hadn't she? Or was he just being polite when he'd suggested she invite him inside? Regardless, someone had let Dr. Weldon and his vampire inside Lifeblood Labs the night Tina and Richard were murdered. Could Axle have done it? Was he working with the mad doctor?

"Who let Weldon and his, um, accomplice inside the facility that night?" she asked.

Gerard arched a brow. "The vampire let him in."

Irritation scraped her nerves. "How did the vampire get in? Can they materialize wherever they want?"

"It can appear that way to mortals because of the speed at which we travel. But we also have the ability to move small, inanimate objects with our minds. So, unlocking a door that requires security access isn't a problem."

Tension tightened the muscles in her neck. Her shoulders bunched. "So, how do I know you didn't kill your employees? You have a security code."

Gerard met her gaze, and then his straight white teeth changed. His incisors grew, stretching into long, lethal fangs. She nearly peed her pants. Pushing to her feet, she knocked over her chair. "What the fu—"

"I didn't kill her. I loved her. But you can see how easily I could have. I'm a vampire. Even if I didn't work there, I wouldn't need a code to get in."

He rose to his feet and came around the table. She took a staggering step back, her hand automatically going to her holster to draw her Glock and aim it at his head. "Get out of my house."

Gerard stood stone still. He didn't even flinch. "Are you really going to shoot me? Again?" He crossed his arms.

Could she? Even if it didn't kill him, could she intentionally inflict pain when he wasn't posing an immediate threat? Her pulse jumped. "Second time's the charm."

"If I wanted to hurt you, I would have done so already—without warning. Just like the vampire who attacked you in Germany."

She felt the color leach from her face. Her hands shook. Gerard stepped forward and wrapped his hands around hers, gently forcing her to lower the gun. She didn't resist despite the fact that he'd made no effort to exert his influence over her. When her arm dropped limply to her side, he slipped the gun from her cold fingers and laid the weapon on the table. Amber stood weak and silent, her body shaking.

"I didn't think it was real," she whispered. "The doctors convinced me it was PTSD."

Gerard led her from the kitchen and into the living room. He circled the coffee table and eased her onto one end of the sectional sofa. Then he sat beside her. She fell limply against the cushions and closed her eyes.

"I'm sorry I invaded your thoughts yesterday, but I had to know what you knew about the murders," he said.

She kept her eyes squeezed shut, refusing to open them. Maybe this was a nightmare. If she didn't acknowledge him, the dream would change. Or she'd wake up.

"Imagine my surprise when I discovered your prior exposure to vampires," he said with a touch of irony.

"I don't know what you're talking about." Liar! Weird thoughts had flashed through her mind yesterday, fuzzy distorted images from crazy-ass dreams that seemed to overlay actual memories. Most likely, looking at crime scene photos and reading autopsy reports of punctured arteries and trocars draining blood had triggered long-forgotten memories—memories best left in the past.

"The images I saw in your head were distorted and random," Gerard said, reading her damn mind again. Or maybe not. She didn't feel disoriented like she had before. "But what's actual memory and what's nightmare, Amber?"

She raised her lids, challenging him with her eyes. "Why not jump inside my head again and find out?"

"Because I don't like to do it. C'est mal poli. It's rude."

"Then don't do it. Ever again. Not to me. Understand?"

"Oui. I understand."

Man, that accent got to her. It made her toes curl. So did his smile. And she hated it. She didn't want to relax her guard or cozy up to Gerard Delaroche. She should treat him like a murder suspect. Or a witness. She shouldn't get all friendly with him. But the man had such an easy going nature when he put his mind to it—and he was damn easy on the eyes too. What gal wouldn't be drawn in?

"I'm probably bat-shit crazy to think vampires are real."

"Do you want to see my fangs again?" he asked with a smile—a smile that looked perfectly normal and human.

Before she could respond, a chill shivered over her skin and the hair on the nape of her neck stood on end. Gerard rose to his feet, sniffing the air like a predatory animal.

"Stay here," he said. Then he vanished.

Chapter 5

Like hell. Amber ran to the kitchen and retrieved her Glock. Comforted by its weight, she returned to the living room. Gerard was gone. He'd disappeared into thin air. She closed her eyes, forcing herself to replay that split second in her mind. There was still no memory of seeing him move, but there was a near simultaneous memory of sound—the sound of her front door slamming shut.

Her shoulders sagged on a sigh. Gerard hadn't actually vanished. He'd just moved faster than her mortal eyes could see. If he'd disappeared, he wouldn't have needed to use the front door. Relief flooded her veins. The realization wasn't profound, but it kept her functional. As long as she could function, she could make rational sense of what she'd just witnessed.

Yeah. Right.

She took a deep breath and stepped toward the foyer holding her weapon angled across her chest with the barrel pointed toward the ceiling. The fine hairs on the nape of her neck stood on end. Seconds before Gerard did his disappearing act, she'd had the sensation of being watched. It was the same sensation she'd experienced in Germany moments before she and Andrew were attacked. Most of that night was a blacked-out blur, but she remembered being thrown against a headstone. Unable to move or scream, paralyzed with fear, she'd watched in horror as a vam—as something or someone ripped open Andrew's throat and drained him of blood. Then, the creature had turned toward her, and Nicolas had saved her. Just as Gerard...

Was saving her now? Hardly. Most likely, a more primal instinct had compelled him to dash out the door sniffing the air like a wolf on the scent of a frightened rabbit. Taking a deep breath, she steeled her nerves. Fear would never hold her immobile again. She would react with courage, and she would react quickly.

She held the Glock close to her chest and stepped off the beige Berber carpet onto the hardwood in the entry hall. Dark stains dotted the oak—blood droplets where Gerard had dripped onto the floor. A twinge of guilt made her flinch.

Had the wound caused him pain? Had it healed completely?

Her fingers tightened on the Glock's textured grip. Frenzied thoughts of vampires and vampire legends filled her thoughts. Then another memory came rushing to the forefront—a memory from her childhood—deeply buried but never completely forgotten. Germany wasn't the only time Nicolas had saved her from attack. He'd rescued her once before when she was a child.

Nausea roiled up from the pit of her stomach. Was Gerard a threat?

"Nicolas?" she whispered.

"No. It's me."

Amber yelped and spun around. Years of training and experience saved Gerard from a second bullet. She lowered the Glock, forcing her rational mind to overrule her fear. If Gerard wanted her dead, he wouldn't have announced his presence.

"Do you know how close you came to buying the farm?" she snapped.

His lips twitched, but he didn't smile. "I'm not interested in farmland."

She scoffed, trying to pretend she didn't find the combination of his quick wit and attractive exterior appealing. Then he leaned against the doorframe between the living room and foyer and folded his muscled arms over his wide chest, and a rush of heat twisted her insides into warm sensual knots. A defeated sigh escaped. It was pointless to ignore the facts. Vampire or not, Gerard was sexy as hell.

The steady throbbing in her skull intensified, and her head felt as if it were going to explode. If vampires were involved in the Lifeblood murders, how would law enforcement ever bring the killers to justice? How would she ever explain any of this to Reid? An image of her partner sneaking through cold, dank catacombs at high noon with wooden stakes and silver crosses flashed through her mind and she nearly snorted aloud.

"Who are you planning to shoot with that thing?" Gerard asked as his eyes focused on the gun she'd lifted without conscious thought. She'd forgotten she was even holding it.

Heat burning her cheeks, she holstered her weapon. "No one. As you've already pointed out, bullets won't stop a vampire."

He smiled faintly. "Silver bullets are rather effective."

"Great. I'll make a note of that the next time I put in a requisition for ammo." Did munitions companies even make silver bullets?

She glanced at Gerard's shirt. His wound no longer bled. And the way he moved—besides being inhumanly fast—indicated a complete lack of discomfort. "If it wasn't for the blood on your shirt, I wouldn't even know I'd shot you."

"Que puis-je vous dire?" he said with a shrug. "What can I say? I'm a vampire. The wound still aches and I'm sure I have a bruise but by tomorrow, there won't even be a scar."

"A bruise?" She'd frickin' shot him. "It wasn't a through and through or a flesh wound. There's still a bullet inside you."

He shrugged again. "You missed my heart, and it's a foreign body. The bullet will work its way out through the original wound track when I fall into the regenerative sleep. When I awaken tomorrow night, I'll find the bullet in my bed."

Teetering on the edge of hysteria, she tried embracing her anger but could only manage impotent sarcasm. "Not your coffin?"

"No," he replied with a touch of annoyance.

Meds. I need Meds. She bent down to retrieve her purse from where she'd dropped it on the floor earlier. Then she brushed past him and into the living room. She needed to be on something a hell of a lot stronger than Ativan and Trazadone because this was way more than post-traumatic stress—a hell of a lot more. This could push her over the edge—if she wasn't there already. Until then, Ativan would have to suffice, and Trazadone at bedtime to help her sleep—despite the nightmares.

Her thoughts raced as panic ebbed and flowed, leaving her jumpy and unable to focus. She dropped onto the sofa, frantically searching her purse like a junky in desperate need of a fix. Gerard stood in the doorway, leaning negligently against the frame. Amber ignored him. Where the hell are my pills?

Taking deep, controlled breaths, she snagged the bottle, opened it, and poured a pill into her palm before popping it into her mouth. Then she swallowed with nothing more than spit.

"You think it's a good idea to take that after drinking beer?" he asked, coming closer.

"Probably not." Most likely, she'd have one hell of a headache in the morning. But the Ativan would calm her nerves and help her cope with this new version of reality—a reality she wasn't ready to face. "Okay, who or what was lurking outside my door?"

"I don't know, but he didn't smell mortal."

"Smell?" Was the man a vampire or a blood hound? She had a damn fine sense of smell herself, but Gerard didn't smell like a vampire—not that she knew what vampires smelled like. Musty and old, she supposed, but he smelled good. Real good. But it was the smell of masculine skin and cologne. Not some moldy vampire scent.

A chill washed over her, sending gooseflesh dancing along her skin. She shook it off, determined to face her fears. She had combat experience. She wasn't going to fall apart. Not this time. If a vampire had been lurking outside her door, she'd find a way to deal with it. She pressed two fingers to the side of her pounding skull and prayed. Lord, don't let me be going crazy.

Gerard sighed, sounding more tired than annoyed, as he dropped down beside her on the sofa. He shifted his hips and angled his legs toward hers. Their knees bumped. So did her heart. He was too damn close and way too sexy.

"It was definitely a vampire," he said, "but I didn't recognize his imprint."

"Color me stumped, but I have no clue what you're talking about." Yep, that's me. The crazy, hysterical female cop.

"Both vampires and mortals leave behind psychic imprints of themselves that linger long after they're gone. It's like a scent, but different. And mortals leave fainter imprints than vampires." He sniffed once and then frowned. "You, however, have a strong imprint for a mortal."

"Maybe it's my perfume." Except, she wasn't wearing any. She'd just gotten home from work, and she didn't wear perfume to work. She cleared her throat, avoiding eye contact. "So, are there a lot of vampires in the world?"

"Probably more than you'd think, but most keep a low profile."

"Yeah, so low your friend Sonia doesn't even have a last name."

A flush crept up his neck to stain his cheeks. "She's not my friend, but if you check your electronic records again tomorrow, you'll find both a last name and an address for her on file."

Anger stirred the ashes of a simmering resentment. She fisted her hands in her lap and glared. "I have paper copies that show nothing on her. Copies obtained through long hours of old-fashioned police work. "

His flush deepened. "Your records are inaccurate."

"What records? We found nothing."

Gerard shrugged, unable to maintain eye contact. "Well there's something there now. If you look again, you'll find a Sonia Dalca in Bat Cave, North Carolina."

The fury burned brighter. Amber embraced it. Anger was safer than fear—or attraction. Anger could keep her alive. Fear could get her killed. She didn't want to think about the other.

"We expended hours of man power in a fruitless search for Sonia because you and Maxwell refused to provide anything useful. Captain Stratford even searched local and FBI data bases without success. So, you better not be lying because I intent to go to that address to question her, and if no one by that name lives there, you'll definitely regret it." Yeah. Right. If a bullet didn't stop him, she seriously doubted her impotent threat would shake him. And what if Sonia was a tech savvy vampire with the power to manipulate public records? She could easily disappear without a trace, effectively erasing all evidence she'd ever existence.

Gerard nodded, casually crossing an ankle over his knee—not the least bit defensive. "She's expecting you, and she will cooperate."

Amber's gaze flickered over his warm, sympathetic expression. He wasn't judging her or trying to manipulate her. He even seemed to understand her anger and frustration. Her fury faded. "Okay. Fine. So, why couldn't we find anything on her before?" As if she didn't know. Some kind of freaking vampire hocus pocus, no doubt.

His lip curled. "Sonia is a master at keeping our existence a secret from mortals."

Amber met his gaze. "So, why don't you like her?"

His eyes widened a fraction before he schooled his expression. "What makes you think I don't?"

"You wouldn't make a good poker player either, Delaroche. Your eyes give you away every time."

"But I was a spy during the French Revolution," he said, a note of incredulity in his voice.

Seriously? His lips might lie but his eyes were a dead giveaway. "You're kidding. Right?"

"Non. It's true. I fought with the Marquis de Lafayette here in America and in France."

"You fought in the American Revolution—with Lafayette?" Well, at least that was something they had in common. He'd been a soldier too—over two hundred years ago.

"That's how I met Vincent. During the war. After Cornwallis's surrender, I returned to France and posed as a supporter of our king to gather information for the Marquis. But the radical Jacobin's didn't want moderate change. And evidently, I wasn't good at subterfuge," he added with a self-deprecating smile. "A Jacobin spy learned I was plotting against them."

"Is that how you died?" Not a typical interview question, but her world had unexpectedly taken on the surreal atmosphere of a cult video game.

"I never technically died. After the Jacobin slit my throat, Vincent arrived. Before I took my last breath, he took what remained of my blood and fed me his. To save me," he added when he seemed to notice her horrified expression.

"He made you a vampire!" The bastard turned his own friend, and Gerard was defending him.

His jaw bunched and a muscle jumped in his cheek. "Don't judge what you can't understand."

If she'd had Vincent's abilities, would she have let Andrew die? Would she have chosen an immortal mother over no mother at all? Her righteous indignation fizzled and died. "You're right. I shouldn't judge. So, help me out here, Frenchie."

"Frenchie?" His lip curled. "Merde! I'd rather you call me vampire."

"Okay, Vampire," she said, half smiling. "How can you so easily forgive Vincent for making you what you are, but you dislike Sonia for relishing her nature?"

Was there something between Sonia and Gerard? Unexpected jealousy burned like acid in her stomach.

"I don't dislike her," he said as if carefully weighing his words. "I just don't understand her. She goes to great lengths to keep our existence a secret from mortals and yet, she flaunts her nature as if being vampire was a privilege instead of a curse." He ground his teeth. "Her wardrobe is designed to draw attention and she hangs out in Fang Clubs, drinking the blood of willing donors who believe she's a pretender rather than the real deal. She's a security risk."

Revulsion made her nauseous. "She turns her donors into vampires?"

Gerard waved a hand as if shooing a fly. "Of course not. Drinking mortal blood doesn't convert them. Blood must be exchanged before conversion occurs. The way Vincent exchanged his blood with mine. It's a bit like the AIDS virus that way."

Was Sonia willingly spreading the disease? "Is she dangerous?" Duh. The woman was a vampire. Of course she was dangerous.

"She definitely has the potential. Not all vampires are as sweet and loveable as me," he said with a sexy smile before his expression turned serious. "Some are deadly."

"I'm a cop. Remember? I'm used to dealing with scumbags." But not scumbags with supernatural abilities.

He met her gaze, staring intently, as if trying to decide whether or not to share some deep dark secret. But seriously, what could be deeper or darker than what she already knew? The cat was out of the bag...or rather...the vampire was out of the coffin. She might not be completely sane, but she could no longer deny the truth. Vampires were real.

The silence stretched. So did her taut nerves. She bit her lip, nervously twisting her fingers together. Besides being inhumanly fast and practically indestructible, vampires lived in almost total obscurity. And they had the power to manipulate witnesses and make evidence disappear. Hadn't Gerard done that very thing?

He cleared his throat, as if he'd reached a decision. "For the most part, vampires don't pose a threat to civilized society. We're no different than the mortals we once were. Some are good. Some aren't. We're just trying to survive eternity the best we can without losing our sanity."

"Mortals don't survive off the blood of others," she said, stating the obvious.

"Mon Dieu! You think we chose this life?" His voice sounded hollow, his eyes so miserable she wanted to bite back the words—no pun intended. But she could no more unsay them than she could un-fire the bullet lodged in his chest.

Her voice softened. "You can choose whether or not to take a life."

"Did you choose to kill in Iraq?" Even though there was no judgment in his voice or eyes, she flinched, as horrific images of blood and death flashed through her mind.

"It was kill or be killed. But you admitted vampires can survive without killing. You drink stored blood. Sonia takes from willing donors without killing. So, if a vampire kills, it's a choice. Not survival."

His shoulders sagged as if burdened by a heavy weight. "Being immortal takes a toll on the soul. Eventually, some lose touch with the last vestige of humanity. Once that happens, some vampires relieve the tedium of living by blending into the most violent of mortal societies, posing as drug dealers and mob bosses. Still, other vampires cling to their mortal roots, watching over their—descendants—protecting them—directing their lives."

His gaze turned serious, penetrating, as if trying to gage her thoughts without reading them. "I think the vampire outside your door tonight has been watching over you. Perhaps he's your ancestor."

Fear settled like a rock in the pit of her stomach. For years, she'd sensed something unseen in the dark, something waiting. Watching. She'd blamed her tour in Iraq for the paranoia. But what if she was wrong? What if something watched at night? She shivered.

Yep. Definitely time to up the meds. Even with the beer kicker, the Ativan just wasn't cutting it.

"There're no vampires hanging from my family tree. Before you flashed those wicked fangs, I didn't even believe in vampires. I thought I made Nicolas up to cope with my friend, Andrew's death." But buried memories from her past were rising up to haunt her days as well as her nights. The nightmares she'd suffered for years were more than just dreams. They were memories—memories she'd desperately tried to suppress.

"How did Andrew die?" His compassionate tone drew her in, encouraging her to confess her darkest secrets.

A tremor shook her. Her pulse pounded, heavy and hard against her ribs. "He was murdered. I was with him when—" Her voice cracked. Swallowing past a near-overwhelming lump of emotion, she added, "It was easier to let the Polizei, the MP's, my commander, and the army doctors convince me we'd been attacked by a drug-crazed Gypsy. It made a hell of a lot more sense than the truth."

He held her gaze. "And what's the truth? Tell me about Germany. And Nicolas."

She wanted to rebel. To push him away. But it would be such a relief to unburden the guilt she'd shouldered since coming home. She needed to tell someone about Iraq and that night in Germany—someone who wouldn't think she was crazy.

A tear escaped. She brushed it aside and held a fist to the painful ache in her chest. "Andrew and I were both specialists with the 615th MP company stationed in Grafenwöhr. Then our unit was deployed to the Nineveh Province in Iraq. We were supposed to return to Germany after twelve months, but our tour was extended as part of the 'stop-loss' program. Most of us handled the extension well." Everyone except Sergeant Morrison.

Morrison had never been what Amber considered an exemplary field officer, but after his wife filed for divorce, he lost control. And her respect. His way of dealing with stress was to alternately revile or hit on women and verbally abuse his soldiers. "One night, our squad was called to protect an Iraqi police station from insurgents. I was in one of three Humvees sent out to reinforce the station. I usually drove, but that night, I manned the exposed 50-caliber machine gun." And she'd killed at least two Iraqis. Maybe more. Their deaths did not sit well on her conscience. Her nails dug into her palms. She took a deep breath, grinding her back teeth. Her jaw ached. Gerard watched her closely, his gaze inviting her to continue.

She exhaled, forcing her shoulders to relax. "Every convoy going into that part of Baghdad had been attacked. It wasn't a question of whether we'd get hit but when. And I had a bad feeling about our mission from the moment we got the call. Tensions were running high and nerves were already frayed when the first mortar struck. We couldn't even move because two of the Humvees were disabled." The fear came back as real and fresh as if it had happened yesterday. Images flashed through her mind. Her pulse raced as she nervously bounced her heel on the floor.

"There was this sergeant from Wisconsin," she said, recalling Morrison's glassy-eyed stare. "He cowered when he should have taken command. He ducked behind a Humvee and just kept screaming for us to stay down. Then another soldier, Hodges, ordered us to lay down cover fire until our sharpshooter could get into position. Morrison went ballistic. He ordered Hodges to rush the sniper—without waiting for confirmation on the sniper's location. Hodges died.

Then Morrison ordered another man to charge. The sniper got him too. I wanted the sniper to get Morrison. I didn't want him dead. Just injured so someone else could take command. Then Morrison told Andrew to rush the sniper. Andrew refused. He said we should follow Hodges' plan and give the sharpshooter time to find the target. Morrison pulled his revolver and stood. The sniper got him before he could shoot Andrew."

Bile burned the back of her throat. Her vision blurred. Gerard loomed closer, his big warm body giving her comfort and strength. Knowing he listened without judgment made it difficult to continue. She swallowed, forcing the words from a throat gone dry. "Afterwards, no one talked about that night. It was like we'd made a silent pact. Morrison was awarded the Purple Heart posthumously. But once we were back in Germany, I started having nightmares. When I ran into Andrew, he said he was having trouble sleeping too. He felt as guilty as I did."

She blinked to clear an embedded image of Morrison from her mind—his head snapping back before jerking forward, his eyes widening as the sniper's bullet found its mark, piercing his forehead below his helmet. The back of his head exploded, spraying blood and gray matter onto the Humvee. His body twitched as if jolted by a thousand volts of electricity. A single crimson ribbon trickled from the wound, rolling over the bridge of his nose to pool in the corner of his left eye just before his knees buckled and he dropped to the sand.

Amber covered her mouth with cold, numb fingers. The image refused to fade. She took a deep breath, bringing her emotions under control before dropping her hand to her lap. "Andrew and I started talking. Then we started dating."

Gerard's expression changed. Amber wasn't sure what emotion flashed behind those eyes because he quickly masked it. "Were you in love with him?"

Pain and loss tugged at her heart. God, she missed him. His friendship. His understanding. He'd been a friend with benefits. But love?

"No," she said honestly. "I cared for him deeply. We shared a traumatic experience that bound us in ways a husband and wife never connect, but we were dysfunctional. It wouldn't have lasted even if he'd lived. But we did date. We went to Nuremberg one night and visited the St. Rochus cemetery. We were attacked. I know now it was a vampire. It—killed Andrew. And I—froze. But Nicolas saved me." Just like when she was little. She swallowed that painful memory, unable to deal with it.

"Don't blame yourself, chérie." Gerard leaned closer; his eyes filled with understanding and something deeper. Something far more dangerous. "The vampire who attacked your friend entranced you. He would have killed you too if Nicolas hadn't shown up. The question is why? His arrival couldn't have been a coincidence. "

His compassion drew her in, tempting her to relax her guard, but she needed to put some distance between them. He was a vampire—a potential killer. And she was a cop.

"I don't know. I don't know anything anymore."

Chapter 6

Gerard stayed away from Amber the following evening, giving her time to deal with her newfound knowledge—knowledge he hated dumping on her—knowledge she'd need to find Tina's killer. He spent the next night wrestling with his conscience, wondering if he shouldn't erase all memories of the truth from her mind and continue the search for Weldon without her.

Vincent was more concerned with keeping Megan safe than in justice or revenge. Sonia had given up the search all together. She'd already returned to her frivolous life of clubs and meaningless sex without a second thought. Gerard wanted revenge. Another mark on his soul.

Weldon had gotten away with his inhuman experiments. He would not get away with murder—even if Gerard had to enlist the help of a mortal detective. Determination led him back to Amber's door. He knocked, waiting impatiently as she stared through the peephole at him for what seemed like hours rather than seconds.

"You were supposed to be a nightmare," she said when she flung open the door. Her brown hair was unbound. It hung in soft waves about her shoulders. Her sleeveless red tank showed a hint of cleavage, her denim shorts a half-mile of tan, smooth legs.

Mon Dieu! Unwanted heat rushed to his groin, hardening him instantly.

He cleared his throat and tried to look at her eyes instead of those high, firm breasts. "Sorry to disappoint."

She harrumphed. "Not as sorry as I am." Then a smile touched her lips. "So, I guess I should invite you in. Huh?"

"I don't actually need an invitation to enter, but we really do need to discuss the case, and I'm trying to show manners. So, please, Amber. May I come in?"

She arched shapely brows. "Great. This is just what I needed after a stressful day of evading my partner's questions and trying to think of ways to investigate without mentioning vampires."

Doubts and second thoughts plagued him. Was it fair to drag her into his dark world? Fair to come between her and her partner? "Maybe this was a mistake," he said turning to leave.

She touched his arm. "You're here now. And I do have more questions."

Heat shot straight to his groin again, and he almost groaned aloud when she held open the door for him to enter. Whether instinct, the need for revenge, or inappropriate lust led him, he wasn't sure. And he wasn't sure he wanted to find out. Knowing he'd surely live to regret it, he crossed the threshold. Amber closed the door and turned toward the living room. He followed, watching the swing of her hips until she dropped down onto the sofa and curled her feet under her bottom.

With a resigned sigh, he sat beside her, angling his body toward hers. "I came here tonight to ask for your help. I shouldn't have. Tina died because of her association with vampires. I don't want the same thing happening to you."

"Don't worry about it. It's my job to investigate crimes and search for the truth—even if the evidence points to vampires," she added with a reticent smile.

Her fear was obvious, but Gerard sensed she wouldn't let it prevent her from doing her job. Backing down didn't seem part of her nature. "You could be in real danger—danger you can't handle with that gun of yours."

"I'm a big girl," she said, trying to sound tough.

Gerard smelled her fear as keenly as he smelled the clean, floral scent of her shampoo. The woman was too damn stubborn for her own good.

Frustration tightened his jaw. "Night before last, a vampire was outside your door. It could happen again when I'm not here to protect you."

"I can protect myself," she said with determination. "Besides, I thought you said Nicolas was watching over me. If that's not the case, then why was he here? What kind of threat does he pose?"

Aside from taking her blood? Gerard wasn't sure. But the vampire he'd sensed didn't seem as interested in Amber as in checking out Gerard. Not that Gerard had seen him or gotten a good whiff of his scent. It was just a mental impression from the faint imprint the vampire had left behind.

Amber had survived a vampire attack before. If Nicolas was still keeping tabs on her, he might have watched outside her door to ensure Gerard wasn't a threat. Then again, Gerard had no way of knowing it was Nicolas.

"I said I thought you were his descendent," he said, closely watching her reactions. "You're the one who said his name was Nicolas. I never saw him.

For all I know, the vampire who attacked you in Germany found out you were investigating our kind and came back to finish the job."

Fear flashed behind her eyes. She quickly masked it and stiffened her spine. "Seems I'm in danger whether I work with you or not. So, I guess I have to work with you. It's not like I can share this information with Reid."

Excluding her partner obviously bothered her. And for some reason, that bothered Gerard. "Don't do me any favors," he grumbled. "Tina kept me at arm's length but at least she trusted me." And damn it, he wanted Amber's trust too.

He could have manipulated her thoughts the way Vincent manipulated her partner's. One mental push had convinced Detective Sheridan to leave Megan alone. That shit probably wouldn't work on Amber—at least not for long. She'd had her thoughts scrambled before. The memories were returning, but Amber was fighting them—just as she'd fought Gerard when he invaded her mind to look for evidence.

She looked thoughtful and just a bit suspicious. "If Tina trusted you, why would she avoid you? Was she afraid of you because you're a vampire?"

"No," he grumbled. "She was afraid for her child."

A flush stained Amber's cheeks, but her apparent embarrassment didn't stop her from slipping into detective mode. "Then why did she go to work for vampires? Why get involved if she feared for her daughter?"

Silence stretched between them as Gerard considered the best way to answer. He wanted to be honest, but truth was subjective and open for interpretation. Anything he said in defense of vampires could be twisted and used against him. It was as if he were back in France, pretending allegiance to the Jacobins, knowing one misspoken word could send him to the guillotine.

"Tina knew about Weldon's vampire research," he said at last. "When she left Baldwin Industries, he smeared her professional reputation. Colonel Timmons was still a threat, and Weldon had ruined her chances of future employment. So, we offered her protection and a position at Lifeblood. She accepted. She even helped Megan with the vaccine. But she didn't want to expose her daughter to vampires. It didn't matter how she felt about me. She wanted to protect her child." Not that it had done a damn bit of good. Tina was dead, and Emily no longer had a mother. But at least the child was safe, and she now lived with her father.

Amber's concentrated gaze studied every nuance of his face as if she were searching for signs of deceit. "Did that piss you off?"

His heart slammed against his ribs. "You think that was my motive for killing her?"

"No…" she hesitated. Her face flushed. "It's a routine question. I'd appreciate an answer."

Routine? Merde! She was treating him like a suspect. He ground his teeth, fighting useless frustration. A cop would never trust a vampire. "I didn't kill her."

"Did you love her?"

The question jolted him. He straightened, his thoughts turning inward. Was he in love with Tina? Or did he see a relationship with her as my one shot at having a family? "I don't know," he said at last.

"Did you sleep with her?"

Anger returned, burning like acid in his gut. He'd taken a monumental risk telling Amber the truth—and she was using the knowledge to build a case against him.

"I said she kept me at arms' length. Did you expect me to force myself on her because I'm a vampire?"

"No. But—"

"Did you expect I'd ignore her motherly concerns and use glamour to get her into bed?" Contempt tightened his jaw. "You might as well accuse me of rape."

"I didn't accuse you," she shouted over his growl. She squared her shoulders and straightened her spine. Red splotches stained her cheeks but her voice was cool—professional—when she added, "I'm searching for a motive. Charles Peterson might not have known you weren't sleeping with his ex-wife."

It was his turn to flush. He opened his mouth to apologize for jumping to the wrong conclusions but snapped his jaw shut before uttering a word. Seconds ago, she'd practically accused him of killing Tina. Night before last, she'd wanted to believe drug dealers committed the crime. Now, she was just throwing spaghetti at the wall to see if it stuck.

Peterson was a trou du cul—an asshole in any language, but he wasn't a murderer. "Peterson wasn't interested in Tina's love life. If he'd suspected her of sleeping with me, he would have found a way to use it against her in the custody battle. Besides," he said with a shrug, "Peterson's remarried."

"That doesn't mean he wanted his ex-wife hooking up."

"Hooking up?"

"Screwing. Having sex," Amber said. "Even if he wasn't jealous, he could have killed her to avoid a nasty custody battle. He could have convinced her to let him into the facility on the pretext of talking about their daughter. It's as good a motive for murder as Reid's drug connection theory. Maybe vampires had nothing to do with it."

The hopeful expression in her eyes tempted him to lie. Amber didn't want vampires to be responsible. She wanted mortal criminals committing mortal crimes. Gerard wished he could give it to her. But he needed her help. So did the Asheville PD. Without it, they'd likely charge an innocent mortal for the Lifeblood murders.

As much as Gerard didn't like Charles Peterson, he didn't want him arrested for a crime he didn't commit. "Have you forgotten about Richard? A trocar didn't kill him. A vampire did."

"I wish I could forget everything you told me and everything I remembered from my past," she said with a resolute sigh. "I wish I could pretend vampires aren't real and that this was a normal case committed by mortal criminals. But I can't ignore the evidence—even if it leads to the brink of insanity."

He'd teetered on that brink himself—the night he woke up a vampire in the wine cellar of a French chateau after a Jacobin spy cut his throat and left him for dead. "You're not crazy. A vampire killed Richard Baxter, Dr. Weldon killed Tina, and I need your help finding him. I'll worry about the vampire later."

"Well, it's not like I can investigate vampires anyway. But until I can prove Weldon committed murder, everyone's a suspect."

"Even me?" he said in a lighthearted tone, despite the hitch in his pulse.

She snorted. "It's not like being undead clears you."

He jerked his head to the side, meeting her gaze. Mischief danced in her eyes. Her lips quivered upward at the corners. Relief sluiced over him. His stiff shoulders sagged. "Well," he said with a smile. "One can hope."

Amber was a lot like Tina. They didn't look alike. Amber was athletically built with dark hair and light gray eyes while Tina had been petite, busty, and blonde with big baby blues. Both women had an inner strength and tough outer shell they used to hide their insecurities. But Amber found humor in life during the darkest of times. It was a quality he found irresistibly attractive.

"Relax," she said with a real smile. "I'm dropping you from my suspect list. The credit card receipts prove you were in Alexandria that night."

Unease settled in the pit of his stomach. He shifted, unwilling to perpetuate his lie, no matter the consequences. "About those receipts..."

Shapely brows snapped together. "Please tell me that wasn't a lie."

He didn't need to confess for her to know the truth. *What is it about my damn eyes?* "I didn't lie about being in Alexandria. That part was true."

"What part isn't true?" She clinched her teeth. Blood rushed through her veins, heating her skin. He smelled the iron metallic aroma. The antivirus prevented him from craving a taste. "I was standing outside Charles Peterson's house that night."

She slid away from him. Dark blue leather creaked beneath her bare thighs. Her eyes flashed fire. "So, your alibi is a lie. A provable lie."

The accusation stung, even if there was a ring of truth to it. "It's not provable. Thanks to Sonia, Lifeblood's credit card records verify what's on the receipt. And if asked, the concierge at Morgan Suites will swear he remembers seeing me check in. And Dr. Guinness will swear we met in the lobby around nine o'clock that evening."

"Vampire hocus pocus," she countered.

"Glamour. And Sonia's incredible talents with a computer." He didn't particularly like Sonia, but she would do anything for Vincent. And she had helped save his ass from Dr. Weldon's lab.

"Maybe you're the vampire who helped Weldon." Her words cut like glass. She was once again the investigator, and he was the suspect.

Just to see what she'd do, or maybe because he was a bâtard and wanted to see if it would scare her or anger her, he flashed his fangs.

"Watch it, Frenchie. I have a gun." She nodded toward the far corner of the room. Her weapon was in a shoulder harness hanging on the back of her computer chair. "It might not kill, but I bet it'd hurt like hell if I spray-painted the walls brain matter gray."

She had a point. A regular bullet could kill him if it lodged in his head. But her gun wasn't close enough to do her a damn bit of good.

He smiled. "Woman, you have more balls than brains."

"I also have a sterling silver letter opener." She tossed her head toward her desk again. "I'm well-armed for vampire slaying," she added with a smile designed to cover her fear.

She had every right to be afraid. She might have served in Iraq, but she was naïve when it came to dealing with vampires. "Giving a mortal criminal the chance to surrender is commendable. Giving a murderous vampire fair warning is a death sentence. Don't ever forget that."

"We're so screwed," she said with a sigh, her head falling back against the sofa cushions. "I can't kill in cold blood and you're a vampire with integrity."

"We're not screwed," he argued, not sure he believed it himself.

"Oh yeah?" She raised her head, "Then we're going to have to do a bit more sharing in the future."

He'd just shared his darkest secret with her. What more did she want? "Like what?"

"Like the truth, for a change. What were you doing outside Charles Peterson's house the night Tina died? Who are you protecting?"

"No one." He blew out a frustrated breath. "You know I didn't kill her. And I wouldn't protect the vampire who did."

Her eyes narrowed. "Then tell me the truth."

"I was spying on Tina's ex."

She raised her head, meeting his gaze with interest. "Why?"

"She was afraid of losing the custody hearing. I wanted to help. Charles is a lobbyist for the Wireless Association. A few months back, he took a bribe from Quasar Cable. Quasar wanted to stop the merger between TriCast Mobile and Horizons Wireless. The cable company wanted to ensure the merger never happened. Charles made sure it didn't. It was more than just a conflict of interest. It was illegal. I wanted to get the evidence Tina needed to use against him. But I knew she wouldn't like my methods. So, I stood outside his house, watching."

"Why didn't you get Sonia to manufacture the proof you needed?"

Another bullet couldn't have hurt more. His pulse tapped against his throat. "We utilize Sonia's talents to protect ourselves from mortals who would hunt us down and destroy us if they knew we existed. Or to put away mortals who would experiment on us the way Colonel Timmons and Dr. Weldon did. We don't frame the innocent, and we don't manufacture evidence against the guilty."

"But you have manufactured evidence," she insisted. "You provided the police with false documentation. And you lied about the missing vaccine."

He snorted. "Would the police believe Weldon stole a serum used to create a vampire vaccine?"

"No, but—"

"Of course not. Most vampires live in the shadows on the fringes of society, and most mortals are oblivious to our existence. For our own protection, we'd like to keep it that way. So, when Tina was murdered, Sonia created a credit card trail to protect me from suspicion. Since I'm innocent, no one was harmed. And Vincent manipulated the head of the Senate Oversight Committee so Colonel Timmons would lose funding for his black ops military project."

Amber's gray eyes widened. "A couple of years ago, Stars and Stripes ran an article about Colonel Timmons' involvement in government research to improve a soldier's endurance in the field. The army was against the project and after he was granted funding, nothing else was mentioned until his court-martial. Another article reported he was serving a fifteen-year sentence at Fort Lewis for misappropriation of funds and defrauding the government. There was no mention of vampires."

"Even if army officials knew the truth," he said, "they'd keep it quiet. If the public knew vampires existed, it would be worse than the Salem witch-hunts. In that respect, vampires can rely on the military for protection."

"That's what the army does," she said with a quirky smile. "It protects the public from all enemies, foreign and domestic. Andrew gave his life for the cause. And no one but me knows how he really died."

Sympathy tightened his chest. He understood her dilemma all too well. He'd lived with secrets for centuries. He blew out his breath on a tired sigh.

He felt—ancient. Too many years of living. Too damn much drama. "I'm sorry for your loss."

"You've lost more than me—everyone you've ever loved is dead. Everyone you will ever love will die before you." Her voice hitched. Leaning closer, she whispered. "I'm so sorry."

He leaned in. Their hands touched on the cool leather. Her skin was soft, the pads of her fingers slightly rough. She didn't lock herself in the lab for hours on end the way Tina had. Amber's job was physically demanding.

Remorse filled him. If Tina had stayed in Alexandria instead of accepting the job at Lifeblood Labs, she might still be alive. Then again, she knew vampires existed. And so did Amber.

I failed Tina. I won't fail Amber.

"Tina is dead because of me," he said, silently vowing to protect Amber with his life. "And there are some vampires who'll do anything to prevent humans from knowing we exist."

Amber stared at their joined hands. "I don't imagine they'd want us mortals knowing we're not at the top of the food chain like we thought."

"Not all vampires kill for their survival. I don't."

"What did you do before Lifeblood? I don't think you'd kill to survive, but you needed to—eat." Her gaze met his, not in challenge or righteous indignation, but with curiosity.

He was no angel. He'd suffered greatly over the years, trying to live with what he was and not take the blood of innocents. And he had killed. Just as she had. "You were a soldier. You know what it's like on a battlefield. Now imagine the Second World War. Or earlier. The dead. The dying. That's a lot of blood, and a regular feeding frenzy for vampires."

A shiver wracked her trim body. She released his hand and wrapped her arms around her elbows. "I guess that's why Nicolas stays in Germany. It's close to so many war-torn countries."

Apprehension filled him. "Isn't Germany his homeland?"

Darkness shadowed her eyes. "I doubt it. He sounded American."

Tension radiated down his spine. There was more to Nicolas than Amber knew. "Tell me again what happened in Germany. There are pieces missing to this puzzle. Pieces a vampire has made you forget. Parts of it are coming back, but if you don't remember everything, it could get you killed."

She pushed to her feet and stepped away from the sofa, taking staggering steps to lean against a small wooden mantel over a gas log fireplace. "I don't know anything about vampires that you haven't told me. I suffered a mental collapse in Germany. Combat fatigue. Post-traumatic stress. Whatever you want to call it, but I did not see vampires."

He rose to his feet and was beside her in a blink. She backed away, stumbling until she bumped into the sofa and dropped back to the cushions.

He slowly stalked her. "Then explain the attack, Amber. You know what you know. You knew it then. Your anxiety and stress were caused by denial not the truth."

She closed her eyes and fisted her hands in her lap. He eased down beside her and captured her hands in his. His fingers brushed her bare thighs. She shivered. So did he. She was in pain and so very vulnerable. And he wanted so much to help. She needed him. And it wasn't a betrayal to Tina. He was only offering comfort and support.

Sliding his hands up her bare arms, he cupped her shoulders and pulled her to his chest. She laid her head on his shoulder, her momentary stiffness giving way to surrender. Her sigh tugged at something deep inside. If he'd had a heart, he would have lost it.

"Nicolas saved me," she whispered, her words muffled against his shirt.

Pulling back, he dipped his chin and cupped her cheek in his palm, raising her face to meet his gaze. "I know. So, it's important you tell me everything, chérie." The endearment slipped unexpectedly past his lips. Amber didn't seem to notice.

She swallowed her tears and stiffened her spine. Sitting up straight, she leaned away from him. She was strong, independent, and stubborn as hell. The woman did not like to acknowledge weakness.

"Germany wasn't the first time he saved my life," she said with a catch in her voice. "I think he saved me when I was a child too."

"You think?" Childhood memories were seldom reliable, but if Nicolas saved her when she was a child, she should have remembered—unless the incident was so traumatic she'd blocked it from her mind. Or maybe, Nicolas had made her forget.

She twisted her fingers together, averting her gaze. "It was my fifth birthday. My father was stationed in Beirut, and that same day, he was injured in a terrorist attack on the barracks. I know he was in a hospital in Germany because I remember talking to him on the phone. I didn't know what was going on then, but I knew my mother was afraid. We didn't live far from Emerald Isle, so, a day or two later, she took me to the beach. It was unseasonably warm. We stayed late. And the sun set early."

Terror filled her eyes. "On the way home, our car broke down. It was near the cut off where we turned to go home. So, Mom picked me up and we started walking." Her voice cracked. Her body quaked. Gerard wanted to take her in his arms, but he was afraid to touch her. Afraid she'd come apart if he did. Afraid he'd give into unwanted, smoldering desire.

Guilt niggled deeper. Memories of Tina hovered at the back of his mind. He took a deep breath and forced himself to stay unmoved by Amber's pain.

"I thought it was the boogieman," she whispered, her voice raw. "He just appeared on the road, ripped me from my mother's arms, and tossed me like a rag doll into a ditch. I remember being wet and cold. I crawled from the ditch and saw the monster lower his head to my mother's throat. She went limp in his arms. I cried. Then this beautiful man rescued me. He said his name was Nicolas. He picked me up and we soared over the salt marshes. And my nightmare turned into a beautiful dream about flying. Then I woke up in my own bed the next morning and learned my mother was dead."

Chapter 7

"You still pissed at me?" Reid stared at Amber through dark sunglasses from the passenger side of her car.

The morning sun glinted off the windshield, scalding her eyeballs. She squinted, trying to fight off a killer headache. Gripping the steering wheel, she refused to think about vampire boogiemen or sexy vampires with French accents. For now, she refused to think about anything vampire-related unless it figured into the Lifeblood slayings.

Of course, she'd tried that same tactic for two days without success. Seeing Gerard again last night had only added to her confusion. If only she could talk to Reid, but he'd probably think she was crazy. Hell, it sounded crazy to her, and she'd seen the truth with her own eyes. Vampires were real.

"I'm not pissed," she said without glancing at her partner.

Reid huffed impatiently. "You're gritting your teeth, and you've hardly spoken since picking me up this morning. Yesterday, you walked around like a zombie. Today, you're acting pissed."

"I'm not pissed." Confused. Scared. Vulnerable. She didn't know what to do or how to act, and she hated feeling unsure. So yeah, maybe she was pissed.

"You were sure acting pissed at the station," Reid said. "You gave me the cold shoulder and didn't say a word when I was filling Captain Stratford in on our progress with the investigation."

"What progress? We're fresh eyes on Daniels and Tanner's case, and so far, we got squat." It wasn't as if she could tell her partner or their captain the truth. Tina Gallagher had known vampires were real, and working with Dr. Megan Harper on a cure had gotten her killed. Richard Baxter had been in the wrong place at the wrong time and wound up on a murderous vampire's dinner menu.

Megan Harper was still alive because she hadn't been at work that night, but that didn't mean she was safe. If she was Weldon's intended target, he might go after her again. But what about Axle Travers? Was he a victim? Or an accomplice?

She needed to talk to Gerard again. As much as Amber wanted to avoid him—and not for the sane, obvious reason of him being a vampire—she needed to learn more about real vampires and their supernatural abilities. Searching the internet for information hadn't helped—too many flakes out there claiming to be "living" vampires.

She should have asked more questions last night, but after Gerard took her in his arms and she'd melted against him like warm butter on a hot French roll, he'd started to feel more like a lover than a witness or a suspect. And that scared the crap out of her. So, she'd freaked. And sent his ass packing. And he obliged. Without question. In the blink of a frickin' eye.

Maybe guilt over Tina's death drove him away. Or maybe he'd felt it too—that same disturbing, undeniable attraction that drew her to him like an addict to crack. Vampire glamour? Or the real deal? Either way, she did not want to get burned by Gerard's immortal fire.

"Okay, so if you're not still pissed, why aren't you talking?" Reid grumbled.

When he wasn't being arrogant, Reid was a nice guy. Nice. But paranoid. Or maybe he was still feeling guilty for driving off in a snit the night before last. Or for waiting until today to ask what was wrong. He was right about one thing. She wasn't herself and hadn't been since Gerard accosted her in her driveway two nights ago.

Maybe accosted was the wrong word, but she had been scared enough to shoot him. Thank God, he didn't die. But weren't vampires already dead?

Her body recalled his hard chest pressed against hers as he took her in his arms. His breath had fanned her neck, his heart steadily beating against her palm. No dead man had ever felt so alive.

Shaking off thoughts of Gerard, she turned left when instructed by her GPS and reassured her partner. "I'm not pissed. I'm just thinking about the case."

As much as she wanted to share what she knew with Reid, she couldn't. He'd never believe her. If Reid couldn't see it, touch it, taste it, or smell it, it didn't exist. Despite his arrogance, she trusted him with her life. Just not her secrets.

"Okay. Good. Because I shouldn't have acted like an ass the other night, and I should have asked what was bothering you yesterday. I guess I just enjoyed the quiet for a change."

"Bite me," she said with a smile, enjoying the camaraderie she shared with her partner. If she told him about vampires, the dynamics of their relationship would change. Reid would push her to get the help he thought she needed. On the off chance he believed her, he'd want her removed from the case—for her own protection.

She didn't like either scenario. So, she had to run with what she was willing to share. As an investigative team, they were so freaking far off the mark it was laughable. But why would any detective suspect vampires? It wasn't as if vampires left evidence behind.

Or did they?

She glanced at Reid. Her GPS instructed her to turn right. "Did the tech guys ever finish enhancing the surveillance videos?"

One of the killers was vampire. That's how he avoided the cameras. But a blurred image had briefly flashed across the digital screen on a single frame. If it was Dr. Weldon, she could legitimately investigate him without mentioning vampires. Daniels and Tanner, the original investigators, didn't know one of the suspects wasn't human. They thought there was a glitch in the digital video recorder. When the department techies couldn't get a better image, they'd sent a digital copy from the hard-drive to the SBI crime lab in Asheville for digital enhancement.

"They didn't get anything either. Just a fuzzy image of the back of a man's head."

Weldon. But she couldn't prove it. So, she had no reason to bring up his name as a possible suspect—unless she could find a stronger link to Baldwin Industries. Even if she and Gerard found Weldon and the vampire responsible for Richard Baxter's murder, how would she prove it? A vampire could make the evidence disappear.

She nearly choked on an indrawn breath. How did one go about arresting a vampire anyway? Or explaining to one's colleagues their suspect was a creature of the night?

"Here we are," she said as she pulled into a bougie subdivision in Albemarle Heights, a small community outside of Asheville.

Brit Travers' residence was the largest house on the block—a big, white-columned structure that looked as if it belonged on a plantation instead of a quarter acre lot in a crowded suburban neighborhood.

"He expecting us?" she asked.

Reid nodded. "Captain called last night to tell him we were coming and ensure Travers' cooperation."

After she parked the car, she and Reid climbed out and walked up the brick sidewalk. They mounted the steps and stood on a long, narrow porch. Six white rockers sat in front of six tall windows, three each on either side of a wide oak door. Tara in the burbs.

"Smells like old money," Reid said with a sneer as he lifted the brass lion's head knocker and rapped three times.

A large man in his late forties to early fifties with skin the color of Columbian coffee answered before Reid could lower his fist. He'd obviously been expecting them.

Reid gave Amber an "I told you so" look before flashing his badge. "Detective Reid Sheridan, and this is my partner, Am...Detective Amber Buckley."

The large man nodded. "Captain Stratford said you'd be stopping by."

"You the butler?" Reid asked in a snarky tone.

Round dark eyes narrowed to predatory slits. "No. I'm Brit Travers." His voice rumbled like softly rolling thunder before a storm.

Reid turned red. Amber had never seen her partner flush with anything other than anger. If the situation hadn't been so precarious, she might have taken a moment to enjoy his discomfort, but Travers' face darkened, and they couldn't afford to piss him off. They couldn't legally force his cooperation either.

Before Amber could say anything to smooth over Reid's social gaff, her partner curled his lip in distaste and said, "You were married to Shannon Travers?"

"Reid..." She wanted to duct tape his mouth shut and push him off the porch before he said something really stupid.

What the hell happened to him letting her lead the interview?

The muscles in Travers' shoulders bunched. He looked about two seconds away from throwing a punch. "Are you surprised because she's white?"

Reid huffed. "I'm surprised because she's a crack whore."

"Reid!" Where's the damn duct tape when you need it? He was going to frickin' ruin any chance they had of questioning Travers.

Reid barely spared her a glance. "Well, she is." He turned his full attention back to Travers who'd turned purple with rage. A vein throbbed in his forehead. "And what I can't figure is why a decent, hardworking fellow like yourself married her."

Purple faded. The vein disappeared. Travers shook his head and sighed. "Her family had money. Mine had brains and determination. Neither approved. Her folks didn't want their angel marrying a black man, and my family thought Shannon was redneck trash with money."

"Huh." Reid grunted. "Guess your parents were right. Your ex-wife is a junkie."

Amber tensed, but a slow smile spread across Travers' broad face. "Yeah. But she gave me a son, a son I love dearly no matter what his mother says." His face tightened. "Is there...Is there any word?"

Dark rings rimmed bloodshot eyes and deep creases furrowed his brow. He looked haunted. Scared. Pity tugged at Amber's heartstrings. She reached up and patted him on the arm just above the elbow.

"We're doing the best we can, but we do have some questions if you wouldn't mind inviting us in."

"Fine." He took a deep breath and let it out in an exhausted huff. "I'll do anything to help find my son. Just remember I'm an attorney. I won't tolerate any questions that could be used against me or my wife in a criminal investigation. Understood?"

"Neither of you are suspects," Amber assured him.

Travers opened the door and stepped aside. "So..." He swallowed thickly. "Do you have any idea what happened to Axle?"

"We have a few leads," Reid said, as they crossed the threshold into the foyer.

Leads my ass. They had squat. Amber knew more than her partner but not even Gerard knew what had really happened to Axle Travers. Just because they hadn't found his body, didn't mean the vampire who killed Richard hadn't taken Axle home for a midnight snack. Or maybe, Dr. Weldon was holding him hostage.

Most likely, Axle had been transformed and didn't want to be found. Then again, if Axle had witnessed a vampire attack, he could have gone into hiding, convinced he was either crazy or doomed because no one would believe him. She knew what it was like to doubt your own eyesight. If the mind wasn't ready to accept what it had seen, it sometimes shut down or searched for other, more logical explanations.

Axle had grown up around drugs. If he'd smoked something before going to work that night and then witnessed a vampire attack, he might have thought it was a hallucination. If he'd escaped with his life, he could have checked into a rehab facility believing he'd finally destroyed his last, remaining functional brain cell. Or he might have gone in search of the nearest drug dealer to fry the rest of his brain so he could forget what he'd seen.

As questions formed in Amber's mind, she followed Reid and Travers into a formal living room. A thin woman with almond-colored skin and straight, shoulder-length black hair perched on the edge of a wingback chair like a nervous bird sitting on a branch.

She rose on trembling legs when Travers approached. He wrapped an arm around her shoulders and pulled her close. "This is my wife, LaDonna. Sweetheart," he said gently, "this is Detectives Sheridan and Buckley."

Mrs. Travers raised her narrow chin and spoke in a surprisingly steady voice. "Have you found my husband's son?"

"No ma'am," Reid said.

"Not yet," Amber added. Travers' wife might look like a frightened sparrow, but she had the steady gaze of a hawk.

She nodded once. Then she took a deep breath and spoke in clipped tones. "Well, you find him. My son, Jerome, only recently met his brother, and this is breaking his heart. So you find Axle. You find him for Jerome, and you find him for Brit. You got that? You find him, and you find him alive."

"Mama...Don't." A preteen boy entered the room and crossed to his mother. She reached for him, pulling him into her arms.

He hugged her once and then turned to face Amber and Reid. The top of his head barely reached her chin. His father stood beside his wife, his hand on his son's shoulder. The young man resembled his father, but he was thin like his mother. His skin was some color between the two.

"Hey," he mumbled.

"The boy doesn't need to be here for this," Reid said with a touch of compassion. "He doesn't need to hear the details or the direction of our investigation. All he needs to know is that we're doing the best we can to find his big brother."

Amber could have hugged Reid. She'd never been more proud to be his partner.

The boy nodded. "Axle's alive. Please find him. Okay?"

Mrs. Travers kissed the top of her son's head. Brit Travers squeezed his shoulder. "Go to your room, son," he said. "We'll call when you can come back down."

"Yes sir." And just like that, the boy left. No pouting. No argument. No stomping off in a snit. And no sagging pants and high-jacked boxers to flash them when he walked out. Just a clean cut kid in loose-fitting jeans and a Carolina sweatshirt.

"Polite young man," Amber said.

Mrs. Travers nodded, her eyes affixed to the door her son just exited. "Thank you. He was an only child for so long, it was hard not to spoil him. It's another reason you have to find Axle. He's..." She covered her mouth. A lone tear slid down her cheek. "He hasn't had such an easy life," she whispered. "And Jerome loves him as if they'd been together since his birth. So, you have to find him—alive."

Guilt washed over Brit Travers' face. He hung his head and pulled his wife closer. "Let's sit down."

He edged around an oval coffee table decorated with magazines and a floral centerpiece. He sat on the sofa, pulling his wife down beside him. Amber and Reid sat across from them in matching wingback chairs.

Amber looked at Reid. He nodded, apparently willing to keep his word and let her take lead. "Did Axle do drugs?" she asked.

"No!" Mrs. Travers' eyes blazed with righteous indignation.

Brit Travers jerked one large shoulder in a half-shrug. "He didn't do drugs under my roof, and there were no needle marks on his arms. I checked before letting him stay here. I'm not a hard-ass, no matter what Shannon told you, but I wasn't about to let Axle expose Jerome to drugs. Axle's my son too, but I hadn't seen him in years, and I had to protect Jerome."

Amber nodded, her heart aching for the big man. He looked worn by guilt and a pain so deep it shadowed his weathered face. "I understand. You can't sacrifice one child for another, but do you think Axle was doing drugs before he came to live with you?"

"He was clean," Mrs. Travers insisted.

"LaDonna." Her husband's voice was gentle but firm. She flushed. Her eyes watered. "I don't know," he said to Amber.

Mrs. Travers caught Amber's gaze and held it. "As much as I wanted Brit reunited with his son, I was afraid Axle was like his mother. I didn't want him in this house if he was into drugs. So, I took him for a drug test, and the only thing that showed up in his system was pot."

"I know it's illegal, but he's twenty-six." Brit held up his palms in a helpless gesture. "Young men his age smoke pot sometimes. I told him it was unacceptable."

"But that wasn't enough for me." LaDonna glanced at her husband and then back at Amber. "I made Brit search Axle's bags. He didn't find anything, but after Brit got him the job at Lifeblood, I asked Vincent to do a monthly drug test. I didn't trust him. And I never warmed up to him. Now—it's too late."

Her face crumbled. Tears fell. Her husband pulled her to his chest, muffling her quiet sobs against his white polo shirt. Travers swallowed convulsively and looked over the top of her head. "Axle was clean. He didn't even light a joint while he was here."

But he'd grown up around drugs. "Did he ever use LSD?" Amber asked.

"No." Travers' voice was emphatic.

"Could the pressure of staying clean have been too much for him? Is it possible he just left and wasn't even at Lifeblood when the murders occurred?"

Reid looked at her sharply. This wasn't the approach they agreed on, but Reid didn't know about vampires.

"I wish that were true," Travers said with a deep sigh. "At least then I wouldn't worry if he'd witnessed a brutal murder and was running for his life. But he wouldn't just leave without telling me. Not voluntarily." His voice cracked.

Amber pushed. "He might if he didn't want to disappoint you." Or if he was scared out of his freaking mind.

"Don't even think of blaming the murders on my son," Travers said in a voice as loud as a thunderclap. "Axle didn't have a flashback from some bad LSD trip, kill two people, and then disappear to live on the streets. That's bullshit." He rose to his feet. "If you're taking your investigation down that road then you can get the hell out of my house."

He glared down at her as if she were a cockroach he wanted to squash.

Reid jumped up and snarled. "Wait just a damn minute!"

Amber rose slowly and held up her hands. "Everyone calm down. Reid. Sit. Mr. Travers, I'm not trying to pin the murders on your son."

Reid narrowed his eyes but didn't move. Brit Travers took a deep breath and eased back down onto the sofa. His wife patted his leg. Amber sat and looked at Reid with brows raised. He grumbled but lowered himself back onto the wingback chair across from her.

Brit Travers seemed calmer. His wife held his hand as she perched on the edge of the sofa like a hawk, ready to swoop if an unsuspecting rabbit hopped by—and Amber felt like the bunny.

She shifted her hips and locked gazes with Brit. "I'm not accusing your son, and there's no evidence to suggest he was doing drugs. It was just a theory, but I do think Axle witnessed the murders. Tina Gallagher bled out by the door, yet Richard Baxter's body was drained of blood. There was barely a drop left at the scene. If Axle witnessed the murders, he might have seen what the killer did with the blood, and it might have been more horrifying than the actual murder."

Was there anything more horrifying than seeing a vampire snack on a friend?

Travers' face turned purple again. His chest rose and fell on rapidly indrawn breaths. "So instead of helping his buddy or calling 911, you think my son ran?"

Amber shook her head and spoke calmly. "I think he was terrified, and I think it's possible he wasn't sure if what he saw was real or not. I've been in his shoes." She met Brit Travers' anguished eyes and told him about Andrew's murder. "I felt guilty for not saving him, but when I tried I was thrown against a headstone. I thought it must be some monster with supernatural powers that attacked us. But the polizei shot a drugged-out Gypsy the next night as he was about to attack another man. Andrew's blood was still on his knife."

And the polizei's story about the gypsy was what convinced her she had PTSD. Now, she knew a vampire must have put that knife in the gypsy's hand and used glamour to make him attack.

Reid's eyes bore into her, but she couldn't meet his gaze. Other than her doctors, she'd never shared that story with anyone...except Gerard.

Travers scrubbed his face with large hands and slumped against the sofa. "So, you think my son might be suffering from some form of post-traumatic stress?"

"It's possible." Amber dared a glance at Reid. His eyes filled with sympathy. She wanted to barf. He'd never treat her as an equal now.

"This all revolves around drugs," Reid said. "Your ex is sitting in a Richmond jail because of drugs, and it's her third strike."

"I'm aware of that," Travers said, his tone harsh, though not rumbling. "But my son isn't like his mother."

"But she's going to do hard time." Reid was pushing now, convinced this drug angle was the right one. Amber wasn't about to tell him he was wrong. If he and the rest of the Asheville PD were looking for drug connections, then maybe she and Gerard could look at vampire connections. That meant late nights. A vision of late nights with Gerard flashed across her mind, and it had nothing to do with crypts or blood or anything else vampire related. Her skin tingled with unwanted anticipation.

Crap. I've been celibate way too long. She forced the erotic images from her brain and concentrated on Reid's voice. It was a pleasant tenor, easy on the ears. Reid wasn't too hard on the eyes either. It was just his sexist, arrogant attitude that sometimes made her want to kick him in the nuts.

"We need whatever information you can give us on your ex-wife," he was saying to Travers. "How you met. People she might know. Places Axle might feel safe. Solving the murders isn't as much of a priority right now as finding your son."

"I appreciate that," Travers said with a quick nod. Then his eyes hardened. "I assume Shannon isn't cooperating with the investigation. Let me guess," he added, his voice filled with sarcasm and suppressed rage. "She's more concerned with the charges pending against her and whether what she told you could be used against her in court."

Reid shrugged. "Like I said, the woman's a junkie."

And Reid had pissed her off. No way, she'd cooperate now—not that they'd actually need her. Drugs had nothing to do with this case. Still, if Axle was hiding out... "Where did your ex-wife live after the divorce?"

"A hotel," Travers said. "We were still living in Durham at the time. I'd just graduated from NC Central and was studying for the bar. I was working nights as a bartender and trying to hold my family together. Shannon hated being married and resented the hell out of me. Said I cramped her style. One day, she just left."

"And took the kid," Reid said, his voice tinged with anger. "So, while you were studying and she was partying, who took care of Axle?"

Travers held his wife's hand as if it were a lifeline. She gave his fingers a quick squeeze but remained silent.

"We took turns," Travers said with a sigh. "And I hired a college student to help. Even after Shannon moved out, I kept Axle on weekends, but Shannon wanted me out of her life. She said I was just like her father, always telling her what to do. So, I filed for divorce and sued for custody. Shannon was arrested on drug possession charges and lost the custody hearing, but Axle wanted equal time with his mom. He said she needed him. We were trying to work out a visitation schedule when Shannon left town and took my son with her. I didn't see Axle again until he showed up on my doorstep last year."

"You never tried to find him?" The anger in Reid's voice intensified. A thin line of sweat beaded his upper lip. "You knew she was on drugs and you let her take him?" The judgment in his voice hinted at a past—a past Amber knew nothing about. But she had her own secrets.

Travers' face fell. He glanced at his wife as if needing her understanding. She smiled and he continued. "I hired a private investigator, but he lost Shannon's trail in Asheville. That's why I moved here and why I've stayed. It was the last place anyone saw my son." Travers took a deep breath. "Then about a year ago, Doug Brinkley, the PI I'd hired all those years ago contacted me. He'd finally located Shannon in Richmond. Apparently, she'd met a man named Jefferson Cross here in Asheville and changed her name to his—even though they never married. She and Axle followed him to Richmond and moved in with him. Doug found her in county lock up in Richmond. Axle was visiting. I got a call from Doug that afternoon, and Axle was on my doorstep the next day."

For a brief moment, the shadows left his eyes and Brit Travers smiled. When the smile faded, Amber pulled a notepad from her purse. "Where's Jefferson Cross now?" she asked. Knowing more about Axle's past and the people in it could help them locate him—if he was still alive—and not a vampire. "With his mom in jail again, is it possible Axle went to him for help?"

Brit scowled. "Not a chance. Besides, Cross died of a drug overdose shortly after they moved to Richmond, and Axle and his mom lived on the streets for a time. It's why Doug had such a hard time finding them."

Amber looked up from her pad. "What about your parents? Or Shannon's folks? Would Axle contact them if he thought he was in trouble?"

Travers exhaled a shuddering breath. "My relationship with my parents suffered when I married Shannon. They never met Axle, and they didn't speak to me again until after I married LaDonna. So, I doubt they care one way or the other what happens to him. They seldom even see Jerome. My choice now. And Shannon's parents disowned her. Even if Axle wanted to contact them, they wouldn't give him the time of day."

Amber exchanged glances with Reid. "Locating him won't be easy, especially if he doesn't want to be found, but we'll do our best."

She only hoped that when they found him, he was still human.

Chapter 8

Amber pulled into her driveway and shut off the engine. She dropped her head against the headrest and sighed. Reid's sympathy was going to drive her over the edge. When they left Travers' house, Reid had been more interested in discussing her past than the case. She responded by asking about his past.

That shut him up. But changing the subject hadn't solved anything. There was still nothing to connect Dr. Steve Weldon to the murders. He'd worked with Tina Gallagher and Megan Harper at Baldwin Industries, but there was no proof he was involved in Gallagher's murder, and there was no evidence to suggest vampires. Even if she found evidence, she couldn't share it. Who'd believe it? Gerard was the only one she could talk honestly with about the case, and he was a vampire himself.

Can we say "conflict of interest?" With a frustrated sigh, she slid from behind the steering wheel and slammed the car door. Then she turned into a solid wall of muscle.

"Whoa!" Gerard gripped her arms to steady her, his hands sliding upward until his warm fingers curled over her shoulders. His face was just inches from hers, his mouth close enough to kiss.

Need jolted her. Her body flamed. "What the hell are you doing sneaking up on me like that?" she snipped, irritated with the inappropriate hot rush of desire that nearly cooked her insides. "You're lucky I didn't put another bullet in you."

His smile was sexy enough to tempt an angel. And she was no angel. "Mon Dieu, woman. Do you always react so violently when startled?"

The open collar of a pale blue polo revealed the strong, thick column of his neck and that sexy little notch at the base of his throat where his collarbones met. Her mouth went dry. Muscled forearms flexed and bulged when he gently squeezed her shoulders before releasing her.

"Well?" he asked.

She blinked. "Well what?" Get your mind out from between the sheets and concentrate.

His brows came together. "Is your first reaction always to shoot first and ask questions later?"

Now, that just pissed her off. Any lingering lust she'd felt from having his hard body pressed against hers faded. "If it was, you'd be dead. Again."

He threw back his head and laughed. The low rumble sent hot tingles racing down her spine. "Touché chérie," he said in a husky voice that made her melt.

Despite her annoyance, she smiled. She was used to the prickly banter she shared with Reid, but Gerard's easy nature and sense of humor not only surprised her, it was a delicious aphrodisiac.

Weren't vampires supposed to be dark and brooding? Like Maxwell? She shook her head and tried lightening her tone. "Didn't anyone ever tell you not to sneak up on an ex-soldier? It can be hazardous to your health."

His smile faded as if she'd insulted him when all she was trying to do was make a joke to ease the tension between them. "I wasn't sneaking," he said. "I was waiting patiently by the tree for you to get out of your car. When you just sat there, I came over to tap on your window, but you jumped out, slamming into me so hard I was afraid you'd fall. So I caught you."

His grudging admission made her feel safe, and that scared the hell out of her. She didn't want or need his protection. She'd been looking after herself for a long time. So, why did she feel all warm and tingly?

Her heart jumped. I'm in deep shit now. A man like Gerard could make a girl feel special...if he wasn't a vampire.

"I'm sorry I snapped. I had a rough day." Rough wasn't the word for it. A depressing waste of time more aptly described how she felt about her job at the moment. She glanced toward the street, looking for a distraction. "Where's your car?"

Another smile tugged at the corners of that lush mouth. "I don't drive. I could if I wanted to. I know how. I mean...I've driven before, but why bother when I can get where I need to go faster on my own."

"That's right. You fly." A chill shivered over her skin raising the fine hairs along her forearms.

"Not really." He glanced around the yard, checking out the street and the neighbors' houses. "Can we take this conversation inside please?"

Why hadn't she thought of that? She didn't know her neighbor's well, but Mrs. Vanderbeek was nosey as hell. No telling what the woman had witnessed over the past couple of days. She turned and marched toward the house without replying. Gerard followed at a human pace.

"You are in a mood today," he said as he entered the foyer behind her and shut the door. "Want to talk about it?"

Yeah. Right. Like I'm going to talk about my sexual attraction to a creature of the night. "Not particularly."

She headed for the kitchen and went straight for the fridge, reaching inside for a dark German beer. "Could I have one?" Gerard asked.

Rising slowly with beer in hand, she turned to face him. "I thought you could only drink red wine and bl..." She couldn't even say it.

"Apparently, the anti-vampiric injections have alleviated yet another symptom of the virus. Vincent told me last night he was able to drink beer again. I tasted his and then waited, but I never experienced the pain I used to get when I tried to eat or drink as if I were still...normal." His face flushed.

Amber dropped her gaze. "What about food? Besides red meat and pork, can you eat real food again?"

A soul-deep sigh made her lift her gaze once more. "Apparently, I still lack many of the enzymes needed to digest most foods. But at least I can eat meat."

His own variation of the Atkins' Diet. Fighting a tug of sympathy she didn't want to feel, she reached back into the refrigerator and pulled out a second beer. He took it almost reverently, holding the bottle and staring at the liquid through the dark glass. Then he uncapped it with his bare hands and turned it up. A deep appreciative groan sent heat pooling between Amber's thighs.

She watched his Adam's apple bobble as he took another long hard pull on the bottle. He looked and sounded like a man in the throes of an orgasm. Her stomach cramped. She could almost envision those full, firm lips on her breasts—tasting them as heartily as he pulled on that bottle. Her nipples hardened. A hot flush scalded her cheeks.

She turned away, groping the side of the refrigerator for the bottle opener. The second she popped off the cap, she turned up the beer and guzzled it like a dehydrated sailor on shore leave. Gerard wiped his mouth with the back of his hand and gently placed the empty bottle on the counter. "Bon sang! That was good."

Amber took another long drag from her beer before replying. "Glad you liked it." Her voice cracked. Her flush deepened.

Damn Gerard. His eyes sparkled as if he knew exactly what she was feeling. So did the smile he bestowed upon her.

"Thank you," he said in a deep, husky murmur that sent a shaft of heat straight to her middle.

Amber coughed into the neck of her bottle and took another sip. She lowered the beer, looked at Gerard's sexy face, and turned it up again, drinking the last of the dark brew in one long, swallow. "Yeah. Whatever."

She picked up the empties and put them in the glass recycle container beside the trash. Then she brushed by Gerard and walked on unsteady legs to the living room. She would have glanced over her shoulder to see if he followed but she was afraid he'd mistake her curiosity for a come-hither look. And she didn't want him to come-hither. Hell, she didn't want him coming hither or otherwise. Otherwise raised intriguing possibilities. She swallowed hard and sat on the sofa.

Gerard eased down beside her, keeping his distance. "So, explain this flying thing to me," she said, trying to pretend his presence wasn't a heady distraction.

He raised a brow. "I told you. We don't fly. Vampires just move at incredible speeds. Our feet do occasionally leave the ground, but it isn't flying."

"No wonder you don't have a car," she said with a smile. "You probably save a fortune in gas, and you could book vacations without worrying about airfare."

She was rambling like a love-struck teenager. She should be concentrating on the case, but she'd never been so physically attracted to anyone in her life, and she didn't like it. Or trust it. Her skin flushed. Her breasts ached to be touched. For all she knew, her physical response to Gerard was some manifestation of his power over mortals.

"I don't really take vacations," he said with a frown. "If I did, I'd probably go back to France—see how much it's changed since I left." His voice echoed with a soul-deep longing.

How long had it been since he'd seen his homeland? Did memories of his past haunt him? Did watching those he'd loved age and die keep him away? Surely, everyone he'd ever loved in life had long since passed away.

Compassion squeezed her chest. Her heart thumped. "How long has it been since you left?"

He shrugged. "A half-century, give or take a decade."

"So, why not just go? It's not like you have to book a flight."

"I wouldn't fly commercially. Too risky," he added with the briefest of smiles. "But I couldn't get there on my own either. Vampires can't sustain flight or move over large bodies of water. When I first came to this country after becoming vampire, I traveled by ship. A servant protected me during the day while I was in the regenerative sleep."

Had he bitten some poor sap's neck and turned him into a mindless zombie?

Images of black and white vampire films sprang to mind. She shivered in revulsion. That was one way to turn down the lust. It was like throwing a bucket of ice water over her head.

Not wanting to insult him or falsely accuse him, she said, "I thought you'd never turned anyone. So, how did you get him to—um—cooperate?"

"I didn't enslave him, if that's what you're implying," he said with disgust. "A vampire's bite cannot turn a mortal into a zombie. Subtle mind control works but not well enough to mentally enslave anyone for any length of time. That's a Hollywood notion with no basis in reality. I bought Etienne's loyalty with cold hard cash."

Embarrassment flushed her skin. She was still relying on memories of old movies for vampire facts instead of asking Gerard. Obviously, trust was still an issue. In her heart, she wanted to trust him, but some deeply ingrained instinct warned against it. The Hollywood influence? Or something more reliable?

She swallowed her pride. "I'm sorry. You've done nothing to warrant my antagonism, but this isn't easy for me. I'm trying to accept the impossible as not only plausible but real. At the same time, I'm trying to solve a murder. If I find the vampire who helped Weldon, how will you react?" She met his gaze and held it. "Will you try to make me forget what I know? Or will you help bring the creature to justice? What if the vampire is someone you know—someone you want to protect? I have to know how far you'll go to guard your secret."

"Fair enough." Gerard leaned forward, resting his forearms on those muscled thighs. He glanced at the floor between his feet. Then he snapped his head to the side and looked at her with such intensity her pulse skyrocketed. "I want justice for Tina. I want to see Weldon put away or put down, and I want to stop the vampire who's helping him. But—I will not allow you to expose Vincent or me as vampires. If I have to manipulate your thoughts or your words to stop you from ruining the lives we've built here, I will. Otherwise, your mind and thoughts are safe."

But what about her body? Her skin tingled when he looked at her with those hooded blue eyes. Oh yeah. Gerard was a threat. He just didn't know the kind of threat he posed. "If you're not a threat to humanity, I don't see any reason to expose you. It's not like anyone would believe me without evidence, and I can't even find enough evidence to solve this case."

Gerard smiled. "So, we'll solve it together."

And leave her partner out of the loop. Her stomach knotted. "When? I can't quit my day job, and you can't venture out until sunset."

"We'll figure something out," he said with an understanding smile. "Thanks to the anti-vampiric injections Megan—Dr. Harper—created, I can move about before sunset and stay up an hour or two beyond sunrise—as long as I use sunblock."

"Could other vampires acquire this ability if they started taking the injections?"

He frowned. "I suppose—but other than Vincent, I don't know any other vampire taking the vaccine. No one has contacted us despite Sonia getting the word out in the vampire community."

She couldn't deal with knowing a secret society infected with the vampire virus lived in darkness among mortals. Anarchy in the shadows—an entire population living outside the norm—a population unfettered by the rules of society. A total loss of control. She swallowed her fear, forcing herself to concentrate on the case. Weldon was continuing Colonel Timmons's research. He wanted to create vampires—not cure them. But if he'd been bitten, he'd want to find a cure.

"Does curing a vampire weaken him?" Imagine the possibilities if vampires could venture out in the sunlight, move at the speed of light, and survive bullet wounds to the chest. The perfect soldier. Or an unstoppable enemy.

"The vaccine isn't a cure," Gerard said with a heart-wrenching sigh. "It's just a treatment to help alleviate some of the symptoms. The nutrients every vampire needs to survive are in blood, but since starting the treatments, I only need about eight ounces a week."

"And before the injections?" Her heart beat against her ribs. How much human blood had Gerard consumed over his very long life?

His gaze slid away. "I needed four to six ounces a day, but a vampire who engorges on warm, fresh blood can go weeks between feedings."

Revulsion turned her skin to ice. "Like a damn bedbug." She shivered, feeling queasy. "Or like the monster who killed Richard Baxter." And my mother and Andrew.

He dragged his gaze upward from the floor. A deep sadness filled his eyes. "The fresher the blood and the larger the amount consumed, the longer a vampire can go between feedings. In ancient times, it allowed vampires to move from city to city without raising suspicion."

"And now?"

His shoulders rose and fell on an indrawn breath. "It's a matter of fear and control. In this day and time, there's no other reason for a vampire to kill."

"Not even for survival?" Not that she'd accept that defense. But would Gerard?

Sitting up straighter, he looked her square in the eye. "Why kill that which we can control? If I wanted to, I could taste your blood tonight and make you forget you ever met me. I don't because I wish to live among mortals. But a vampire who kills so violently has no desire to live as human."

"What about Sonia?" She lived on the fringes of mortal society. Could she be working with Weldon? She'd dealt with him in the past. "If she's not a threat, then why isn't she taking the antivirus?"

Gerard shrugged. "Like I said before, she relishes her nature."

"Enough to kill to protect her secret?" There was no evidence to prove the vampire was male. Hell, there was precious little evidence at all. "Maybe she wants to stop production of the vaccine. Maybe she let Weldon inside and then killed him after she got the vaccine. Is it possible she's the perp we're looking for?"

Gerard scrubbed his face with his hands before meeting her gaze. "If she is, you'll never prove it. Sonia's too good at manipulating both minds and evidence. She's a genius with computers and anything electronic."

"That makes her a suspect." The intensity in his blue eyes drew her closer. She leaned in, inhaling the crisp clean scent of some sexy, masculine cologne.

"I've thought of that," he said in a low tone that heated her insides. "But Vincent would know if she'd been in contact with Weldon. He would have sensed it. Unless..." He sighed and clenched his fists. "No. It's not possible. Vincent wouldn't protect a killer, and Weldon wouldn't trust Sonia. She helped destroy his lab at Baldwin Industries."

The cadence of his voice drew her even closer. Their shoulders touched. Heat shot straight to her womb. She swallowed, trying to coat her suddenly dry throat. "What else have you thought of?"

"This." And without warning, he touched his lips to hers.

Lightning struck inside her chest. Her pulse quickened. She gasped, inhaling his very breath. And when she didn't protest or push away, he slid his arms around her shoulders and slipped his tongue past her lips. Flames licked her skin, setting her body aflame. She melted against him, not just accepting the kiss but returning it with a smoldering passion.

His tongue plunged deep, tasting her, tempting her beyond reason. She slid her fingers into his thick hair, holding him close, savoring his mouth's caress. Their lips mated, his kiss robbing her of thought, emptying her mind of everything but the delicious sensations he stirred. His arms banded around her more tightly, his hands sliding over her back in an erotic rhythm that sent her senses spiraling out of control.

Gasping, tasting, licking, she slid her hands down the sides of his neck and over his shoulders to feel the hardness of his chest. "Dear God," she whispered against his mouth.

Gerard gentled the kiss and pulled away. She felt as if she'd been abandoned in combat. Lost. Desolate. She hugged herself. Heart pounding, eyes taking in every inch of his face, she said, "That shouldn't have happened."

"I'm sorry." With a sigh, he dropped his head back against the sofa and closed his eyes. "I feel like I'm cheating on Tina, and we never really dated."

Her heart plummeted to her stomach. She was about to go up in flames, and he felt guilty. Her burning lust fizzled and died. "I'm sorry I enticed you to sin," she whispered.

A smile teased the corners of his mouth. "You'd entice a saint to sin."

Dear Lord! He still wanted her. She felt it with every breath she took. "Then why apologize?" The way she said it sounded like an invitation to sin again.

I've gone off the deep end. Officially. I'm trying to entice a vampire into my bed.

He opened his eyes and met her gaze. "Trust me. You don't need me in your life, Amber. I'm a soulless, blood sucking vampire."

Pity filled her. He looked so lost and lonely in that moment she couldn't resist raising her hand to cup his cheek. "The eyes are the window to the soul, Gerard. And no one with eyes as expressive as yours can be soulless. I see your heart in yours every time you mention Tina. And I see your concern for me now."

He kissed her palm. Warmth filled her. Not the hot rush of desire she'd felt only moments ago, but something deeper—and much more dangerous. She shivered.

"This has to be about the investigation," he said. "I don't want you giving into desires now and blaming vampire glamour later."

"Is it glamour? Is what I felt when I kissed you part of your vampire charm? Or is it real?"

She watched the slide of his Adam's apple when he swallowed. His eyes burned hotly. "I guess that depends on what you felt."

Her insides curled into delicious knots. Had she ever wanted a man as badly as she wanted Gerard?

"Confusion," she whispered. "I don't trust what I feel."

Sadness seeped into his smile. "I understand. And I don't blame you." He sighed and straightened. "I want you Amber, but I'd rather have your trust."

Chapter 9

"Maybe you should leave," Amber said. A mixture of relief and regret shone in her eyes.

Gerard's heart pounded. What was he thinking? Amber deserved so much more than he can give. Guilt stabbed him like a stake through the heart. "I'm sorry. I shouldn't have tempted you."

"You'd tempt a saint," she said with a smile, throwing his words back at him.

A chuckle escaped. Then he sobered. "Still, I should never have dragged you into my dark world."

"You didn't drag me into anything. The blood sucker who committed the Lifeblood murders dragged me into this nightmare."

At least she wasn't going to make him feel guilty for almost seducing her. His momentary relief faded. Did she consider him a bloodsucker too? Even if there had never been a murder at Lifeblood, he was still a vampire—a soulless bloodsucker—and she was mortal.

He slowly rose to his feet. Conflicting emotions tugged at his conscience, torturing whatever glimmer of humanity passed for his soul. He didn't have to worry about dying. Not because he was immortal, but because he'd already died and gone to hell. God was punishing him with glimpses of a life he could never have. First with Tina. Now, with Amber. Whatever hope he had for a normal life withered and died.

"You're right," he said with a quivering sigh. "We come from two different worlds. Merde! We come from two different centuries."

Amber's hand froze as she was smoothing her hair. Their gazes met. Held. Her face was an expressionless mask. "There's no need to explain," she said in an equally expressionless tone. "You feel as if you betrayed Tina's memory. I understand. No problem. It was just a kiss."

It was more than just a kiss. A hell of a lot more. He took a deep cleansing breath and let it out slowly. "I cared deeply for Tina, but it couldn't have been love. I was never as attracted to her as I am to you."

Amber threw up her hands with an exasperated grunt. "It was just a kiss—a kiss that won't happen again. You're not on my suspect list any more, but you're still a potential witness. You shouldn't even be in my house. It could jeopardize the case."

She was using her job to protect her heart. He knew that, but it still hurt that she could dismiss him so easily when he still ached for her touch. "You deserve better than a one-night stand with a vampire. If I didn't believe that, I'd be inside of you right now."

A gasp escaped her parted lips. Her pulse drummed in her throat. He could see the pounding as plainly as the flush in her cheeks. "I decide what I deserve," she said, her voice raspy.

Her desire heated his blood. He ignored temptation. "Getting involved with me drags you in deeper. It changes our relationship."

That arrogant chin notched up, her eyes blazed. "What relationship?"

Her challenging tone stung. So did her refusal to acknowledge their mutual attraction. "You said it, Amber. I'm a witness. Making out with me like a horny teenager could damage your credibility."

Her eyes bulged and her mouth gaped. She sputtered, moving her hands erratically before dropping her gaze. "It was just a kiss. We didn't make out, and we didn't have sex."

"But we both wanted to," he said softly.

Her chin snapped upward; her eyes widened. "It won't happen again," she said with a slight tremor in her voice. "It was just raging hormones. I got it under control now."

Not hardly. He could smell her desire—and her fear. His pulse jumped. "It was more than a kiss, Amber. You felt it too. We're drawn to one another like—"

"Two horny teenagers?" she said with a sad smile.

Another laugh escaped—bitter and harsh. "Yeah. Just like that."

Sadness crept into her voice. "And that's all it can ever be."

Harsh reality doused his desire. Despite centuries of practice, he'd never experienced a kiss as heartfelt as what he'd just shared with Amber. Just thinking about it made him ache for what could never be. He was immortal, and Amber wasn't. "I understand."

"It's not that. I mean..." She flushed. "I'm a cop. I don't get involved with witnesses or anyone else involved in a case. But I did with you, and I can't let it happen again. I can't jeopardize the case. Please understand."

"I do. Getting involved with a vampire isn't safe." And he'd never do anything to intentionally put her in danger. "But it was a great kiss. Wasn't it?"

Color stained her cheeks. Her pulse jumped. He could see the rapid pounding in her neck and smell the increased flow of blood through her veins. He'd never felt such profound relief.

"Good or not, it can't happen again." She eyed him suspiciously. "It won't happen again."

Was she trying to convince herself? Or did she suspect him of using glamour?

"I didn't manipulate you, Amber," he said softly. "Not physically, emotionally or mentally."

Tension drained from her face. "I know. I participated. Hell, I probably instigated it. Now, we have to move on and pretend it never happened. So, don't come to see me again unless it pertains to the investigation."

The attraction between them was undeniable—and impossible to ignore. He'd still keep an eye on her—protect her—but she was right. He couldn't see her alone again.

"Call if you need me?" He reached into his wallet and pulled out a business card—the one he gave to hospitals and members of the Organ Procurement Transplant Network. He was still in charge of Lifeblood's organ procurement and the OPTN maintained the only national patient waiting list for organ transplantation.

Her hand shook when she reached for the card, her fingers brushing against his, sending a hot rush of desire straight to his groin. Mon Dieu! His chest cramped as he leaned in and gently kissed her forehead. "Good-bye, Amber."

"Bye." Her smile was hesitant. "I'm sure I'll have more questions for you. So, we'll see each other again. It just can't be like—this."

"I know." Why was he delaying his departure? Just get the hell out before you break your resolve and make promises you can't keep.

He walked to the door. She followed. Slowly. "I will call. But it'll be official police business."

"I know." Merde! Just leave already.

"I wish things could be different. But it's not possible. You're a—well, it's just not possible." She smiled to soften the blow. It didn't help. Whatever was between them was too damn powerful to just walk away and not look back.

Unable to resist, he leaned forward to kiss her one last time. Their lips connected. Heat stirred him to life, hardening him instantly. He pulled her closer. She didn't resist.

Plowing his fingers through her silky dark hair, he bent her backwards over his arm as he kissed her with every ounce of passion he possessed—marking her. Branding her. Ensuring she'd never forget him. He sure as hell wouldn't forget her. Even if he lived to be a thousand.

Her hands entwined around his neck. Her tongue dueled with his for dominance. She pressed closer until he thought he'd lose control and take her right there in the foyer. Gasping for breath, he raised his head and slowly pulled her upright. Dazed and flushed with desire, she inhaled deeply. Her pulse beat erratically in her throat. She swallowed and offered a quivering smile. "Maybe this won't be so easy after all."

"It'll be impossible," he said in a breathless rumble, feeling himself strain against his zipper. He wanted her. But he couldn't have her. Then with one last smile, he kissed the top of her head and got the hell out of her house.

#

Amber looked at the woman standing under the porch light and felt the blood drain from her face. Sonia Dalca's cottage in Bat Cave resembled a small castle. Amber avoided her direct gaze, fearing the Gothic vamp would peek inside her head.

She looked at Reid. He was completely dumbstruck. His eyes bulged. His mouth gaped. Sonia all but purred in reaction to his lustful stare.

"Well, well. What brings the Asheville PD to my door?" Her voice was sultry and slightly accented. Her long red hair flowed passed her shoulders as she struck a seductive pose in black leather pants, spike-heeled boots, and a shimmering gold blouse that plunged to her navel. A thin gold chain connected the cups of her bra together, pushing the full swell of her generous bosom upward for Reid's slack-jaw gaze.

Amber frowned. "We have some questions about the night Tina Gallagher and Richard Baxter died."

"I'll bet you do." Her mouth inched upward in a sly smile. "But it seems you already know more than you should."

Amber's mind grew fuzzy. She shook her head, breaking eye content. Sonia touched the doorframe as if to steady herself. Her smile widened. "Yes, you definitely know more than you should."

A chill crept up Amber's spine and settled in her chest. Her heart pounded. The bitch was threatening her. She swallowed the burgeoning fear and steeled her nerves. "And I know your weakness too. Let's not forget that."

"Nu ma ameninta." The vampire's voice was cold enough to freeze lava. "Don't threaten me. You'll live to regret it. Or not."

Amber pulled her gun, attempting a bluff. "Silver bullets kill. Don't they?"

Her body shook. She looked at Reid. What the hell was the matter with him? He stood stone still, his mouth slightly parted—his eyes glazed over.

Sonia laughed but didn't sound amused. "An empty threat, mortal. But you bluff well. Still, I think I might actually like you. You're more than you seem."

"Reid." Amber kept her eyes on Sonia but snapped at her partner. He didn't respond. She dared another glance in his direction. He still wore the same silly expression on his frozen face.

Amber could barely discern his breathing. "What the hell did you do to him?" she growled, her attention and her gun swinging back to Sonia.

The vampiress chuckled. "Relax, mortal. He's just entranced. I wanted to talk to you without his hearing. He doesn't know. Does he?"

"No." Amber's heart pounded. Sweat slicked her palms. Her hands shook. She steadied her aim, but Sonia raised a brow and nodded to the gun as if it were a toy.

"I called your bluff. Now put that damn thing away. Shooting me will only piss me off."

Heart still beating like a frightened rabbit's, Amber holstered her gun and nodded to her partner. "What will he remember?"

"Me answering the door and him lusting after me like a love-sick school boy." Her smile widened as she skimmed her hands over her narrow waist. "Men can't resist me. It has been this way since before I was immortal."

Amber started to make a wisecrack but something dark and forbidden flashed behind Sonia's eyes. She smiled seductively, but her eyes reflected something else—a dark secret that had nothing to do with her being immortal. Sonia Dalca might relish her nature, but she definitely had issues. She reminded Amber of Jack-Kay—a transvestite hooker sexually abused by his own father. Jack-Kay preened and seduced, but he was filled with self-loathing. And Sonia's eyes reflected the same inner turmoil.

"You're Romanian?" Amber asked.

The vampire's eyes darkened. "Da. I am Romuini."

Besides spawning vampire legends, Romania was once a feudal country. Even less than a century ago, a beautiful woman would not have had an easy life if she were poor.

"What century?"

"What does it matter, Catea?"

It only mattered in how Amber handled the vampire. Sonia's attitude could stem from a deep hurt. Was it possible she wasn't as dangerous as she appeared?

Amber swallowed a lump of fear and met Sonia's gaze. The vampiress nudged at her mind. Amber allowed it—until Sonia went digging into memories Amber didn't want exposed. Fighting an uber-invasion of privacy, Amber forced her mind to go blank. Sonia swayed and broke contact.

"Clever trick, mortal, but I saw enough. You're no stranger to our kind."

"And you're not as heartless as you want people to think. Gerard said you were hurt by Maxwell's marriage. Did you go to Lifeblood looking for Dr. Harper?"

Sonia leaned closer. "I wouldn't harm Megan, despite the risk to Vincent."

Amber stood her ground, ignoring the pounding in her chest. "What risk?"

"She's mortal." Sonia spoke the word as if it were an insult. "And mortals and immortals don't mix."

Gerard had said as much. But he suspected Weldon of killing Tina. Was it a ruse to throw Amber off track? Would he lie to protect Sonia? It wouldn't be the first time he'd manipulated her. Whether he did so with his mind or words hardly mattered. The end result was the same. "Is Tina dead because she broke your 'rules' and got involved with Gerard?"

Sonia's lips spread into a slow sensual smile. "Ah. So, it's like that is it? You got a taste of vampire loving and fear he manipulated you."

"No." The denial was weak and ineffective. Sonia didn't have to read her mind to know she was lying. "Did you kill Tina because she'd been with Gerard?"

Sonia laughed. "I did not kill Gerard's little plaything, and I do not care for your lover. But rest assured. He would not use glamour to seduce you. He is cocky, that Frenchman. He likes to woo women the mortal way."

Amber ground her teeth. Pain radiated from her bunched jaw to her brain. She would not discuss Gerard with a vampire who was quite possibly an ex-lover. "Did you meet with Megan Harper the night Tina died?"

"Da. I saw her. She wanted to invite me to a celebration of her second wedding anniversary to Vincent. I declined and warned her not to hurt him. Since I created him, I feel responsible for his life. His happiness is important to me. But she's dragging him into a world between worlds and weakening his power. If she continues, he'll be defenseless."

"So, you're against a cure for your condition." It was an accusation not a question. Sonia could be working with Weldon to destroy any hope of curing the condition he was trying to clone in some sort of race...or rather...species war.

"There is no cure," Sonia spat, and her eyes flashed red like two glowing hot coals. "Vincent can eat steak. So what? He's still a vampire who requires blood. He's just weaker and more vulnerable to mortal attack."

Amber met her gaze and then lowered her lids, shielding her eyes. "Most mortals don't even know you exist."

"The world is changing," Sonia said, her voice low and cryptic. "I live among immortals—and mortals who are posers. The posers think they are vampires—the fools. And others do not believe vampires—real vampires—exist. But technology is bringing our worlds closer whether we wish it or not. There is no cure for damnation. Only false hope. A vaccine won't protect us from those who wish to experiment with our blood in an effort to gain our powers without the negative side-effects."

"You're talking about Weldon." Cold slithered over Amber like a second skin. Sonia wasn't working with Weldon. She despised him as much as Gerard did.

"Dr. Weldon is merely a puppet who continues to work without a master. I was referring to the bastard who hired him. Without the colonel, the good doctor will simply flounder until he is exposed. Then, I will take care of him the way I did the colonel."

"Colonel Timmons is dead?" Had Sonia just confessed to murder? Did it matter if she had? Amber couldn't arrest her. The woman could probably escape a pair of handcuffs without breaking a sweat.

Sonia's knowing-smile did not reach her eyes. "I visited him in the brig two days ago. He didn't survive the encounter." She waved Amber off before she could protest. "Gerard doesn't know. Yet. I imagine the story will make the news soon enough."

"What did you do?" Amber's voice was a hoarse croak as she imagined the horrifying scene. Memories of Andrew and her mother bombarded her.

"Nothing too violent. I entranced him. He felt nothing when I drank from his wrists before slashing them with the sharpened edge of a spoon handle. I left enough blood in his veins to make a nice little mess on the floor. Before leaving, I dropped the shank beside him. The authorities think he committed suicide."

"Why?" Colonel Timmons had kidnapped Gerard—not Vincent. Was Sonia in love with both vampires?

"Because he was a threat," she snarled. "Your mortal laws did nothing to stop his evil. Even from his prison cell, he was paying Dr. Weldon to continue his research. So, I stopped him."

"But you didn't stop Weldon. He's still out there."

"For now," she said in a dark and threatening voice. "But he will reveal himself without my putting forth much effort. Then, I will end his research once and for all."

"Why don't you use your vampire voodoo?" She'd done it before. Why not now?

"I tried." Pouting, Sonia folded her arms under her breasts and slouched against the door jam. "But Weldon is smarter than I thought. He communicated with Timmons using an alias and a post office box. His letters were written in code so the prison warden didn't know they'd been in contact. Timmons read them and then destroyed them. I couldn't get my hands on a single one."

A lead at last. Hope buoyed Amber's spirits. "What name did Weldon use? Where was the post office box? It would have to be nearby for him to check it regularly."

Sonia twirled a strand of hair around her finger. "Not necessarily. Weldon hired someone to make contact with Timmons. That person mailed the letters to someone in Raleigh who then forwarded the letters to Timmons. There wasn't a return address on any of the letters, and he never met Weldon in person."

"But he met someone. Who did Weldon send to make the initial contact? Who paid him?" Amber glanced briefly at her partner to make sure he was still breathing. Reid stood completely still, his face now a blank mask.

Sonia sighed, shaking her head. "I don't know. The bastard's brain was fried."

Chapter 10

"Miss Dalca confirmed Dr. Harper's alibi," Reid said, as Amber pulled into the parking space in front of his townhouse. "And did you get a load of that outfit?" He whistled appreciatively. "She's gorgeous, but she looks like a stripper. I bet the real reason she wouldn't see us until late is because she works nights and sleeps all day. That story about having just flown in from Alaska and being jet-lagged was bullshit."

If he knew what really happened during the interview, he'd have a coronary. After Sonia released Reid from his trance, she'd answered his questions. Not that he'd noticed. He seemed to remember her outfit more than the actual words. Which hardly mattered. Most of what she told him was bullshit.

Guilt flushed her cheeks. "Yeah. She looks like a stripper." A stripper who could rip out a man's throat and bleed him dry.

She threw the car in park, unable to meet Reid's gaze. While Reid had stood on the porch, eyes glazed over in a trance, Amber had interviewed the vampiress alone. How could she claim a true partnership with him when she'd allowed such an atrocity? He'd been violated. And he didn't even know it.

He touched her arm. She jumped. "What's wrong, partner?"

The sympathy and concern in his voice was enough to gag her. "I'm tired. This investigation isn't going anywhere."

"Not true," he said, sounding more optimistic than the situation warranted. "We know where not to look. And the more questions we ask, the closer we get to proving what you and I already know. Shannon Travers' drug connection is the key to solving this case. And that's what we're going to start looking into on Monday."

"Sure." She barely listened. If only she could talk honestly with him. She needed his input. His opinions. But Reid had a hard time believing in God. He'd never believe vampires were real.

"Don't look so down." Reid patted her knee, startling her. "Relax. Enjoy our three-day Labor Day weekend. We'll get a fresh start on Monday."

"Can't wait," she quipped, but the cynicism she intended was lacking.

Chuckling, Reid slid from the car. Before he shut the door, he leaned in and studied her face. "Stop stressing. You look like shit."

"Gee. Thanks Reid. You really know how to swell a girl's head."

He flashed a cocky grin. "Seriously, Amber. You look tired. Get some rest. Okay?"

"I will." Rest my ass. "I'll see you Monday."

She glanced at the dashboard clock as she pulled out of the neighborhood. Twenty-three fifteen—quarter after eleven. Would anyone besides the security staff be at Lifeblood of America? She needed to talk to someone about Sonia, and she wasn't sure Gerard or Vincent could be objective. Dr. Harper might be biased, based on her husbands' past relationship with the vampire, but Amber had nowhere else to turn. She didn't want to waste time chasing leads if Sonia wasn't reliable.

Could she seek out Dr. Harper without Gerard knowing she was in the building? Was he even working tonight? Neither he nor Maxwell had a set schedule. They came and went as they pleased or worked from home. But Dr. Harper reported to her lab at least four days a week. Would she be there now? It didn't get dark this time of year until quarter to eight or so. Did that cut into Vincent Maxwell's work hours? Or did the anti-virus injections allow him to keep a regular nightly schedule?

Vampires must hate summer and daylight savings time.

She pulled onto interstate forty and headed west. Then she took the Sweeten Creek Road exit and drove toward Bolton Boulevard and Lifeblood of America. Florescent lights illuminated the parking lot, but as she approached the front entrance, the hair on the nape of her neck stood on end. She glanced over her shoulder. The lot was empty. She walked faster. Light from inside the facility shone through the large plate glass door. A security guard sat at the desk.

Amber knocked to get his attention. He remained seated, glaring at her from across the lobby. She flipped open her badge and held it up to the glass. He grudgingly rose to his feet, came around the desk, and took his own sweet time unlocking the door.

"Can I help you?" His tone said, "Go away."

"I'm Detective Amber Buckley. I'd like to come in and ask some questions about the murders last spring."

With an irritated grunt, he moved aside, allowing her to enter the lobby. Then the muscle-bound security guard stepped in front of her as if barring further entrance into the facility. He watched her drop her badge into her purse, his expression belligerent. "What kind of questions? I didn't even work here then."

"Dr. Harper did. I'd like to ask her a few questions. Is she in?"

Mr. Happy smiled. It wasn't pleasing to the eye. "No."

It took supreme effort on Amber's part not to jack the man up against the wall and threaten to arrest him for obstruction of justice. That would knock the smirk off his face.

She tapped her foot. "What time will she be in?"

"Don't know." He glanced at the clock on the wall behind him and shrugged as if to say he didn't care.

Her foot stilled. "Is Mr. Maxwell in?"

"No."

She stood on tiptoes and got in his face. The guard jumped back, his eyes bugging out of his head. "I don't have time for this shit," she snapped. "When I ask a question, I expect complete answers spoken in complete sentences. Now. Let's try this again. Is Mr. Maxwell in and if not, when do you expect him?"

"He's not in. He took his wife out of town on vacation. I don't know when they'll be back."

Vacation my ass. He was avoiding the investigation. Or protecting his wife. Maxwell was no dummy. Weldon had taken the serum but that didn't mean he knew how to turn it into a vampire vaccine. Dr. Harper knew the vaccine's side effects and limitations. And she'd know how to create more if that was Weldon's goal. If his goal was to destroy the vaccine, then she was in danger, and Maxwell wouldn't want her anywhere near Lifeblood of America.

Amber stepped back and forced a note of civility into her tone. "Thanks." For nothing. Then without another word, she turned and left the building.

The sensation of being watched persisted. Her low heels clicked against the pavement as she hurried to her car. A shiver snaked down her spine. She touched the door handle and froze. Something or someone watched from the shadows.

She slipped a hand inside her jacket, unsnapping the thumb break on her Glock. Sweat clung to her back and pooled beneath her arms—not just from the heat. This felt like Iraq all over again. The air was thick with danger. She could feel it, though its source remained elusive, like a terrorist strike with no clear direction. She turned in a slow circle. Nothing stood out. No one lingered in the parking lot. No movement stirred in the shadows. Then she turned back to her car—and collided with strong arms.

She grunted. A low growl emanated from a broad chest. She raised her chin. Light shone from behind, shadowing the man's face, but his eyes glowed a predatory red. Her heart slammed against her ribs. Choking back fear, she reached for her Glock. He grabbed her wrist and jerked her arm over her head before her fingers made contact. Then his lips peeled away from his teeth revealing razor sharp fangs that glistened in the dark.

Before she could scream, the nightmare vanished in a blur. Air whooshed by her—the force strong enough to knock her to the ground. Her purse slid from her shoulder. She let it go, clawing at the pavement, reaching for her gun as she pushed to her feet.

Two figures tussled on the ground, moving inhumanly fast. One rose and vanished. The other snarled and turned. Heart pounding, palms slick with sweat, she raised her weapon, but couldn't pull the trigger.

Dark eyes held her captive. Her fear abated. "Nicolas."

\#

Gerard sat at his desk, responding to Lifeblood emails when fear pierced his heart. His body tensed. Amber was in danger. He sensed it.

"Mon Dieu!" How was that possible? He'd never made love to her or taken her blood, and she had never been exposed to his. How could there be a psychic connection?

He pushed back his chair and stood. Where the hell was she? Closing his eyes, he tried sensing her again, but the connection was faint. His mind hummed. His skin tingled. Then...nothing. Amber's fear abated. Or, he'd lost whatever tentative connection they shared. But why was he able to connect with her at all? It made no sense. Unless...

Vincent shared a supernatural connection with Megan. Gerard always thought it was because she'd injected herself with Vincent's blood to create the anti-virus. Megan could feel Vincent's emotions, but she'd had his blood in her veins. But what if it was something more? What if engaging a vampire's heart created the connection?

Merde! Am I in love with Amber?

He most assuredly felt her fear. Or he had until he'd felt...nothing. Was she unconscious? Or... Terror seized him. He couldn't think of other possibilities and maintain his sanity. He shoved his feet into his shoes and disappeared into the night.

#

Amber rubbed her temple and tried to blink the world back into focus. The parking lot at Lifeblood didn't re-appear. Nicolas had transported her to a large room with hunter green walls and dark wood trim. Books lined inlaid shelves above a large mahogany desk in the corner opposite leather furniture and matching side tables. The faintly sweet aroma of expensive cigars hung in the air.

She dared a glance at her savior. Or was he her doom? "Where are we?"

"Cedar Plank, near Mount Mitchell State Park." Nicolas held out his hands, encompassing the richly decorated room. "Welcome to my home."

They were still in North Carolina, but miles away from Asheville.

"How did we get here?" Her voice faded to a whisper as the shock faded. She vaguely recalled the pounding wind and blur of scenery zipping passed. Memories assailed her. "You saved me. Just like before when I was little."

Traveling with Nicolas when she was a child had felt like a gravity-defying thrill ride—so fast, so fierce, she'd clung to him as if her life depended on it. But now, everything was different. This time, she was in shock—barely aware, barely breathing. The truth slammed into her, impossible to grasp. Her legs gave way, useless beneath her. She would've crumpled to the floor if Nicolas hadn't dragged her to the sofa. Collapsing onto the cool leather, she shut her eyes, trying to anchor herself in a reality that refused to settle.

"Not all vampires are hedonists and reprobates," Nicolas said, a smile in his voice. "Some of us take care of our...of others."

Anger roused her, incinerating her misery. She ground her teeth. "I guess the vampire who killed my mother and Andrew didn't get the memo."

He bowed his head, fists tightening at his sides. "I was too late. I'm sorrier than you'll ever know. But I did what I could. I took you home, buried the memory of that night, and replaced it with dreams of flying. I've been watching over you ever since."

Her breath caught. The idea that someone—or something—had been watching her all these years wasn't comforting. It was chilling.

"Why?" she asked, voice low. "Why would a vampire protect me? Why would you?"

He shifted, inching away, as if the truth itself might burn. His eyes avoided hers, fixed on the floor. "Let's just say... I'm family. The kind you don't remember. The kind you weren't supposed to know."

"Let's not," she said, locking eyes with him. "I'm not fragile. I can handle the truth."

His gaze snapped to hers, sharp and unflinching. "Can you?"

She'd already accepted vampires as real. What could be worse? Werewolves? Banshees? Demons? She folded her arms and leaned back against the cushions, bracing herself. "You owe me answers. Why are you protecting me? More importantly—why do vampires keep coming after me?"

"Because you're investigating them," he said, his gaze slipping away again.

No. That wasn't enough. The vampire tonight wasn't the same one who'd murdered her mother and Andrew. And what if the vampire who'd attacked her mother had been after her instead? Her heart constricted. Her chest tightened.

"I wasn't investigating vampires in Germany," she said, forcing the words past the painful knot in her throat. "I didn't even know they existed. And neither did my mother when she was killed."

He stared at his shoes. "Your mother did know about vampires."

She'd braced herself, thinking she could handle anything. She was wrong. Her heart beat painfully in her chest. It hurt to breathe.

"Someone would have told me," she whispered. Her father. Her grandmother. "Someone would have warned me the boogieman was real."

"I'm sorry," he said again, his anguish as real as her own.

She swallowed the tears clogging her throat. "How did she find out?"

Nicolas rose to his feet, turning his head away from her as if he could no longer bear looking at her tear-streaked face. "Your father was injured in the marine barracks bombing back in eighty-three. He was buried beneath the rubble for hours."

"I remember," she said, speaking softly through her tears. "It was my birthday."

He spared her a quick glance. "Your fifth."

She swiped at her eyes and sat up, stiffening her spine. "Dad called from the hospital two days later—a hospital in Germany. And two days after that, a vampire killed my mother. And twenty some years later I was attacked, and my friend was killed—also in Germany. And you saved me both times just as you did tonight. Why? What's the connection?"

"I'm the unidentified soldier who pulled your father from the rubble."

Amber stood, slowly backing away from him. It felt as if someone had stuck an eggbeater inside her head, scrambling her brain. "Why would you save my father? Why me?" she demanded again.

"I knew your parents when I was mortal," he said. "Greg was my best friend. He joined the marines when I joined the army. So, I knew he was in Beirut, and when I heard about the bombing, I—"

"Stop." Amber's world tilted even further off its axis. Nicolas wasn't an ancient. He was her father's age, but he looked like a man in his early thirties. He looked younger than she did. "When did you die?"

Since meeting Gerard, the absurd question had become a routine part of her investigation.

A frown marred Nicolas' handsome face. "It's complicated."

"Then use small words. I'll keep up."

He smiled. Then sobered. "I was injured in a live training exercise while stationed at Grafenwöhr in seventy-eight. They medevac me to Landstuhl—a US Military hospital—but my injuries were fatal. Before I died, an ancient vampire converted me. He made the army—my family—everyone believe I was dead. So, I stayed in Germany until—I stayed for years before returning to North Carolina."

"Then you were already a vampire when you rescued my dad. Did he recognize you? Did he know you were a vampire?" Did that explain her father's estrangement? Did he keep his distance to protect her?

"No. I manipulated his mind," Nicolas said, remorse roughening his words. "He thought I was nothing more than a morphine-induced dream."

So, her father's neglect had nothing to do with his wanting to protect her. He was just avoiding her because she didn't get along with his new family.

She inhaled sharply, fighting a fresh wave of tears. "Then how did my mother learn about vampires? If my father didn't tell her, how did she know?"

Nicolas turned to pace; she jumped in his path. "You better start talking because I'm about two seconds away from doing something really stupid—like arresting you."

A ghost of a smile flashed across his face. "That would be stupid. Unless you have silver handcuffs."

"Please," she pleaded. "I need answers."

He sighed as if resigned. "After I saved Greg, I went to see your mother. I knew she'd be glued to the television, watching the horrific images flashing across the screen, choking on fear while she awaited word from the military. I couldn't put her through that." He lowered his chin, avoiding her gaze. "Naturally, she was shocked to see me. She thought I was dead. So, an explanation was in order. She didn't like it."

Amber scoffed. "I don't reckon she did. Dead men don't usually make social calls."

Pain etched his face. "I should have manipulated her thoughts—made her forget the way I did Greg, but she was so sad—so vulnerable. I—I left her to her misery. The next day, she called my former sergeant demanding he do something about the vampires preying on mortally wounded soldiers."

Her pulse quickened. "That's how Timmons found out. Isn't it?"

"He wasn't a colonel then," Nicolas said, "but it was the beginning of his obsession with vampires."

Gerard had been kidnapped because of her mother. She'd started this chain of events when she ignited Timmons' compulsion to create the perfect soldier. And a vampire killed her to stop her from telling anyone else. Tina Gallagher and Richard Baxter were also dead—and who knew how many others. So much tragedy because her mother tried to do the right thing.

No good deed goes unpunished.

"Why is Timmons still alive if my mother is dead?" It didn't seem fair. Her mother had been a kind, generous woman. Colonel Timmons was obsessed with power and advancing his military career at the expense of innocent people.

Nicolas grimaced. "Timmons kept his knowledge a secret, but your mother was on a mission to expose vampires. One of Surratt's fledglings killed her."

Amber's heart slammed against her ribs. "Who's Surratt?"

Nicolas jerked as if she'd shot him. "It's not important."

"He's the ancient who turned you. Isn't he? That's how he knew my mother called the authorities—through his connection to you."

"Let it alone, Amber."

Amber's hands curled into fists. "Not a chance. He's responsible for my mother's death. Did his little buddy kill Andrew too? What was his excuse—protecting their kind from discovery? Andrew didn't even know vampires existed."

"But you did." Nicolas' eyes shone with sorrow. "We can implant false memories, twist thoughts... but complete erasure? Tragic memories resist. A sliver always remains."

"So Surratt got tired of wondering if I'd remember and decided to kill me? Is that it?" Her voice dropped. She didn't doubt anymore—vampires were real.

"Surratt was there that night, but Klaus attacked you and Andrew."

Knowing the name of Andrew's killer didn't ease the pain. The bastard who'd killed him was still alive—and immortal. "Did he kill my mother too?"

"Yes." Nicolas' voice barely carried. His eyes were shadowed, haunted.

Amber hardened. "You didn't try to stop him. You let him go. Why? Because Surratt created you both? Is Klaus your blood brother or something?"

Nicolas had saved her life—twice. But how could she trust him after this?

"Saving you mattered more than chasing your mother's killer. Later, when I confronted Klaus, Surratt shielded him."

"Then Surratt is responsible." Her voice turned razor-sharp. "He sanctions the killing of mortals."

"No. Vampires need humans to survive. Killing them depletes our supply—and draws dangerous attention."

Amber's blood began to burn. Her fists clenched tighter. "So you see humans as nothing more than food? Saving me was just like saving a farmer's chicken?"

He reached for her. Amber stepped back, fury pulsing in every heartbeat. If looks could kill...

Dropping his hand, he sighed. "You matter to me, Amber. More than you'll ever know. And Surratt isn't the enemy. He's trying to prevent war—between mortals who know we exist and vampires who kill indiscriminately."

"His methods suck. Klaus got away with murder. Twice." Even the name clawed at her throat.

"Klaus learned of our existence when he was mortal so Surratt erased his memory, but there were computer files Surratt didn't know about. Computers weren't as prevalent then. When Andrew rediscovered the files, his memory returned, and he began his investigation again, armed with the knowledge that vampires could alter memories. So Surratt turned him. Klaus then vowed to protect vampires from mortal discovery—just as Surratt wanted. But after he killed your mother, Surratt restrained him. Then you showed up in Germany—where Klaus lived."

"The army sent me to Germany," Amber argued.

"But they didn't send you to the cemetery—the cemetery where Klaus was supposed to be buried. He thought you'd remembered. He thought you were gathering evidence to use against him."

Had she subconsciously remembered something? Visiting the cemetery had been her idea, but not to find vampires. Since her mother's death, cemeteries brought peace. After Iraq, she clung to peace wherever she found it.

"I didn't even know Klaus's name," she whispered. But had she walked over his grave?

She stepped closer, locking eyes with Nicolas. "I wasn't looking for vampires—but I am now. Is Surratt connected to the Lifeblood Labs murders?"

"No. He wants that rogue vampire stopped just as much as you do."

"I doubt it."

"Let it go, Amber," he said again. "Let vampires handle their own. Mortals have plenty of crimes to solve."

Seriously? He expected her to just walk away and let vampires handle it? That would be like putting terrorists in charge of punishing those responsible for the 9-11 attacks. "I don't think so. I'm a cop. It's my job to investigate crimes, no matter who commits them."

"This investigation is going to get you killed." He ground his teeth like a father lecturing a teenager. "And you can't go after Klaus. He's dead."

A hollow ache settled in her chest. Her mother's killer was dead. Her need for revenge should have been appeased, but the pain didn't go away. "Who killed him?"

He exhaled slowly, deflating. "I did. Despite the blood we shared, I defied Surratt and ended him"

She met his dark gaze. Memory flickered—concrete cracking her skull, the hot, metallic scent of blood, her scream echoing as Klaus tore into Andrew's throat as cleanly as if he'd sliced it with a blade. After drinking his fill, tossed Andrew aside like a rag doll and turned toward her.

His approach had been slow. Methodical. She tried screaming but heard nothing but the roar of blood in her ears. Paralyzed, sprawled against a crypt where Klaus had thrown her, she watched death approach—until Nicolas appeared. Shielding her, he fought Klaus. Saints and angels carved in stone bore silent witness. She woke in the hospital days later. Memory fractured. PTSD intact. "You erased my memories," she whispered as the visions faded.

Nicolas clenched his fists. Tension rolled across his shoulders. "Let it go. Klaus is dead. Surratt didn't punish me for killing him. He only demanded I leave you alone—as long as you remembered nothing. So walk away. Forget. Stay away from vampires. Do I make myself clear?"

She crossed her arms. "I can't forget. Not again. I'll do whatever's necessary to protect and serve—whether it's in an army uniform or on Asheville's streets."

"If I thought it would help, I'd make you forget. Again. But something else would bring it all back. And you'd hate me for it." His expression softened. "So there's only one option left."

Then he pulled her into his arms and the world went fuzzy.

Chapter 11

Gerard snatched up Amber's abandoned purse, his eyes scanning the dimly lit parking lot outside Lifeblood. He inhaled sharply. Her scent still clung to the air—faint, but unmistakable. But beneath it, the sharper notes of an immortal presence. Two of them.

No blood. Thank God. The idea of her turning vampire chilled him to the core. Immortality was a curse he wouldn't inflict on his worst enemy, let alone someone he might actually care for.

Care for? Hell, who was he kidding? This wasn't friendship. He would've felt her even without the purse or the empty car. Her presence thrummed beneath his skin—her fear, pulsing and raw. He'd never sensed anything like that from a mortal. While Weldon was busy carving Tina's throat, Gerard had been in Alexandria, tailing her ex—oblivious to the terror she'd endured.

The rush of emotion made his past obsession with Tina feel like a flicker compared to the blaze raging now. Guilt burned hot across his skin. He'd failed Tina. And now Amber was gone. No clue where she'd been taken. No trail to follow.

Paralyzed by indecision, he stood adrift in a world of shadows—powerful, yet powerless. The darkness inside him beckoned, whispering promises he didn't trust. Desperate, he reached out with his mind, letting the dark tendrils stretch. Somewhere in that haze, he mentally called Vincent.

Vincent materialized beside him in a heartbeat, eyes narrowing. "What's wrong?"

"Amber's missing," Gerard rasped. The words felt like glass in his throat.

Vincent's scowl was immediate. "Since when are you on a first-name basis with Detective Buckley?"

"It doesn't matter. She's been abducted." Exposing her to the truth had put her in danger—just as it had Tina. "I don't know the vampire who took her, so I can't track him. I couldn't track him the other night either, but I know he was watching outside Amber's house."

Vincent's brows climbed his forehead before snapping down over disapproving eyes. "I won't ask why you were at her house—or why you're hugging her bag."

Gerard lowered his chin and stared at Amber's purse, unwilling to meet Vincent's gaze. "She dropped it." That explanation was easier than revealing why he'd been at her house—more than once. Or why he'd kissed her. She was a cop—a potential threat to their kind—especially since most vampires lived behind layers of forged identities. But Vincent probably knew how Gerard felt. Gerard hadn't blocked their mental connection.

Vincent furrowed his brow. "Why would a vampire be interested in a mortal detective?"

"To protect her? To protect himself? Je ne sais pas." Not knowing was killing him. How could he protect Amber without knowing from what? Or whom? "I think he might be her ancestor."

Gerard tried not to dwell on the second vampire he'd sensed in the parking lot. Some strange psychic tether linked them. Weak—yet undeniable. He felt the creature's desire to kill but couldn't decipher its motives or pinpoint its location. Something was off about him. Alien. And yet, somehow familiar.

Vincent closed his eyes, nostrils flaring. He swayed and then snapped upright. His irises glowed red. Pupils dilated. "There was another vampire here. He vanished before the one you believe is Nicolas took her."

"But where did he take her?" The other vampire wasn't an immediate threat. Nicolas was.

"The connection is weak, but the other vampire seemed to be...you." Vincent sounded puzzled rather than accusing.

Apprehension skittered down Gerard's spine. "What if it was my clone?"

"You think Dr. Weldon perfected cloning to the extent the creature is functional? Recognizable?"

Earlier versions of the clones Dr. Weldon created from Gerard's DNA were grotesque—exposed muscles and tendons, incapable of thought or speech. Creatures of suffering. Gerard had felt every pang.

Emotion tightened his gut. "Yes."

Vincent's face paled to the complexion of a vampire in the regenerative sleep. "He's made another you."

Gerard forced a wry smile. "Good thing you can tell the difference. Means the copy isn't as good as the original, huh?" Flippancy was easier than fear. But fear crawled under his skin. He shuffled his feet, unable to stand still.

"Vampire DNA replicates quickly," Vincent warned.

"Mon Dieu. There could be a half-dozen me's running around out there." How many mortals would they attack? Kill? How many of his associates would believe him responsible?

"Megan." Vincent's eyes went wild. Dangerous. "She knows Weldon is working with a vampire, but if it's a clone—your clone—she won't be able to tell the difference if he approaches. Not like I can."

"No one will be able to—until it's too late." Paranoia spun out terrible possibilities. A clone could use Megan as bait. Or worse—force her into Weldon's lab. She'd created the sedative and the antivirus. What could Weldon do with her research? And why Amber? Had the clone sensed Gerard's link to her? Smelled him on her skin? The how didn't matter. Weldon had used his DNA to craft a monster. "Where's Megan now?"

"I put her on the company jet last night. She's at my New York residence. I couldn't protect her and chase Weldon, and now he's working with a vampire, and not just any vampire. It's your clone." Vincent raked a hand through his hair. "How do I keep her safe?"

If Weldon could clone vampires and command them, he was unstoppable, especially at night with a vampire protector. Maybe the antivirus was Weldon's shield for daylight. Maybe he'd become a vampire himself. That could explain everything. The serum hadn't been ready for injection, but he was a scientist. Even without Megan, he'd figure it out. That's probably why he took Axle—to turn him and then test the vaccine. The possibilities were endless. None of them good.

"We have to find Weldon and stop him—before he reaches Megan again." His lungs squeezed tight. "Or Amber."

Vincent's expression turned ashen. "I'm sorry. I need to get to New York. I have to protect Megan, and you have to find your detective."

"Go," Gerard said. "I'll call if I need you."

Vincent vanished, leaving Gerard alone in the parking lot—his arms wrapped tightly around Amber's purse.

#

Nicolas returned Amber to Lifeblood as swiftly as he'd whisked her away to his hidden cabin. Her head spun. Her legs faltered. He steadied her, holding her close until her equilibrium returned.

She blinked, clearing blurred vision—only to find herself staring at her own reflection. Wide, frightened eyes met hers in a mirror above a row of sinks. Disinfectant and ammonia stung her nostrils as she drew a shaky breath.

"If this is the ladies' room," she croaked, "you better hope no one walks in."

Their eyes met in the mirror. Nicolas smiled. "We're alone and back at Lifeblood, but I had to transport you to the ladies' room to escape notice. It's midnight. Shift change for the security guards. I couldn't risk the parking lot—too many people."

She nodded, unable to speak. She'd been to some cabin near Mount Mitchel and back in just over an hour. Un-freaking-believable.

In the mirror, Nicolas' dark eyes shone with concern. "I see your reflection," she said in a choked whisper. Just like Gerard's in the glass of her kitchen table.

"I thought it might comfort you." His voice was low, almost reverent. "Some vampires learn to bend perception. Few master it. The legend says we cast no reflection—but that's only half true. Belief shapes reality. We're real, so we reflect. If you believe, the mirror agrees."

"I see." No...the hell she didn't. Gerard had filled her head with vampire lore, and still none of it made sense.

"Do you trust Gerard?" Nicolas asked, as if reading her mind.

She turned to face him. "I'm not sure. I want to."

He nodded again. "I don't know him—but he's outside now. His thoughts are burning with fear."

A thrill shivered over Amber's skin. "He's here?"

"He's waiting by your car, but I think you should avoid him. I think you should avoid all vampires. So, let me take you home. You can come back for your car tomorrow."

"I..." Did she want to see Gerard when she was so confused? He'd only muddle her thoughts more. Not that Nicolas was helping. He knew more than he was telling, but she wasn't thinking clearly enough to figure it out. She couldn't even think of coherent questions to prod him into talking.

"I don't think he's a threat," Nicolas said with a grudging sigh. "But he's still a vampire. You know how I feel about that."

Head games. Cryptic comments. Secrets. She still didn't know if her memories were real—or engineered.

"Maybe I should talk to Gerard." Despite everything, she trusted him more than she trusted Nicolas.

Nicolas gripped her shoulders, staring into her eyes. Her heart fluttered. There was a connection here too. She shared some sort of link with this man. Was it because he'd known her parents? Or was it something more?

"There's much you don't know, Amber," he said softly. "And I'm hesitant to tell you for fear of endangering your life further. My best advice is to go to Florida. Spend time with your father. Get to know your step sister."

Seriously? He expected her to walk away from a murder investigation so she could get to know a fifteen-year-old drama queen?

"I told you, I have a job to do. I don't have time for a family reunion." Especially not with a family who didn't consider her a member.

"Then go to Florida. Or take a cruise. There aren't many vampires in Florida or on cruise ships. Too much sunshine. But mountains block the sun. So do tall buildings. So get out of the mountains and avoid big cities. Avoid vampires. Stop investigating. Stop attracting their attention."

She didn't have a choice. The evidence stacked too high. Ignoring the vampire angle meant ignoring everything. She knew the dangers of such a probe—not just to her professional reputation for investigating mythical creatures, but to her health. If she wasn't careful, she'd end up like her mother and Andrew.

"There's much you don't know, Amber," he warned. "And I'm hesitant to tell you for fear of endangering your life further."

"What could endanger my life more than knowing about vampires?" she asked, looking directly into his eyes.

His gaze softened. "Isn't that enough?" he said. And then—he vanished.

#

Gerard felt her presence before he saw her crossing the parking lot. He met her halfway, thrusting her pocketbook into her arms as he pulled her into a rough embrace. She froze for a heartbeat and then slipped one arm around his waist. A second later, she stepped back and slung the bag over her shoulder. Their eyes met. Locked. Held. A chill of apprehension clawed through his spine. "Where were you?"

"Cedar Plank," she said. "Nicolas, the vampire who keeps saving me from other vampires, rescued me again. Another vampire attacked me here in the parking lot. Nicolas chased him off and then took me to his cabin."

Fear drained the blood from Gerard's veins like a starving vampire. Cedar Plank was almost a two-hour drive by car. How had she gotten there and back so fast, and why had Nicolas intervened again? What was his stake in this?

Despair settled dark and heavy in his gut. He should have been able to get to Amber before Nicolas. Unless Nicolas was stalking her. "Get in the car," he said, his voice sharper than intended. When Amber opened her mouth to protest, he softened. "Please. Not here."

She dug her keys from her purse and pressed the button to unlock the doors. Gerard climbed into the passenger side. Amber slid behind the wheel and remained silent until she pulled onto the highway.

"Buckle up," she said.

Gerard smiled faintly but obliged. Then he took a deep breath and turned to face her. "How did you get to Cedar Plank and back again so quickly?" Mortals couldn't travel at vampire speed. It wasn't possible.

Amber's answer came cool and strange. "I took the Vampire Express."

His heart skipped a beat. "You couldn't—"

"I did." She cut him a glance and then returned her gaze to the road. "Nicolas held on to me. We flew through the trees and over mountains like a freight train. It was... disorienting."

Gerard stared at her. His pulse was loud in his ears. "You shouldn't have survived that. You're mortal."

Unless... but no. He didn't want to name the possibility clawing at the edges of his thoughts.

"Well, I did survive," she said, with brittle defiance. "So I guess it is possible."

Fear gnawed deeper. "It isn't humanly possible. The gravitational force would crush your lungs. Even if you survived, once you arrived at your destination, you'd get the bends, much the same way a diver does when rising too quickly to the surface. And yet, you're sitting here. Alive."

"So?" Her voice quavered beneath its toughness. Her knuckles whitened on the wheel.

A shiver chilled his skin. "You won't like the answer."

#

Amber exited the car before Gerard could circle around to open her door. Soldiers didn't open doors for each other. Neither did cops. In her world, chivalry wasn't expected—equality was. But Gerard was old-school, and damn it, she kind of liked that about him.

His hand landed on the small of her back, guiding her to the door. Her heart pounded with each step. Awareness blazed through her senses. Blood surged beneath her skin. Gerard's spicy cologne mixed with the scent of fear. Sweat pricked her brow. Her hands trembled as she fumbled with the key. Somehow, she shoved it into the lock and pushed open the door. A blast of air-conditioning cooled her flushed cheeks—but not her nerves. She shook like an addict craving a fix.

Inside, she tore off her blazer and flung it toward the sofa. It landed sloppily, one sleeve brushing the floor. Her purse thudded onto the desk, followed by the soft clink of her gun against the wood. In a daze, she slumped beside her blazer. Gerard retrieved the jacket, smoothed its wrinkles, and folded it neatly over the back of the sofa. He sat close, legs angled toward hers.

She inhaled deeply, exhaled slowly. It didn't help. She needed her pills.

"Tell me about your father." Gerard's voice sliced through the haze.

Her pulse stuttered. Family was a raw nerve—too many wounds, too many questions. "There's not much to tell. He was a marine. I joined the army. He didn't like it. We argued a lot and when he retired, he moved to

Florida and remarried. His stepdaughter is fifteen and very obedient. I never was."

His eyes shone with sympathy. "And your mother?"

"You know how she died." Her voice tightened. She hadn't just died—she'd been murdered by a vampire, and remembering felt like losing her all over again.

"I know," he said gently. "But what was she like? How did she meet your father?"

A smile touched her heart and her lips. "They were high-school sweethearts. I think they broke up when my dad joined the marines, but then Mom found out she was pregnant. When Dad came home on leave, they got married." Amber arrived two months later.

"How does Nicolas figure into it?"

She knew only what Nicolas had told her—and she wasn't sure she believed. "He said he knew my dad before he turned. Apparently, they grew up together."

"Then he's not an ancient."

She explained Surratt, swallowing the grief that twisted into rage whenever she thought of her mother's death. Gerard frowned, as seemingly confused by Nicolas' motives as she was. "But he's been watching over you since you were a child. Why?"

Her throat tightened. Nicolas had saved her—more than once. But had he also betrayed her?

"Tell me everything," Gerard said gently, his voice so low and full of compassion it made her want to trust him.

She told him what she remembered and what Nicolas had told her. "He didn't wipe my memory this time. That means his deal with Surratt is off, and Surratt might come after me again."

A cold shiver snaked down her spine. Memories tormented her. Had it not been for Gerard, she would have wished to forget vampires existed.

Gerard clasped her hands, eyes locked on hers. "You have me to protect you now. I won't let Surratt hurt you."

"How?" she whispered. "It's not like you can catch him in his coffin and drive a stake through his heart. When he sleeps, you sleep. And ancient vampires are harder to kill. Aren't they?"

"They're stronger and faster, sure. But the brain and heart are just as vulnerable. Destroy either, and the vampire dies—even awake."

"Might need those silver bullets after all," she muttered. If her aim faltered, she could just keep firing until the twitching stopped.

She didn't tell Gerard her mother had spoken to Colonel Timmons all those years ago. Despite their growing intimacy, she wasn't sure she could fully trust him. But Lord help her, she couldn't resist him. She wished she could blame it on glamour, but she was terribly afraid it was something else. Something more human and less easily explained than lust.

Gerard's eyes grew distant, his voice contemplative. "How was Nicolas able to shield you from the physical pressure exerted on the body when traveling at vampire speed?" His voice sharpened with concern. "There has to be an explanation."

"Why?" she snapped. "There's no scientific explanation for vampires." Maybe it was the cop in her, the part that hated unexplainable things. Then again, not every mystery needed solving.

Gerard searched her face, his eyes darker than before. "There's only one explanation. But it makes no sense."

Irritation prickled her skin. "If it doesn't make sense then it can't very well be the answer, now can it?"

She sounded like a shrew but she somehow sensed what he was feeling and it scared the hell out of her. She stepped back, needing space, needing air.

"You know," he whispered, his voice riddled with the terror she saw in his eyes. "Or you suspect."

"Know what?" A door creaked open in her mind—some deep knowledge she didn't want to examine. But it was there. Waiting. And once she looked, everything would change.

"I didn't think it was possible." He rose slowly, awe eclipsing his fear. "But there's no other explanation."

Fear coiled in her stomach. Her voice barely escaped her. "What are you saying?"

"Your father was a vampire."

Her mind recoiled, refusing to accept his words "My father isn't a vampire. He's up every morning at the butt-crack of dawn."

"The man who raised you might be your father... but I don't think you're his biological daughter."

"I wasn't adopted, and my mother didn't cheat. Greg is my father, and he isn't a vampire." But deep down, she didn't know anything for sure anymore.

Gerard's eyes shimmered—not just with sympathy, but with pity. It made her nauseous. She clenched her jaw.

"What did Nicolas tell you?" he asked.

"To stop looking into vampires." She stepped further back, putting emotional distance between them. Gerard's complex emotions unsettled her.

"You need answers, Amber." His voice was patient. Kind. He stepped closer and leaned in, his breath a warm whisper on her skin. "If Greg is your biological father, then explain how you were able to travel with Nicolas. Can you explain that? Or this?" Then he pulled her into his arms, and she was soaring through Asheville at an impossible speed.

The world rushed by in a dizzying Kaleidoscope of colors. Their feet barely touched ground as he leapt or glided like a flying squirrel over buildings and highways. Amber tried to scream, but the wind swallowed her voice as Gerard dragged her like a rag doll across rivers and through the mountains until finally, they stopped.

Her head spun as she collapsed, dizzy and disoriented. Gerard held her close, and his body trembled. "Dear God, it's true," he whispered. "You're a dhampir."

Chapter 12

Dhampir. The word echoed through Amber's mind like a ghost she couldn't banish. Her throat tightened. She swallowed. Hard. "What's a dhampir?"

Gerard laughed—a low, bitter sound. "Damned. That's what I am. Just when happiness is within my grasp, it slips away. Tina's dead. And you... you were born to be my natural enemy."

Enemy was such a harsh word. But survival wasn't about sentiment—it was about readiness. If a vampire attacked, hope wouldn't save her. Knowledge might. "Because I'm a cop?"

He shook his head. "Because you're a dhampir—the child of a mortal and a vampire." His voice cracked with disbelief. "Nicolas wasn't just your father's friend. I think he is your father."

"No he's not. Greg Buckley is." Her voice faltered, but the traitorous whisper inside her head disagreed.

Amber refused to listen. Her emotions were a wreck—a hot mix of rage, panic, and grief. She wanted to scream or sob or shoot something. But tears were useless, and gunfire would attract company. She needed to escape.

Heart pounding, she twisted to the right and lurched to a stop in front of a brick wall. She turned again. A narrow passage yawned before her, a shadowy abyss covered in graffiti—fading into inky blackness. Something moved in the shadows. A cat? A rat? Or maybe even Batman.

Gerard had transported her to some dank, stinking alley, and he was blocking her only escape. Her shoulders twitched from the heat of his stare.

"There's no other explanation, ma chérie. You're a dhampir, and Nicolas is your father. I just don't know how."

She spun around, coming full circle, fear turning to anger. "Dhampirs are make-believe. Like leprechauns and—"

"Vampires?" he asked softly, bursting her defensive bubble.

Keeping her wits meant expecting the unexpected—doing the unexpected. That meant accepting the possibility Gerard was right, but something in her rebelled, clinging to the view of the ordinary world she knew. Or thought she knew.

Grasping at straws, she said, "If vampires could reproduce, there'd be vampire children. There aren't." At least, she didn't think so. But who really knew what crept through the darkness?

Her skin prickled. This was why she skipped horror movies. Her life had been scary enough.

Gerard studied her face as if he could discern her genetic makeup with the intensity of his gaze. "Balkan folklore speaks of dhampirs. They supposedly lack a vampire's strength but possess other abilities—like detecting and killing vampires."

"Why would a dhampir kill vampires if they're half vampire themselves?" It gave patricide a whole new meaning.

Gerard shrugged. "I don't know. That's why I brought you to New York."

"Wait—we're in New York?" Hell. Why not? She'd already been to Cedar Plank without getting in a car. Why not New York without boarding a plane?

Gerard stepped forward, reaching for her. She raised both hands—warding him off. His touch scrambled her thoughts. Her body betrayed her too easily.

He stopped, arms falling. "I thought you should speak to Vincent. Or Megan. He's originally from Bosnia where dhampir legends originated. And Megan studies vampires. Maybe she can offer a scientific explanation. But if you'd rather talk to Nicolas or your father..."

"I don't know how to contact Nicolas, and I won't drag dad into this." He'd never believe her. Even if he did, he had his new family to protect—a family that no longer include her, even if he was her biological father.

"Can you sense Nicolas?"

"What part of 'no' don't you understand?" Her nerves stretched thin as wire.

"Didn't Nicolas tell you anything? He must have said something." Gerard stared, tapping at her brain, trying to see into her thoughts.

She imagined a brick wall, blocking his efforts. He'd invaded her thoughts before, but this felt like a betrayal. "Stop."

He staggered, eyes clearing. "I swore I wouldn't do that again. I'm sorry. It was the only way to prove my point."

Pulse pounding in her throat, she ground her teeth. "What. Point."

Eying her with sympathy rather than remorse, he spoke softly, as if they were at a funeral. "A mere mortal couldn't block me, Amber. How can you?"

"Adrenalin. I'm pissed as hell." Her heart pounded against her sternum like a jackhammer.

"Pissed or afraid?"

"Back off, Gerard."

"Your life could be in peril if you don't accept what you are," he said, as tenacious as a dog with a damn bone.

A denial sprang to her lips—lips cold with fear. "I'd know if I was something other than human."

Do I look like Nicolas? His eyes were brown. Hers were gray—like her mother's. But the hair... the smile. Thin upper lip. Pouting lower one. Dimples like whispered secrets. Her mouth looked like his.

"How good of a soldier were you? Fast? Intuitive? A dhampir has certain powers—"

"Stop drilling me like I'm a suspect." Memories of Iraq nearly stopped her heart. She had been intuitive. She once warned Hodges of an IED before he stepped on it. The Improvised Explosive Devise was planted in the dirt outside the abandoned house they were clearing. Then there was the night he and Morrison died...

"A lot of soldiers are intuitive," she said, barely a whisper. "They have to be to survive." But she'd known something bad was going to happen that night. Her fear had run deep. And she remembered sensing something in the dark. Something far more sinister than insurgents. Surratt? Klaus? Or something far worse... feeding on fear and blood.

Gerard shook his head. "You've done more than just survive. You've never even been sick. Have you?"

"I'm sure I was sick as a child." Yet, she didn't remember ever having a cold. And she'd never missed a day of school.

"Were you ever injured, even in the army?" He looked at her as if every word out of her mouth confirmed his suspicions.

"I'm on medications, aren't I?" She'd come home a walking basket case. She was still a basket case. "I have horrible migraines," she added, her voice weak. Feeble.

His gaze was sharp enough to cut glass. "How can you be sure the pain is physical and not mental?"

A slap wouldn't have hurt more. "Just because I take anxiety medicine doesn't make me crazy."

He stepped closer but stopped without touching her. She would have fallen apart if he had. Knowing about vampires was enough to push anyone over the edge, and she was teetering above a deep precipice.

"Maybe you get headaches because your mind doesn't want to acknowledge the truth."

She held up her hands, violently shaking her head. "No."

"How old are you, Amber?"

Old enough not to believe in vampires and things that go bump in the night. "Almost forty. What does it matter?"

"You could pass for your late twenties or early thirties."

"I use moisturizer." And maybe it was genetic. Grasping at straws, she added, "Besides, you could pass for thirty-five and you're over two hundred."

His answering smile sent a chill down her spine. "My point exactly. I died when I was forty-two. And before I started taking the anti-vampiric injections, I would have looked younger than my stated age for eternity. Dhampirs don't live as long as vampires, but they age slowly, and they don't get sick."

"So now you believe in the old myths? In dhampirs?" She flung his previous disbelief in his face. Let him deal with confusion for a change.

"You've made me a believer."

"Bullshit. If you shot me, I'd die."

"If I shot you in the heart or head, yes," he agreed. "Even a through and through would do it for you. But if I shot you anywhere else, you'd heal. Much more slowly than a vampire, but with medical care, you would survive."

"You don't know that." Her pulse pounded. She could barely breathe, much less think. So what if she'd never been sick. Her mother had vaccinated her. And maybe she just had a damn good immune system. That didn't mean she was some hybrid freak of nature.

"I can't be sure unless you want me to shoot you with your own gun, but I'd rather not test that theory," he said with a sharp edge of sarcasm. "But I know what the legends say. And it's hard to ignore the obvious. You traveled with a vampire and survived. Three times."

"Maybe it's not impossible. Have you ever taken a mortal on one of your midnight flights to find out?" If her heart beat any harder, it would leap out of her chest. She touched her breastbone, praying it would stay exactly where it was.

Gerard arched a brow. "No one but you. Because it would kill them." Regarding her with understanding, he said, "You need answers, Amber."

She rubbed her temple. "I'm tired. And confused. I don't know what I need any more."

"Nicolas might answer your questions now that you know the truth. Can you call him?"

"Not unless he has a cellphone. And I don't have his number."

A soft smile softened the lines of tension around his mouth. "You're part vampire. You shouldn't need a phone. If you are a dhampir, you should be able to call to him. Or at least sense his presence."

Somehow, during the course of their argument, part of her must have accepted the possibility that she was something other than human. Considering her past, it made a strange kind of sense. She licked her suddenly dry lips and met Gerard's gaze. "How?"

He shrugged. "Concentrate. Send out mental feelers. Think vampire." He raised his hands, palms upward, in a quintessential French gesture. "I don't suppose you'd do it any differently than I do. Look for a vampire with your mind."

"This is bullshit," she said as she closed her eyes and concentrated. "I can't—"

A ghost of an image flickered across her mind, too translucent to grasp. Her muscles coiled. Her blood tingled. And some deeply ingrained instinct warned of danger. "There's a vampire near," she whispered. "About five or six blocks west of here."

Gerard chuckled. She opened her eyes and glared. "You think this is funny?"

"No. I think you just found Vincent."

#

Desperate to help Amber, Gerard sped her six blocks to Vincent's Brownstone. On the stoop, she collapsed against him, staggering like a sailor on a drunken sea.

Staggering, she said, "Moving that fast is disorienting as hell. But at least it didn't take but a couple of seconds this time."

Gerard tucked her close, bracing her with one arm. "You'll get used to it."

"Don't bet on it, Frenchie."

Stifling an unexpected chuckle, he raised his free arm to knock. Vincent jerked open the door before his knuckles made contact.

"I see you found her," he said, his hard gaze settling on Amber. She stiffened. "Detective," he added in a stern voice. Then turning with a snap, he led them down the hall. His military bearing commanded obedience. Without prompting, Amber followed. Inside, the stench of latex and lacquer made Gerard's nose twitch.

After Tina's death, Megan had completely remodeled Vincent's mountain home. Now, she was renovating the Brownstone. The hallway gleamed with fresh paint, and the living room's faded floral wallpaper was gone. Drop cloths blanketed furniture beneath walls tinted blush wine.

Therapy? Gerard met Vincent's eyes. Grief pooled there. Tina's death had cut Megan deeper than she'd admitted.

Amber wrinkled her nose. "If this is a bad time…"

"Unless you've caught Tina's killer, it's never going to be a good time," Vincent replied.

Frustration radiated from Amber like a beacon. Gerard placed a hand on the small of her back, nudging her forward. She hesitated only a second before crossing the room and lowering her lean hips onto a canvas-draped sofa. Gerard settled beside her. Vincent remained standing, eyes glinting. Having read Gerard's thoughts, he knew Amber was a dhampir, and he didn't like her presence in his home. It didn't take a vampire to see that.

Tension rippled the air until Megan entered, drying her hands on paint-spattered jeans. Her smile was warm and welcoming. "Detective Buckley, I presume."

Amber tried to stand but faltered. Her hand fluttered, and then dropped to her thigh. "Yes. But please… call me Amber."

Megan nodded. "Well, Amber. Can I get you anything? Tea? Water? A straight shot of whiskey?"

"There's not enough whiskey in the world," she said, a trace of humor tugging her lips.

Megan's smile widened as she took the chair beside the sofa. Her eyes searched Amber's face with kindness. "So, Gerard told you their little secret."

Amber nodded, words failing her. Gerard gave her hand a gentle squeeze.

"It's a lot to take in," Megan said softly.

Vincent crossed the room and sat beside his wife. His tone turned grim. "That's not the worst of it. Detective Buckley is a dhampir."

Megan blinked. "How's that possible?"

"That's what we came to find out," Gerard said.

Amber didn't speak. Muscles taut as wire, she perched at the edge of the cushion, eyes sweeping the room for escape. Gerard's heart clenched. She'd rather be anywhere else.

Was her fear normal? Or instinct—carved into her dhampir blood?

Vincent leaned forward, examining her with dark, hypnotic eyes. He stared, trying to get past her defenses. He swayed in the chair, a frown tugging the corners of his mouth downward.

"She's a hard nut to crack, isn't she?" Gerard smiled. Amber was tough, even when afraid.

"Don't call me a nut." She turned toward Vincent with fire in her eyes. "And stay out of my head."

Megan shot Vincent a look and then turned to Amber. "I apologize for my husband's rudeness. He doesn't mean to be intrusive."

"The hell I don't," he snapped, his eyes turning predatory. "She's a dhampir—a potential threat."

"I'm not the one probing people's minds," Amber said, her eyes glowing faintly with a light Gerard hadn't seen before. Not in mortals. She was awakening, and she didn't know it.

"She's no threat," Gerard said, steady. Vincent hadn't trusted Amber before—he sure wouldn't now.

Vincent's eyes turned red. His fangs descended. "She's a dhampir. A vampire hunter. I know the legends."

"She's just looking for answers, Vin, and, she didn't hunt you down—at least not intentionally."

Vincent glared but retracted his fangs. He looked at Amber. "Is that true? Did you come here to solve your murders or to hunt vampires?"

Amber slowly came to her feet, her hand automatically reaching for her Glock. She glanced briefly at Megan's frightened face and dropped her hand to her side. Gerard forced himself to relax. Forced himself to trust her. A dhampir.

"My murders?" she hissed. "A vampire killed two of your employees. Doesn't that bother you, Maxwell? Or do you already know who's working with Dr. Weldon? Who are you protecting?"

"No one." He sagged back against the chair cushion. "Even if a vampire is involved, I blame Dr. Weldon. He hasn't given up on his efforts to create the perfect soldier for Colonel Timmons."

Eyes fixed on Vincent, Amber said, "Colonel Timmons is dead. Sonia killed him."

Gerard inhaled sharply. She'd known. And kept it from him. His pulse hammered. She wouldn't meet his eyes. Her gaze lingered near his collar.

She gave an awkward half shrug. "Weldon kept in contact with Timmons through letters, but Weldon used an intermediary to mail them. Sonia looked inside Timmons' head before killing him, searching for Weldon, but the trail was cold—he covered it well. She doesn't know his location, but he's still experimenting."

Mon Dieu. She'd confirmed what Gerard had feared. Sonia had proof—and hadn't shared it. Was she going after Weldon alone? Or had she stopped caring what he did?

Vincent watched Gerard carefully. "Sonia was supposed to monitor Timmons. She should have told us if Weldon made contact. We didn't know about Gerard's clone. Or the colonel. Sonia never said a word."

Amber stiffened. "Clone?" Her voice cracked.

Gerard froze. Rising slowly, he stepped toward her. She tensed—but didn't back away. "Amber—"

"Oh my God." Her voice was a whisper. Her face paled.

His heart plunged. "What?"

"The thing that attacked me." Her breath hitched. "It was you."

Chapter 13

Gerard's eyes shone with fear. "It wasn't me. It was my clone."

The tortured confession resonated with raw sincerity, but suspicion clung to Amber like a second skin. "You said Weldon hadn't perfected cloning."

"He hadn't," Gerard admitted, his sigh brushing the edges of her defenses. "Not while I was his prisoner. But he had my DNA—and evidently, time enough to finish what he started."

Megan stood. "It only takes one cell," she said, drawing Amber's attention. "And vampire DNA replicates fast—dangerously fast. Weldon could've crafted a full-grown clone in a matter of months."

Amber edged back, keeping the open doorway within reach. She was boxed in by vampires—and the wife of one. Her heart whispered trust. Her mind screamed betrayal. Vampires needed blood. Human blood. They could mold minds like clay and implant false memories. Anyone aligned with them was suspect.

A low growl escaped. "Then how do I know which Gerard is real?" She turned to Gerard, her heart pleading. "How do I know you're you?"

"Trust your instincts," he said, making no effort to manipulate her thoughts. "You know I'd never hurt you."

"I do," she whispered, conviction blooming despite the doubt. "But when you mentioned clones... I remembered something. The vampire who attacked me—when he first grabbed me, I thought he was you." The moment the creature flashed his fangs, her first instinct had evaporated. Gerard would never hurt her. She was certain of that. Wasn't she? But had the creature looked like him?

Her gaze flicked to Gerard's face: short, light brown hair tinged with gray at the temples, swept back from a broad forehead. Deep-set blue eyes—expressive, set just a fraction too close above a wide nose and a square jaw. His slightly dimpled chin added charm to the imperfect symmetry. Masculine. Familiar. But was it the same face?

She squeezed her eyes shut, searching for the memory. The attacker had Gerard's height, his build. But the light had flared behind him, drowning his features in shadow. She hadn't seen his face. Only felt the grip. Only caught a breath of his scent.

Her eyes flew open. "He smelled like you." It didn't register at the time. She'd been too afraid to pay attention to her other senses. But she was paying attention now.

Confusion colored Gerard's expression. "You initially thought it was me because we wear the same cologne?"

"He wasn't wearing cologne. It was his skin. It smelled like yours."

"But I wear cologne. How could you recognize my actual skin scent? Unless you think I stink." He raised one arm and gave an exaggerated sniff.

Despite the tension winding through the room, Amber smiled. Then she leaned in, inhaling deeply. Oak, leather, patchouli... and something rawer. Elemental. Earthy and charged. Her muscles tensed. "You smell fine."

How could she explain her ability to distinguish one man's scent from another's? She'd always had an acute sense of smell. Andrew used to say she had the nose of a bloodhound. It had come in handy on more than one occasion in the field.

"It's your skin," she clarified when Gerard continued to stare as if she were a freak of nature. "Beneath the smell of your cologne, is your unique scent. That—thing—had the same smell." A memory stirred. She frowned. "Only—different."

"Amber," Megan said, "most mortals don't have that keen a sense of smell."

She shifted uneasily. "That doesn't prove anything."

"It proves you have heightened senses. Like a dhampir," Vincent said, his voice smug and yet somehow dangerous.

She ignored his challenging tone and looked at Gerard. "Having a sensitive nose isn't proof beyond a reasonable doubt." Was anything reasonable where vampires were concerned? Certainly not her growing affection for Gerard.

Gerard stepped closer. His gaze was soft, compassionate—but his voice held a note of caution. "You're a dhampir, Amber. You have vampire-like abilities. Heightened senses. Sharper instincts than most mortals. But your powers didn't begin to surface until you were exposed to vampires."

"Why?" Her voice was flat, resisting the truth. She wasn't asking out of curiosity. She was asking because she needed the answer to be something ordinary. Something normal.

Since when had her life ever been normal?

She closed her eyes, fighting to suppress memories of her mother and Andrew—desperate to forget again, to rewind to a time before Richard Baxter's autopsy report had triggered fresh nightmares and warped fragments from the past.

"Blood calls to blood," Gerard said quietly.

"Your blood recognized that part of you which is vampire," Megan added.

Amber opened her eyes again, fisting her hands at her sides. "How can I be half-vampire if vampires can't reproduce? It doesn't make sense." And she needed it to. She needed proof—or at least a semi-believable hypothesis. Something logical. Rational.

Gerard and Vincent turned to Megan, as seemingly anxious as Amber for an explanation. Megan wrinkled her brow. "I've run extensive tests on Vincent and a few on Gerard, and they both have azoospermia."

"Azoo what?" It sounded like a zoology term. Something caged monkeys got. "Not that I have a clue what that is, but what does it have to do with a vampire's ability to reproduce?"

"Azoospermia means there's no sperm in the ejaculate," Megan said, as if it were obvious. "But while I was testing them, I realized—"

"I don't need the details," Amber cut in, raising both palms.

Gerard's gaze locked onto hers. "Would've been easier getting a specimen if I'd known you back then," he said with a mischievous grin, despite the gravity of the moment.

She rolled her eyes. "That is so not funny," but a shiver of awareness curled through her, unbidden—reminding her of Gerard's mouth on hers.

A blowtorch couldn't have warmed her cheeks more than the image in her head. Avoiding his knowing gaze, she turned to Megan. "So, how do you know it's not just these two who're sterile?"

"Because I had a child when I was mortal," Vincent said, his tone edged with irritation, like he was explaining something to a toddler. "And I can't have them now."

"Well, you are pretty damned old. There could be a million reasons you became sterile—including the fact that you died over a century ago." His sperm had probably shriveled into dust long before she was even born.

Megan raised her hands between them, referee-style. "Children, please."

Amber flushed, properly chastised. Vincent looked a little pink too

"I can only guess," Megan continued. "Theoretically, a newly converted vampire might be able to impregnate a woman—if the circumstances were right."

"What circumstances?" Amber asked. "And why does the vampire parent have to be male?" Not that she thought her mother had been a vampire either. If she had been, she wouldn't have died—not permanently at least. An aching knot rose in her throat. She swallowed, pushing the pain down into that deep dark place that tore at her soul.

"Females are born with all the eggs they're ever going to have—mature eggs that die with the body," Megan said. "But a man produces ten to thirty million new sperm a month—sperm that don't mature all at once. So, even though sperm production ceases at death, the remaining sperm could continue to mature once a man turns vampire. And if that newly converted vampire had sex before the body reabsorbed the sperm, it might be possible for him to impregnate a woman. The odds are against it, but—"

"The odds are against vampires too," Amber said with a snort. "They still exist. But my father isn't one. So, how do you explain me?"

Megan flushed, averting her gaze. "Nicolas is a vampire. Could he have raped your mother?"

A sharp denial spawned by fear sprang to her lips. "No." Reason returned, calming her nerves. She lowered her voice. "My mother didn't fit the profile of a rape victim."

"There's always glamour," Vincent said, for once sounding sympathetic rather than challenging. "Your mother may not have known what happened. Or remembered." He lowered his gaze, but not before Amber saw the shame in his eyes. "In some vampires, blood lust triggers sexual aggression."

"But as far as we know, Amber's mother was never bitten," Gerard argued. "And rape isn't about sex. It's about power and control. That kind of aggression would have triggered violent blood lust. If he'd bitten her, he'd most likely have killed her."

Gerard was right. Rape wasn't about sex, and her mother hadn't died that night. But Nicolas could have seduced her. Tears clogged her throat. She swallowed against the pain. "He took advantage of her and then erased her memory."

Had Nicolas lusted after her mother when he was mortal and then used glamour to entice her into his bed once he became vampire? It was the most logical explanation.

Logical? Ha! There wasn't anything logical about the existence of vampires.

"Dhampirs instinctively know they weren't conceived in love," Vincent said, his voice filled with such sympathy it made her ache. "I suppose that's why they hunt vampires."

"Retribution." Yeah. She could understand the need to retaliate. She wanted to drive a stake through Surratt's heart and send his sorry ass to hell. He may not have killed her mother, but he'd created the vampire who had. That bastard was dead. Surratt wasn't.

"When I was a boy in Bosnia," Vincent said quietly, "a woman gave birth ten months after her husband died."

"Babies are late all the time." Amber shrugged. "That's how vampire legends get started." Then again, vampires were real. Maybe dhampirs were too, but that didn't mean she was one.

Vincent nodded. "True. But this child was never sick. She had heightened senses—could hear whispers across a crowded room, see in near-total darkness. I was forbidden to go near her. The village believed she was a dhampir. They feared her father would return to feed on others. They ostracized her and her mother." He paused, voice tightening. "When she reached puberty, she used her gifts to track and kill him. Then she became a vampire hunter. She blamed her father for everything—the isolation, the cruelty—and she wanted revenge. That's what dhampirs do. They use their extraordinary senses to hunt vampires, and you have those same skills."

Amber recoiled. "Even if my father isn't who I thought he was, and I am what you say—I'm not about to go on some vampire-hunting spree." Her voice was sharp with disgust. "Do you really think I have so little control over my own actions?"

"Instinct is hard to ignore," Vincent said, a trace of sorrow in his voice. "Ask any vampire. No matter how fiercely we resist the urge to feed, we never truly win. It's as much a part of us as the color of our eyes."

"But vampirism is a virus," she snapped. "And I don't have a damn virus. I might not control my eye color, but I sure as hell control my actions." Once she solved the Lifeblood murders, she would choose to settle the score with Surratt. It wasn't vengeance—it was justice. She might not have a legal reason to kill him, but she'd do everything in her power to make sure he never converted another mortal or unleashed another murderous vampire on the world.

"I want justice," she reiterated in case Maxwell wasn't paying attention. "But I have zero interest in becoming Amber the Vampire Slayer."

"Amber has a mind of her own," Gerard said with a smile. "She's not going to kill anyone—mortal or immortal—without cause."

Still smiling down at her, he pulled her under his arm and held her close. Feeling like a frightened bird tucked beneath a protective wing, she leaned into him, drawing strength from his quiet presence.

"If Nicolas is her father," Gerard continued, "he didn't use glamour. He didn't rape her mother. I couldn't track him, but I didn't sense any hostility either. And from what Amber's told me, he seems to genuinely care for her."

Every muscle in her body went rigid. "My mother didn't have an affair," she said sharply.

Gerard rubbed her back, his voice soft. "You don't know what happened. You were only five when she died. Just... consider the possibility that she and Nicolas had a relationship. That maybe you were conceived in love."

Was Nicolas her real father? Did he love her? More than Greg did? The childish thought made her bristle. Gerard kept holding her, his arms strong and gentle.

"She needs to locate Nicolas," Vincent said. "He's the only one who knows the truth."

"You won't rest until you hear it from him," Gerard added, giving her a gentle squeeze. But the truth might be something Nicolas didn't want to share—or something she wasn't ready to hear.

"I can't talk to anyone tonight." Her voice was low, drained. "I just want to sleep."

Would a month be long enough? A year? Megan looked at her as if she understood her spiraling emotions and said, "Maybe we can finish this conversation tomorrow."

Nerves tightened Amber's muscles. Her neck and shoulders ached. "I'm not up for another ride on the vampire express. Just call me a cab and I'll check into a hotel."

She avoided looking at Gerard but felt him stiffen beside her.

"Nonsense. We have plenty of room," Megan said, giving her husband a pointed look. "Don't we, Vincent?"

He grunted and glanced at Gerard. "She stays, you stay. Somebody's got to keep an eye on her."

Gerard's lips curved into that familiar half smile. "You're not afraid she can take you, are you, Vin?"

Another snort from tall, dark, and menacing. "No. I just don't want to wake up with a stake poised over my heart."

Amber had to hand it to him—Vincent nailed the brooding vampire persona. All he needed was a cape and some creepy organ music. Handsome as sin, and just as dangerous. "I hate to disappoint you, Vamp, but I left my stake in my other business suit."

A smile twisted Vincent's mouth. Gerard chuckled and said, "You might as well give it up, mon ami. She doesn't scare easily."

"Forgive Vincent," Megan said. "He's not worried about himself so much as me. He's overprotective." She gave her husband a reproving look and then turned to Amber. "The guest rooms are upstairs. You and Gerard take your pick."

"Gerard doesn't need to stay." She'd never fall asleep with him in the house—her body tingled whenever he was near. "He still has time to get back to North Carolina before sunup."

"I'm not leaving you, Amber," he said softly at her ear.

She jumped, turning to meet his gaze. His eyes darkened. Desire twisted her insides into a tight knot. "Afraid I'll go after your clone without you?" she said, trying to ignore the heat rising in her cheeks.

His gaze softened. "No. I'm afraid he'll come after you."

Fear quickened her pulse, but she forced a smile. "I thought I was the vampire hunter."

"You are. But for some reason, my clone wants to capture or kill you."

Despite Gerard's large comforting presence, cold settled in her chest. "You think?" she said. "That damn thing came at me like a rabid squirrel on crack. It's like he was targeting me."

"He didn't track you to Lifeblood."

"Gerard's right," Megan added. "He was there at the normal time I report to work. If he was waiting for me and then saw you, he might have sensed what you are."

"I don't think so," Gerard said, gaze distant. "I think he sensed your connection to me."

Amber stared at him until he met her eyes. "You're not just guessing, are you? You're aware of your clone on a subconscious level. And he's probably aware of you—your thoughts. Your feelings..." But she did not want to think about Gerard's feelings. Not now. Maybe never.

He shifted away from her. "I'm—I don't know. I thought I was just imagining it. But recently, I've sensed... something."

For the second time since their arrival, Vincent's eyes gleamed with something other than anger. "If Dr. Weldon created the clone then we can reasonably assume they're together. Find one, find the other."

"And how do you propose we find Dr. Weldon?" She so needed her Trazadone for a good night's rest. But she'd have to settle for whatever sleep she could get and skip her meds. Her purse was in Asheville. And her meds were in her purse.

Vincent and Gerard exchanged glances. Gerard nodded. "It might work."

"What might work?" Megan and Amber asked in unison.

"I obviously have some faint connection to the clone," Gerard said. He looked at Amber. "And you have the instincts needed to track vampires."

"Why do you need me to track him? Can't vampires track other vampires?"

"Only if we already have the scent and the trail is fresh. We know a vampire when we encounter one, but we can only find a vampire without a fresh scent if we're connected by blood. And despite our shared DNA, the connection I share with my clone is weak. But I think you can help me find him."

"And what if I don't want to hunt vampires?" Would they come after her?

"You want justice. Don't you?" Vincent snarled.

Guilt warmed her cheeks. "Yes. But I can't just storm some mad scientist's laboratory without a warrant. And how am I going to get a search warrant for a cloned vampire?"

Seriously? They'd lock her in a mental hospital and throw away the key. And Reid didn't believe in anything he couldn't prove. And how the hell did one prove vampires existed if they didn't want you to know?

"You'll be looking for a kidnap victim, not a vampire clone," Gerard said. "Dr. Weldon kidnapped Axle."

"Is he still alive? Is he still..."

"Human?" Gerard supplied.

Amber swallowed thickly and nodded. "If he's a vampire, how do we know he's not a blood-thirsty killer?"

Gerard's eyes searched hers, wounded. "Is that what you think of me?"

"No, but..." She let the rest hang in the air. What did she really know about vampires, anyway?

"Relax, Gerard." Megan stepped forward and gently took Amber's arm. "She's got a lot to process. Let her figure out how she feels before expecting her to act."

"She doesn't have time," Vincent snapped. "If Weldon's perfected cloning, the balance of nature is in jeopardy. We have to stop him."

"Balance?" Amber echoed, her voice brittle. The world she thought she knew had fractured. In its place was something darker—hidden from mortals, yet undeniably real. A world of vampires. A world she wanted no part of. "Vampires were never part of my definition of 'natural.' So yeah, my whole world's out of balance—thanks for that."

Vincent rolled his eyes. "Megan didn't struggle this much, and she didn't have any prior exposure to vampires."

Amber's spine stiffened. "Sorry, vamp. I deal in facts and logic. I'm not here to discover a new species or cure some mystery virus. I'm here to protect and serve."

"That's exactly what vampire hunters do," Gerard said quietly, pain flickering in his eyes. "They protect mortals from the ones who kill. And that clone is a killer."

He turned to Vincent, and Amber felt the weight of something unspoken pass between them—like a pact about to be broken. His voice hardened. "He needs to be put down. Blood of my blood or not. The clone dies. And so does Dr. Weldon."

Amber drew in a slow breath, then another. She squared her shoulders. "Then we get some rest. Because tomorrow—we hunt vampires."

Chapter 14

Amber couldn't sleep. It wasn't just the bedside lamp she'd left on to chase away the dark. Her bones ached, and her mind spun like a hamster on a wheel—round and round, faster and faster, getting nowhere.

With a frustrated breath, she threw off the covers and stood. The antique bed groaned beneath her, its high, carved headboard casting shadows like watchful eyes. Her gaze flicked to the marble-topped dresser, where her earrings and necklace lay. She'd removed them to sleep but didn't dare leave them behind. If she had her pocketbook, she'd tuck them away. If she had her pocketbook, she'd have her pills.

She straightened the long white gown Megan had loaned her, catching her reflection in the mirror—hollow-eyed, restless.

What the hell am I doing here? She was a soldier. A cop. Not someone who belonged in a frilly, outdated room in the home of a vampire. But it wasn't just the room. Or the vampire. It was her.

Dhampir.

A chill crawled over her skin. She rubbed the fine hairs on her arms and shivered. She needed those pills. Otherwise, she'd never sleep. Would warm milk help?

She slipped on her pants and then pulled the nightgown over her head. Ignoring her bra, she reached for her blouse. The satiny fabric slithered over her skin, teasing her nipples into tight peaks. Gerard's kiss flashed through her mind—his touch, his lips...

Damn Frenchman is in my head far too often.

Grumbling to herself, she crossed the floor and threw open the door. Gerard stood guard on the other side, as if she were in the witness protection program. Or as if he were a soldier watching a fellow soldier's back. Warmth bloomed in her chest. "What are you doing?"

"Keeping watch." He gazed at her face, as if memorizing every detail. "It's another half-hour before sunrise. Thanks to the injections, I can stay up a bit longer—long enough to ensure no vampire comes near you. So, go back to bed and get some sleep. You're safe."

The warmth spread. She leaned against the door jam. "Can't sleep."

His eyes narrowed. "You weren't thinking of leaving. Were you?"

"My meds are in my purse, and you zapped me here without it. So, yeah. I considered it."

"You take drugs to sleep?" His tone cooled. So much for the warm fuzzies.

"I have a prescription," she said, lips firming.

He drifted toward her, his movements graceful—predatory. "You're much too stressed."

"You think?" Her reality check had bounced, and her anxiety was cashing in.

"I think you need to relax." He touched her shoulder and turned her gently. Before she could protest, his fingers dug into her tense muscles, kneading the knots. Her head lolled. Tension drained from her fingertips. Her body softened

"Feel good?" His voice was a dark, husky whisper.

"Hmm." She sagged forward on a sigh, muscles fluid. Then something shifted. His palms began to caress, not just massage. Awareness shimmered across her skin. Every nerve tuned to his touch. Her brain fogged. Knees weakened. Then Gerard pressed his hardened arousal against her.

A tremor ran through her. Desire pooled hot and heavy between her thighs. She leaned forward, breath hitching as he whispered against her neck, "I know something else that'll feel good."

She jerked upright, reaching back to clasp his thighs, holding him close. His hands slid around her waist, upward to cup her breasts, fingers grazing taut nipples through silk. She gasped, arching into his palms, pressing her bottom against his groin. Nudging her inside, he closed the door with his foot. Then his hands slipped beneath her blouse, fingers skimming bare skin, igniting a firestorm of need.

"Oh God," she moaned, fumbling behind her back for the button on his jeans.

He growled low, spun her around, and crushed his mouth to hers. The kiss was dark. Erotic. Consuming. It nearly engulfed her in flames. Skin smoldering, she unzipped him, shoved open the fly, and slid her hand inside. Her fingers curled around silk-covered iron, pulsing hot and heavy.

He jerked. "Mon dieu, woman!"

Time stilled. Her breath caught. She moved—fingers caressing, lips tasting—telling him with action what she couldn't put into words. He moaned, pressing into her palm, trailing kisses down her neck. Trust had never come easy. Trusting a vampire this close to her throat should've been impossible. It wasn't. She wanted him. Simple as that.

Don't think the "L" word.

He peeled her blouse from her shoulders and let it fall. Cool air pebbled her nipples. His voice rasped, "Where's your bra?"

She tossed her head, hoping it looked sexy, not spastic. "In the chair."

He glanced across the room at the lacy pink bra. "Sexy. Nice contrast to your manly suits."

"Manly?" She withdrew her hand and rested her palm on his stomach. "I'll have you know—"

"Shush." Chuckling, he dipped his head and took one taut nipple in his hot mouth. Her thoughts scattered like leaves in the wind. Electricity arced between them. Her back arched.

Then he pulled away, kicked off his shoes, and dropped his pants. By the time he was naked, her panties lay at her feet. Without a word, he scooped her into his arms and carried her to the bed. He lowered her to the mattress, his mouth fused to hers, kissing her with a hunger that bordered on starvation. And she was more than eager to feed him.

Feasting on his lips was like a banquet to the senses. The salty taste of his lips. The warmth of his tongue and the rasp of his whisker-roughened cheek against hers. His sexy cologne—and his own earthy scent.

Her body thrummed. He straddled her hips, slid a finger deep inside, stroking heated flesh. She moaned, arching into his palm, writhing, pulsing. After endless moments of exquisite torture, he spread her legs and entered her, plunging deep.

She cried out, muscles clenching around him. Body aching, she met his rhythm with fierce urgency, matching every thrust. Burning, she strained for release. Her muscles coiled tighter and tighter until heaven hovered within reach. She raced for it—arched—and shuddered, convulsing around him. When he came seconds later, she felt his joy as if it were her own.

#

Amber woke disoriented, tangled in unfamiliar sheets beside a cool, unmoving body. Panic surged. She'd dreamed of this—waking next to the dead, cold flesh pressed against her skin.

"Shit!" She flung off the covers and bolted upright

Gerard lay curled on his side, his lids heavy—his eyes open. The bedside lamp she'd left burning to ward off the darkness reflected in his red-rimmed eyes.

"Good morning," he said in a gravelly voice thick with sleep.

"Why are you still here?" She'd never spent an entire night with a man. In the past, someone had always gone home.

"Watching over you until sunrise." His eyes fluttered closed, then reopened with effort. He tried to smile. "I told you I'd keep you safe."

She glanced at the window. Heavy brocade drapes and canvas shades blocked the glass, but sunlight bled through the fabric. It was well past dawn. "I don't think you have to worry about vampires again until tonight."

She turned toward the nightstand. A hand-painted porcelain clock ticked softly. Both hands pointed to twelve. She looked at Gerard. "It's noon."

Gerard squinted at the clock, lids drooping. "Not possible," he murmured.

She grabbed the clock and held it inches from his face. His brows shot up. Eyes widened.

"Can't be right," he mumbled, then closed his eyes and didn't open them again.

Amber scooped up her clothes and slipped into the bathroom. By the time she showered, towel dried her hair, and dressed in yesterday's clothes, she felt better. Confused as hell...but clean. Somewhat. She'd kill for fresh panties.

Back in the bedroom, Gerard lay motionless and pale as death. His fangs barely grazed his bottom lip, but he'd been awake—at noon. The anti-vampiric injections allowed him to see the sunrise, but should he be able to stay awake until noon? Megan would know.

Amber slipped on her shoes and padded out. She found Megan in the kitchen.

"Good morning. Or afternoon," Megan said, smiling. "I made coffee."

"Can't start my day without it."

"Cream's in the fridge. Sugar's in the bowl."

"Black's fine." Amber poured a cup and took a long sip, the bitter heat kick starting her brain.

Megan watched her over the rim of her mug. "Sleep well?"

Amber kept her eyes on her cup. The smug look grated. Or maybe she was just feeling exposed. "Well enough."

She didn't want to talk about it. Not Gerard. Not vampires. Not the fact that she'd woken beside someone who shouldn't have been awake—even if he wasn't quite as dead as he looked. What she needed was clarity. She needed to figure out what Gerard meant to her, beyond being another name in her catalog of doomed relationships. At least he wouldn't die like Andrew. Or end up cuffed in a drug bust like George. Different disasters. Same ending.

Megan raised her brows and sipped her coffee, watching Amber over the rim. "Hmm. I see."

Amber groaned and dropped her head into her hands. "Is it that obvious?"

Megan laughed. "Well, I have been in your shoes. Knowing vampires exist is one thing. Knowing you're falling in love with one is something else entirely."

Amber jolted upright. Her pulse pounded. "It's not love. It was just...I mean...It's—it's none of your business."

Too much. Too fast. Her emotions tangled like wires, sparking and shorting out. But Megan didn't push. She just sipped her coffee and waited.

Amber's cheeks flushed. "Sorry I snapped. It's just..." Words failed her.

"It's okay," Megan said gently. "Loving an immortal twists you up inside. But it's not about glamour."

"God, I hope not." Doubt clouded Amber's thoughts. Since meeting Gerard, she wasn't sure of anything—including her own sanity.

"He really cares about you."

"He's a vampire. It'll never work." Regret tightened her throat. She wasn't chasing a fairy tale. Gerard was immortal. But part of her wanted to understand him. To find common ground.

Sorrow flickered across Megan's face. "It's not easy. Tina understood. That's what I miss most about her. She knew vampires were real—and she didn't judge me for loving one."

Amber raised her hands. "Hey, I'm not judging. I just can't imagine the isolation. I mean, sharing your personal space with a man is hard enough. Hiding the fact he's a mythical creature who dines on blood would be impossible. I can't handle mortal relationships. I'm definitely not up for an immortal one."

Megan leaned forward, elbows on the table. "Vampires are nothing like the ones in horror movies."

"Some are." Images of her mother and Andrew's deaths flashed like a slasher reel. She clenched her fists, forcing the memories down

Megan touched her hand. "Not all vampires are like the one who killed your mother and friend."

"No. I guess not." A hesitant smile tugged at her mouth. Her fists loosened. "Some can stay up until noon."

"Not usually," Megan said. "But the antivirus helps."

"Do they usually inject themselves at night or just before sunrise?" Did changing when he took the injection explain why Gerard had still been awake at noon?

Megan frowned. "At night, when they rise. But Gerard missed his dose yesterday. He borrowed Vincent's to avoid skipping it."

Amber leaned forward, gripping Megan's hands. Her pulse quickened. "He was still awake when I got up. At noon. Not for long—but he was awake."

"Oh God." Megan paled. She pulled her hands free and leaned back in her chair. "I followed stimulant dosing protocols for mortals—a single morning dose for immediate effect and extended action into the evening. I just reversed it for vampires, since they're awake at night. I wanted Vincent to stay conscious long enough to see the sunrise, so I suggested he take the injection upon rising. It seemed to work." Her voice faded. Shoulders sagged. She looked like she'd failed him when nothing could be further from the truth.

"Megan, the vaccine worked. He saw the sunrise. Injecting him with an experimental drug was risky enough without improvising the dosing schedule." But Amber understood the disappointment. After every mission in Iraq, she'd questioned her choices and often wondered if she could've done something differently—something that might've saved a life

Megan exhaled a soul-deep sigh. "The antivirus isn't just a stimulant. It boosts immunity to the vampire virus. Reversing the mortal dosing schedule seemed logical. But vampires experience a longer Delta sleep cycle than humans. That's the deep stage of sleep where DNA repair happens. In vampires, it's more complex—cellular rejuvenation actually occurs. I should've considered how that might amplify the vaccine's effects. I should've tried giving it before he entered regenerative sleep."

"Why would you have thought of it before if the vaccine was working?"

"Because it could've worked better," Megan said, her voice tinged with self-disgust. Another thing they had in common—being too hard on themselves.

"You know, necessity is the mother of invention. Assumption is the mother of all screw-ups. And sometimes success is just dumb luck. If Gerard hadn't been distracted, he would've taken the vaccine at the usual time, and you might never have discovered the impact of changing the schedule."

She sighed again. "True."

"So, Gerard being awake at noon wasn't a fluke." Excitement unfurled, filling Amber with hope. If a shot could make Gerard more human....

She stifled the budding enthusiasm. She needed Gerard awake at noon to help locate Dr. Weldon's vampire—not so he'd fit more comfortably into her life.

"I'd need to run tests, but syncing the dose with Delta brain waves makes sense," Megan said, her voice taut. "I should've thought of it sooner, but I was thinking in terms of mortals—not immortals."

Amber recognized the guilt—the weight of responsibility. Failure wasn't an option, but it was always a possibility. "Don't blame yourself. You couldn't have known. It's not like you could run a double-blind study or follow FDA protocols."

Megan straightened, pulling herself together. "I suppose."

"Didn't you use your own blood for the vaccine?" Had mixing her mortal blood with a vampire's given her dhampir-like abilities?

Megan smiled. "Yes. And Vincent let me run my tests—despite the danger."

"Did you have any side-effects from injecting yourself with his blood?" Were her senses heightened? Could she sense vampires? Did she have more in common with Megan than just a lo—liking for vampires?

"I got sick at first, but like smallpox, once I recovered, my blood carried the antibodies needed to create the vaccine."

Smallpox left scars. What metaphysical scars did vampire blood leave? "You haven't noticed any changes?"

"I feel more connected to Vincent—as if we share some sort of psychic connection that wasn't there before. But I'm not going to research it further. Like I said last night, testing vampire blood on humans is dangerous."

"And yet, you tested it on yourself." Amber would risk her life for her country, for her partner, Reid, and for the innocent. She'd lay her life on the line for duty and honor. But for a man? For something as ephemeral as love? Was she even capable of that kind of emotion?

Megan smiled. "I wanted to be with Vincent, but I didn't want to be a vampire. So, for me, it was worth the risk. What about you, Amber? What would you risk for Gerard?"

Heat crept into Amber's cheeks. She looked away, unable to meet Megan's gaze—or face the questions in her own heart. "I'm risking my career. Gerard's a witness in an ongoing investigation. And he's a vampire. I'm investigating vampires—without my partner or supervisor's knowledge."

"And Gerard's risking his life," Megan said, her voice sharpening. "Can he trust you with it?"

Amber's spine stiffened. "I'm sworn to protect and serve. That oath applies to everyone—even the undead."

"I hope there's more to it than that."

A heavy sigh escaped her. "There is. But don't ask me to define it." As if she could. There was chemistry between her and Gerard—volatile, combustible. But if it was more than lust, she wasn't ready to face it.

"Okay. Fair enough," Megan said. "But if we find Axle, promise you won't kill him, even if he's a vampire."

Amber stiffened. The request felt like an insult. "Your husband's paranoia aside, I'm not about to dash off half-cocked on some vampire-killing spree.

I'm a cop, and Axle's a witness, a killer, or a kidnap victim. When the evidence tells me which, I'll act accordingly."

"I didn't mean to offend." Megan's cheeks flushed. "But if he's a vampire, he might be scared or aggressive. I just don't want you to respond with force when there are other ways to subdue him."

"Do you suggest I wear a garlic necklace and splash him with holy water?" Sarcasm didn't suit her, but uncertainty gnawed at her confidence. Just like in Iraq. And Germany. Despite her training, she'd been unable to kill Surratt or protect Andrew. If she'd known about her abilities then...could she have changed the outcome? Could she save Axle now?

Megan sighed. "No. I still have some of the vampire sedative I created. It should work on Axle if he's turned. Just promise you'll never use it on Gerard." She smiled to soften the sting. "Or Vincent. No matter how crazy they make you."

Confused. Crazy. Either way, she was already there. But she hadn't arrived alone. Megan had gotten there first.

"You created a vampire sedative and an antivirus? You're quite the mad scientist. Aren't you?"

Megan bolted upright, defensive. "I created the sedative because it was my job. I created the vaccine because I was in love."

The "L" word hit Amber like a punch. She thought of Gerard—his sleepy gaze at high noon, the sun filtering through the drapes. His smile. His wit. His loyalty. Warmth seeped into her chest. She shoved it aside. She needed to think like a cop—logical and practical.

"There's only so much I can do officially," she said. "But if I'm going to hunt vampires on my own time, I'll need Gerard and Vincent's help. And I can't hunt at night. That would be the epitome of stupid." Like every ridiculous vampire movie she'd ever seen where the hero or heroine carried a wooden stake into the vampire's lair just before sundown.

Megan frowned. "No matter how we adjust the dosing schedule, the sun is still their enemy. It weakens them—or kills them. I don't think a vaccine can change that. But the liposome lotion seems effective. Maybe with additional precautions, they could move about in daylight." Her face lit up. "Maybe they could finally live more human lives."

Not human enough for Amber. And that saddened her more than knowing she couldn't share this case with Reid.

Chapter 15

The women had been awake for hours by the time the men drifted into the kitchen. The summer sun had passed its zenith, but it still shone outside, brightening the heavy shades covering the windows. A thin shaft of light found its way into the kitchen and danced across the floor. Gerard and Vincent gave the errant beam a wide berth as they moved toward the kitchen table where Amber and Megan lingered over cooling coffee.

Megan rose to meet Vincent's kiss—slow, familiar, and full of quiet possession. Amber looked away, her chest tightening. Her gaze snagged on Gerard, who leaned against the counter, flame-blue eyes smoldering with hunger.

Heat surged through her. Muscles clenched. She shifted forward, pressing her hips into the chair as if anchoring herself against the pull. Her arms folded across her waist, elbows digging into her thighs, a makeshift restraint against the urge to reach for him—to drag him back to bed and lose herself in the promise of his body. But it wasn't just lust. His eyes held more than that. They offered permanence. Devotion. A lifetime of love—but his lifetime stretched into eternity while she had an expiration date.

The thought hollowed her. Desire flickered and then guttered, smothered by sorrow. Her shoulders sagged beneath the weight of it.

When Megan finally disentangled herself from Vincent's not-so-casual embrace, Amber reached up and grabbed her wrist, clutching it like a lifeline.

"Tell them about the vaccine," she blurted, desperate to escape the weight of Gerard's stare.

Megan parted her lips to speak, but Gerard cut in smoothly. "Whatever it is can wait. It's Friday afternoon. That gives us three nights before Amber goes back to work Monday morning." His voice was calm, almost clinical—at odds with the bulge straining the front of his jeans.

Amber released Megan's arm and leaned back against the chair, forcing her eyes away from the evidence of Gerard's desire. "Three nights for what?"

Gerard pushed off the counter with predatory grace. "To search the Lifeblood parking lot for any lingering trace of the clone."

The image of Gerard on all fours, nose to the pavement sniffing for skin cells and scent particles, doused the last embers of her lust. She exhaled sharply. "And how exactly do you plan to explain sniffing around like a bloodhound?"

"He shouldn't have to," Megan said. "The facility closes at five today and won't reopen again until after Labor Day."

"And the security guards?" Amber asked.

"We'll handle it," Vincent said, ever the strategist. His tone was clipped, focused on containment. Damage control was his default setting.

Amber understood his caution. She'd watched vampire movies through spread fingers as a kid. Survival depended on secrecy. But finding Axle Travers mattered more.

She stood and turned to Gerard. "What makes you think you can track a clone when you couldn't even find Nicolas—a full-fledged vampire?"

Gerard's brow lifted, offended. "I'd never met Nicolas. I couldn't recognize his imprint—or scent. But I'm linked to the clone by blood. And I'll have your help."

Amber crossed her arms. "You might be able to follow an invisible odor trail, but I need a paper trail." Honestly, he'd be better off with a dog.

Did vampires even like dogs? Did they keep pets? There was so much she didn't know about him and so much she was afraid to learn.

"You're a dhampir," Vincent said, playing that tired tune again. "Tracking is in your blood."

Her head throbbed. She rubbed her temple. "I follow evidence—footprints, credit card receipts—tangible evidence. I don't know how to use whatever skills you think I have."

Gerard stepped closer. "Don't worry. I'll help you learn how to track with your mind. Between my genetic connection and your intrinsic abilities, we should be able to pick up his scent. Then Vincent and I can follow it. If we're lucky, he'll lead us back to Weldon's lab."

Even if that was possible, did he really think she'd play pointer and then go home to await his call? This was her case. She wasn't walking away.

She opened her mouth to protest, but Vincent cut her off. "We can't go in blind. We need time to plan. Once we locate the facility, Amber can pull the blueprints, and Sonia can handle cleanup. We need to cover our tracks."

"My partner would be more useful than Sonia," Amber snapped, though she knew Reid couldn't be involved. "She might know how to ghost through a system, but Reid knows where to look. I trust him. I don't trust her." Too much caffeine and too many unsolicited strategies were fraying her nerves. She wasn't used to taking orders from civilians—especially vampire civilians.

"You don't trust any vampire. Do you?"

""Vincent!" Megan smacked his chest with the back of her hand. He barely flinched.

"Give it a rest, Vin," Gerard said, stepping behind Amber and resting a steadying hand on the small of her back. Confidence surged through her. "Just because she's a dhampir doesn't mean she's going to start killing our kind."

"She might," Vincent muttered, watching her like she was a ticking bomb. "She's a born hunter."

"So are vampires," Gerard shot back.

Technically, vampires weren't born—they were made. But why split hairs? They were predators, refined and relentless. They had to be to have survived for so many years. But she wasn't a natural born anything. Even if she was a dhampir—and she wasn't admitting that without proof—she wasn't ruled by instinct. Her survival skills had been forged in Iraq and sharpened by intelligence and experience.

Then again, she had slept with a vampire. How smart was that?

She forced a smile. "Relax, Vincent. I'm not some mindless beast. I think before I act, and I don't need your vampire girlfriend's help. I just need Weldon's location—and then I go in at high noon, locked and loaded."

Of course, going commando against Weldon and his pet vampire would be easier with silver bullets. Or a crossbow with sterling-tipped arrows. All she had was her Glock, Megan's vampire sedative, and the sterling silver letter opener she planned to swipe from her desk at home.

"Sonia's not my girlfriend," Vincent said, wincing as his gaze flicked to his wife. Guilt radiated off him. It didn't take a detective to see that. At some point, he and Sonia had been lovers. But for a vampire, it could have been a month ago or a century ago.

Megan looped her arm through his and leaned against his shoulder. "I'm not jealous of Sonia." Her voice was calm, but her eyes flashed. She didn't like the vampiress. Not one bit.

Amber smiled. "Either way, I don't need her help."

"You might." Megan ground her teeth as if it pained her to say the words. "I hate to admit it, but she has her uses. And she's not afraid to kill. Vincent and Gerard could hesitate where Sonia wouldn't."

"I'll do whatever's necessary," Vincent said, his tone sharp, as if Megan had questioned his manhood.

Gerard nodded, all alpha resolve. Then his expression shifted from determined to resigned. "Vampires instinctively protect their creator and any they've created. It's a bond stronger than blood or loyalty. I didn't create the clone, but we share the same DNA. And Vincent created me. So if killing is the only option... we might falter. Sonia wouldn't. We need her."

A chill settled in Amber's gut. If a vampire who looked like Gerard attacked, could she kill him? Would she even know the difference?

"Shouldn't a creature created from your DNA share the same instincts?" Megan asked. "If you can't kill him, then he shouldn't be able to kill you. Or Vincent."

"I don't know." Gerard shifted, leaning away from Amber. "I do know destroying a man with my face won't be easy."

"Well, don't think I'll hesitate," Amber lied. "If it's kill or be killed, I'll get the job done." But killing a reflection of Gerard would haunt her dreams. Yet taking a vampire into custody didn't seem like a viable option. Explaining to her captain why she'd staked a suspect with a sterling silver letter opener didn't sound plausible either—assuming there'd be enough left of the corpse to raise the question.

"It's the hunter in you," Vincent said.

"Killing isn't stamped on my DNA like a barcode," Amber snapped. "I'm a cop. I used to be a soldier. It's the training." But had that instinct pushed her to be a better soldier? Had it made her more aggressive?

She'd volunteered to man the guns the night they entered the Ninewah Province in Iraq—the night Hodges and Morrison died. She'd moved before the first mortar hit, killing at least two insurgents. Reid claimed she was a better detective—better with weapons. They both assumed it was due to her army training. But what if it was because she had a genetic predisposition for violence? For—hunting?

"You do have certain abilities," Gerard said. "And you're going to need to hone those skills if you want to survive. You're also going to need Sonia's help whether you want it or not."

"Why? Does she know where Weldon is?"

"No, but—"

"If she can't locate your clone with vampire magic, then there's only one way to find Weldon. And that's through good, old-fashion police work."

"Sonia has resources you can only dream of," Vincent insisted. "We need her."

"Then why hasn't she found Weldon already?" Amber's voice was low, sharp.

Sonia could probably track the researcher if she truly wanted to. Unless she was afraid of losing Vincent if she embraced her darker powers. Or maybe she was clinging to the hope that he'd return to her once Megan aged. The vampiress might revel in immortality, but she hadn't severed all ties to humanity. Like every woman Amber had ever known, Sonia wanted to be loved. Understood. It showed in the way she moved, the way she spoke—or maybe it didn't.

Amber frowned, reconsidering. Maybe she was a damn dhampir after all. Then again, maybe she just had an analytical and observant mind.

Vincent's gaze slid away, and if Amber wasn't mistaken, a faint blush stained his cheeks. "Point taken," he said.

A smile tugged at the corners of her mouth. "What's that, Vamp? You apologizing?"

"Hardly."

Megan elbowed him in the side. "Stop being an ass." Then she turned to face Amber. "So, what do you propose? Talking to Nicolas?"

Amber's stomach knotted. She wasn't ready to hear the truth from Nicolas. Not now. Maybe never. She cleared her throat. "Researching my past isn't the priority. My job is, and for now, I need to find Axle Travers and whoever's behind the murders." Even if one—or more—of them weren't human.

Vincent pulled Megan into his arms as if his touch alone could shield her. "Weldon's responsible. He's still researching vampires, and he has Axle. So, we need to find him before he takes another hostage."

The clone wasn't human. It never had been. Did it even have a soul? A conscience? "The clone has to be stopped, by whatever means possible. But I'm taking Weldon into custody." She wasn't about to violate his civil rights.

Vincent snorted. "If you can find him."

"I will."

"How? You refuse Sonia's help. You refuse to admit you're a dhampir. How are you going to find him? I doubt he has a Facebook page."

Amber smiled. Despite Vincent's skepticism, she was on familiar ground. "Research. Brains over brawn—or vampire hocus-pocus. I just need to take another look at the case files. The evidence is there. I just have to figure out a way to apply it to vampires—and Dr. Weldon."

"The man's guilty. Why was he never a suspect?" Vincent challenged.

The prickly vampire rubbed her the wrong way. She clenched her jaw to keep from snapping back. "There's no motive. Weldon worked with Tina at Baldwin Industries. That's his only connection to the case. If he was involved in anything more illegal than stealing the money Timmons had stashed in the Cayman Islands' account, the evidence was destroyed in the gas explosion that damaged Baldwin Industries before the government shut it down."

"That wasn't an explosion," Gerard said. "The damage was done when Vincent and Sonia rescued me from the sub-basement. Timmons's men set a gas explosion afterwards to cover up the truth."

"He wasn't protecting vampires," Vincent added. "He was protecting his operation."

Timmons had known about vampires far longer than either Vincent or Gerard suspected. He'd been quietly laying groundwork for years, which probably explained why some of Gerard's DNA had survived. From the beginning, Timmons must have had a backup research site. After his arrest, he'd contacted Weldon, who used the stolen funds to activate those contingency plans. Weldon was wanted by the FBI for embezzlement, but Virginia authorities had lost interest, and North Carolina didn't consider him a suspect.

"What aren't you telling me?" Gerard's quiet accusation sent her pulse into overdrive.

If she'd trusted him completely, she would've confessed her mother's connection to Timmons long ago. Swallowing guilt, she couldn't meet his gaze. "When my dad was injured in the Beirut bombing, Nicolas rescued him and—" A thought struck like lightning. Her heart nearly stopped.

The truth had always been there, buried in plain sight. Nicolas had practically confessed. He'd known both her parents. He'd tampered with Greg's memory, erasing the moment he saved him in Beirut. But why hadn't he erased her mother's memory of that visit—of telling her Greg was still alive? He'd claimed she'd suffered enough, but it was more than pity. He'd loved her.

Had she loved him back? Had they been together before she married Greg? It explained why Nicolas saved Greg...and why her mother's memories remained untouched. It also explained Amber. Nicolas wasn't just family. He was her biological father.

"Amber? Are you all right?" Megan's voice cut through the haze.

Gerard laid a hand on her shoulder. The gentle contact nearly unraveled her. "What's wrong, mon chérie?" he asked, his voice a balm to her fractured soul. "Why do you cry?"

Was she crying? She raised a trembling hand to wipe away a stray tear. Her throat ached.

"My mother knew about vampires." Turning slowly, she placed her hands on Gerard's chest—a silent plea for forgiveness. "Nicolas went to see her after saving Greg. She knew he'd died years before, and even though he erased Greg's memory, he left hers intact. Because he loved her. That's when..." Emotion clamped her throat shut. More tears spilled over her lashes.

Fearing rejection, she dared to meet Gerard's gaze. Pity, love, heartbreak—all mingled in the blue depths of his eyes. He cupped her cheeks, lifting her face to his. Then he lowered his head and gently kissed her forehead. "No more tears, mon amour."

She hiccupped. "You don't understand." Pulling away, she hugged herself against the pain. "Nicolas was in the army when he died—when he was turned. My mother must've thought the army was responsible. After he told her Greg was alive, she called Nicolas's former sergeant." She paused, drawing strength from Gerard, praying he'd forgive her silence. "Timmons wasn't a colonel then. He was a sergeant—Nicolas's sergeant."

Gerard and Vincent exchanged glances. Silent understanding passed between them.

"It explains his obsession," Vincent said. "And how he knew we existed."

"He believed her story but kept it to himself," Gerard added. "It was his chance to climb the ranks. If he'd succeeded in creating invincible soldiers, he'd have been more powerful than the president."

Amber dropped her hands to her sides. Her heart ached. Before she could step away, Gerard draped an arm over her shoulders and pulled her close. Swallowing the knot in her throat, she said, "My mother wasn't trying to hurt Nicolas. She must have loved him. And for all intents and purposes, she'd lost him."

"I don't hold her responsible for Timmons' actions." Gerard's sympathetic smile eased her guilt. "And I don't blame you."

"Timmons had more than a few years to plan this," Vincent said. "He had at least decades."

Amber pulled away, straightened her shoulders, and swiped at her tears. Detectives didn't cry. "Timmons had an account in the Caymans. He siphoned funds from his black ops project and was arrested for misappropriation."

"The military knew about the cloning," Megan said. "When Timmons was arrested, he confessed to the senator heading the Oversight Committee."

There was no law against cloning in North Carolina—which was terrifying, given the research at RTP. But Timmons had been arrested in Virginia.

"Only fifteen states have laws against cloning," Amber said. "Virginia's one of them, but he wasn't charged with that. The earlier allegations were dismissed as rumor."

"The military didn't want the public to know," Gerard said. "That's why they charged him with misappropriation. But Weldon escaped. He needs Megan to continue the experiments. And Axle is his next project."

A quiet gasp drew Amber's attention. Megan's hands covered her mouth. Her face paled.

"He probably turned Axle the night he was taken," she whispered. "He's had time to test the vaccine, but if a vampire clone turned him, the dosage might be off. Playing with genetics like that could kill him—or create something unimaginable."

Pity clogged Amber's throat. Axle might prefer death to becoming a vampire.

Her guilty gaze drifted to Gerard. He knew what she was thinking—and didn't judge. He hated his immortal nature. It's why he took the vaccine.

Tension knotted her shoulders. "It may be too late to save Axle, but I'm going to find Weldon. There's got to be something in the case files—something the Asheville PD missed."

Then again, her colleagues hadn't known to look for vampires.

"You can't ask Sheridan for help," Gerard said softly. "Or anyone else on the force."

"I know." And that stung. Reid was her partner. She should have his back. But he'd never believe the truth. And these unsubs weren't the usual suspects.

"Do you really think you can solve a supernatural case using normal police methods?" Megan asked.

"I'm damn sure going to try. As soon as Gerard takes me home."

Megan sighed. "I can't travel at vampire speed. But I'll catch the first flight or drive—whichever's faster."

"You're not going," Vincent snapped. "You're staying here. Where it's safe."

She lifted her chin. "I don't think so, Vin."

"Damn it, Megan. I can't keep you safe if you keep putting yourself in danger."

"You can't protect me by leaving me here alone." She smiled coyly. "Besides, if Axle's a vampire, you'll need me. I may not be a medical doctor, but I'm the only one you know with vampire experience."

Grumbling in a language Amber didn't recognize, Vincent turned to Gerard. "I guess I'll fly down with my wife. Don't get yourself into any trouble, moj prijatelj."

Amber waited for nerves to twist her stomach, but she remained calm. Had she used her medication as a crutch since Iraq? Were the headaches and anxiety symptoms of denial?

Time to stop hiding. Time to accept what her mind had been telling her all along. She was a freak. A hybrid vampire freak.

Time to embrace her freaky side.

Chapter 16

Gerard returned Amber to North Carolina with the same lack of ceremony he'd shown when whisking her off to New York. As soon as she regained her footing, she gathered the case files from her desk and spread them across the kitchen table. Half the stack she shoved toward Gerard.

He raised a brow but said nothing, opening the first file and diving in. For the next half hour, they read in silence, skimming through paperwork.

"Not much here," Gerard muttered.

Amber barely registered the comment, her focus locked on the evidence folder. She combed through it, desperate for anything that might link Weldon to the case. There had to be something.

In homicide investigations, detectives started with those closest to the victim. If that led nowhere, they widened the net to include friends, coworkers, and anyone with a potential motive. Once motive was suspected, they built the case. Means and opportunity came later.

Richard Baxter had lived with his parents and younger siblings. His death shattered the family, and no motive had surfaced for killing the twenty-two-year-old community college student. Tina Gallagher's ex-husband had motive, but he also had an airtight alibi. He'd been schmoozing congressional interns at the Capital Lounge before heading home to his wife and daughter.

Tina's mother was deceased, her father confined to a nursing home with advanced Alzheimer's. She had no siblings, so that left Lifeblood employees.

Tanner had first suggested a sexual relationship between Megan and Gerard. Vincent had been the prime suspect until Tanner and Daniels interviewed him and Megan at their home outside Cherokee. The hour-and-fifteen-minute drive to Lifeblood confirmed Vincent's alibi. At the time of the murders, he'd been on a three-way conference call with Brit Travers and a Hong Kong investment firm.

The original detectives hadn't known Vincent could cover sixty-five miles in minutes. Nor had they been aware of Sonia's ability to manipulate thoughts and memories. But even with those abilities, Amber didn't consider Vincent or Megan suspects.

She tossed the file aside and grabbed the next. A red tab marked Gerard as a person of interest. Lifeblood's private jet had filed its flight plan with the FAA. Reid had even confirmed the data on FlightAware.com. That proved Gerard had flown to Alexandria the night of the murders, but Sonia had tampered with the website, the pilot's memory, and the credit card receipts. No one had shown Gerard's photo to the night clerk at Morgan Suites, and no one had spoken to Dr. Geniss.

Gerard might be innocent, but the evidence was fabricated. If the clerk denied seeing him or the doctor failed to confirm the late-night meeting, Gerard had nine unaccounted hours—enough time to rent a car, drive to Asheville, and commit the murders.

The police wouldn't accept Gerard's fabricated xeroderma pigmentosum diagnosis as proof he couldn't drive after sunrise. They'd argue he used skin protection and rented a car with tinted windows, and Reid would be the first to accuse him. He already distrusted Gerard. He wouldn't hesitate to get a search warrant, despite Sonia's forged receipts.

Amber scanned the address listed for Gerard in the files. She hadn't known what to expect, but a luxury home in Black Mountain tucked among upscale vacation rentals caught her off guard. "Is this your real address?"

Gerard was hunched over, reading one of the files she'd handed him. He straightened and glanced at the page in her hand. "Yes."

"Do you own or lease?"

"I own it. There's a privacy fence and no permanent neighbors. Vacationers don't stick around long enough to snoop, and the homeowners have primary residences elsewhere." He paused. "There's also a panic room in the basement. It's secure, soundproof, and safe during daylight hours, when I'm most vulnerable."

Amber hesitated. "Is the panic room fixed up like a bedroom?" Her cheeks flushed. She would not ask if he slept in a coffin

"Yes. And I sleep in a bed," he said, smiling wide enough to reveal dimples. "There's a fridge for stored blood, my computer, and personal records from a very long life. Don't worry. No one will find it, even if your partner gets a warrant."

She hated it when he read her mind. Even when he didn't, he had an uncanny knack for knowing her thoughts. Rolling her eyes, she reached for another file. Weldon's name leapt off the page. Her heart fluttered. "This is it."

Gerard leaned closer, his shoulder brushing hers. Warmth pooled in her stomach. She ignored it and focused on the file.

After Timmons' arrest, Weldon cleaned out the Cayman Islands account and vanished. Since the stolen funds had backed a government project, the Feds wanted them returned. Both the Army and government wanted to avoid ties to Baldwin Industries and allegations of cloning experiments. So, Virginia investigators dropped all but the embezzlement charges. Once Weldon left the state, the case was handed to the Fugitive Apprehension Unit.

North Carolina wasn't even looking for him.

Amber lowered the file and looked at Gerard. "If Weldon wasn't on a federal watch list, I could search public real estate and tax records. But if I run his name for so much as a parking ticket, it'll send up a red flag to the FBI, and Federal Marshalls will be knocking on my door within twenty-four hours."

Gerard's brow furrowed. "We can't involve the feds. If they uncover anything about vampires, we won't be able to protect our existence. And manipulating that many minds..." He trailed off. "It's not worth the risk."

It didn't matter where Weldon lived. Amber wasn't after his home address. She wanted the lab where he was holding Axle and conducting experiments. There had to be a way to find him without alerting the authorities.

"Timmons set this up years ago. Weldon was part of it," she said. "He didn't stop researching when Baldwin Industries collapsed. He just moved to another location."

"He's a fugitive and a pariah in the research community," Gerard said. "I don't think anyone would hire him."

"But he has all that stolen money," she said, a spark of inspiration lighting her voice. "He doesn't need a job. He's not seeking accreditation. He could set up a lab in his basement or in some abandoned building somewhere. But he wouldn't risk generating property records purchasing something, so he's most likely renting."

She pushed away from the table and headed to the living room. Gerard followed.

"What are you looking for?" he asked as she sat at her desk and powered on her department-issued laptop."

"Abandoned buildings where Weldon could set up a lab."

Gerard leaned over her shoulder as she exited the Asheville PD home page and opened an internet search engine. "Why not look through police files or databases?" he asked. "You have secure access to the department internet on that thing. Don't you?"

She looked up and met his gaze. "There's no database for abandoned buildings. I figured we'd do a broad search—see if anything on the East Coast looks promising. Maybe seeing pictures of what your clone sees will give you a mental connection or something. If you get a hunch, I can check real estate records, find the owner, and ask if they've rented to someone matching Weldon's description."

The odds of locating Weldon through Gerard's mental connection to the clone were next to nil. But she had no other leads. Apparently Gerard didn't agree. He retrieved a chair from the kitchen and pulled it close, leaning forward with his forearms on his thighs. "Once we locate Weldon, you should let Vincent and me handle it."

She glanced over her shoulder. "Not hardly—not when you admitted you can't destroy a vampire created from your blood."

"But I could make Weldon pay for his crimes without dragging you into it. Vampires have the power to exact retribution without fear of detection or reprisals. It's a power few mortals will ever realize. And yes. It corrupts."

Did he feel corrupted? She stared into his eyes, and images from his life flickered through her mind. She gasped, her nails digging into her palms. Was he sending her visions? Or was she somehow reading his thoughts?

He had killed—violently, like the vampire who murdered her mother. But he wasn't a murderer. The men he'd taken down were already dying, or they posed a threat to society. If he'd worn a badge, he would've been forced to shoot. If he'd been a soldier, it would've been just like Iraq had been for her.

Yes, he'd killed. And living with those deaths was as hard for him as pulling the trigger had been for her.

She touched his knee. "Some deaths are unavoidable, and some men deserve it. But I can't condone violence unless it's in the line of duty." Her voice softened. "Even then, it's never easy. So, if we find Weldon, I'm going to arrest him. Not kill him."

Their gazes locked. She saw the ghosts in his eyes still haunting him. So did his need for revenge.

"You're not like those other vampires," she added. "You still possess a soul—a conscience. If you kill Weldon merely for revenge, it will haunt you."

He dropped his gaze, his sigh slicing through her. "I'm not so sure. Without the regenerative sleep, I wonder how easily I'd rest."

She squeezed his knee. "You did what you had to do to survive. The fact that you feel guilt proves you still have a soul."

"Then you'll trust me to handle this?"

She smiled. "Not a chance."

Turning back to the computer, she hesitated. Weldon didn't need an entire facility—just a couple of rooms. He'd want somewhere remote, away from major cities. Somewhere that wouldn't raise suspicion if lights glowed through the windows at night. She typed "abandoned US laboratories" into the search engine.

"This is interesting," she said. "If a university professor quits without properly disposing of hazardous research materials, the lab is listed as 'abandoned'—even if it's still usable."

"I don't think he's working in a university lab," Gerard said. "Too hard to blend in on campus."

"I know. But it proves an abandoned lab doesn't have to be unusable." She clicked on a site showing photos of an abandoned biochemical lab. "Hmm. It looks like they left behind files. And equipment."

"Broken equipment," Gerard said. "Refurbishing a lab costs money, with or without FDA approval. So does renting or purchasing real estate like that."

"He has the money. Or he could get his vampire to use his hocus pocus tricks to gain access to the building without money exchanging hands." Saying it aloud made it sound ridiculous—even to her. But the idea took root. Weldon was using an abandoned facility. Every instinct she possessed—cop, soldier, dhampir—agreed. She was on the right track.

Frustration tightened the tendons in her neck as she kept searching. Most sites about abandoned labs led to gaming pages: Undead Avengers, Lethal Contagion, Mad Science II.

Were any of these games based on real vampire encounters? In one, the vampires were the heroes. "Maybe I should be looking for abandoned hospitals instead of deserted labs."

Her skin tingled at the thought. She could almost see the vampire clone with Gerard's face walking down a narrow hall with peeling green paint.

She typed "abandoned US hospitals" and got dozens of hits. Some buildings had been deserted for over a century. Third on the list was a link to an urban exploration database.

Urban decay had ignited a quiet revolution. Photographers, psychics, ghost hunters, and history-seekers documented their exploration of abandoned manmade structures through online websites. The practice was risky and often illegal, but its allure seemed to be growing. Even amateur photographs stirred something visceral. They captured an odd beauty in the unlikeliest of places—a glimpse of a forgotten past—a portent of the unpredictable future. Despite creeping kudzu and decades of neglect, the architecture of some buildings endured. It felt wrong not to restore them.

Shaking her head, Amber navigated the Urbex website until she found a link to abandoned hospitals. The oppressive, haunting pictures touched off a firestorm of images in her mind—brief mental flashes too illusive to grasp.

Over-active imagination? Or some sort of paranormal, psychic ability? Driven by instinct, she clicked an abandoned hospital link.

"He's not in South Carolina," Gerard said, referring to an image on the computer monitor.

The third floor of the abandoned asylum looked more like a ballroom with crown molding, stained glass, and dusty planked floors. In contrast, windowed doors on the patient rooms locked from the outside and bars covered the windows. Even without the grime and moss creeping in from a leaking roof, the room would have been depressing.

A century ago, the mentally ill had been locked away, sedated, and restrained with no hope of recovery. Amber shuddered and kept searching. Nothing about the South Carolina asylum triggered a psychic reaction. Just an emotional one.

"Some of these hospitals are used for horror movie locations and paranormal investigations." Nearby residents would be used to temporary renters. Weldon could set up shop and post guards. Only the vagrants would be disturbed.

"That would suit Weldon's needs," Gerard said with an almost imperceptible shiver. "He definitely fits the criteria of mad scientist."

There were abandoned hospitals in every state. Most were TB sanatoriums, asylums, or condemned mental institutions shut down decades ago. Some were small-town hospitals that had simply outgrown their rural locations. She clicked another link.

Oppressive images filled the screen. In one, light from a broken window spilled across a rusted gurney—a haunting spotlight. A ghostly echo. Gerard's hand settled on her shoulder. The contact sent a jolt through her brain. A vision shimmered—just out of reach.

"You can sense him too. Can't you?" He leaned closer, peering over her shoulder.

The image sharpened—not on the screen, but in her mind. "We're definitely on the right track." She loathed admitting the truth. Doing so meant acknowledging her abilities.

"My touching you is like an antenna," he said, awed. "You've been in contact with my clone. His imprint should be familiar. Since I share his DNA, it boosts your ability to connect. Try linking your thoughts with mine—then concentrate."

She nodded, unable to speak. Her mind spun, the images in her head intensifying with each breath.

"I feel it too," he whispered, almost reverently. "A connection to my clone. I can't be sure where Weldon is, but my clone is sleeping in an abandoned hospital in Western North Carolina."

"He's asleep? Now?"

"Yes."

Amber looked toward the darkened window. "Why's he asleep in the middle of the night? Isn't that prime hunting for a nocturnal creature?"

The moment the words left her mouth, she winced. Embarrassment surged hot across her cheeks. "Sorry," she murmured, flicking a glance at Gerard. "I didn't mean anything by it. It's just that, well—"

"It's okay, mon chèrie." His voice was gentle. "We are nocturnal by nature. Since vampires are only dangerous after dark, I imagine Weldon's using the garlic-extract sedative to keep him subdued until he needs him."

Her heart thudded. She swiveled fully in her chair to face him. "Maybe he'll still be sedated when we find him. Then it's just Weldon, and I can arrest Weldon."

But for what? Unless they found Axle or uncovered evidence linking Weldon to Tina and Richard's deaths, she had no grounds. Still, the embezzlement charges would be enough to hand him over to the Feds.

A cold knot settled in her gut. Weldon had created a cloned vampire—a creature he used as a bodyguard. "What if the clone's not asleep when we go in? What if—"

"Shhh." Gerard touched two fingers to her lips Heat sparked between them. He leaned in, eyelids drifting shut. Their lips met and—

The doorbell rang.

They sprang apart like lovers caught mid-sin, both turning toward the foyer. Gerard's eyes narrowed. "Expecting someone?"

"Vincent and Megan." She rose to her feet.

"It's too soon. They had to catch a flight," Gerard said, rising beside her.

Amber grabbed her gun, holding it low at her side, barrel angled toward the floor. As she approached the door, she motioned to Gerard. "Stay back."

He mumbled something in French. Casting a quick glance over her shoulder, she said, "What was that, Frenchie?"

"No way in hell, mon chèrie."

Despite the chill of fear snaking down her spine, she smiled. Leaning toward the door, she peered through the peephole. Reid stood on the other side.

Her heart dropped to her toes. "Well, shit."

Chapter 17

Reid Sheridan didn't wait for an invitation. As soon as Amber opened the door, he strode inside like he owned the place. The smile on his face curdled into a scowl when he spotted Gerard.

"What the hell is he doing here?" Sheridan's hand instinctively reached for the gun he usually wore beneath his suit jacket. But tonight, he was dressed in jeans and a polo shirt. Casual wear. For what looked like a casual visit.

Jealousy flared in Gerard's gut. He stepped forward. "I was invited. Were you?"

Amber moved between them. "Enough." She shot Gerard a reproving glance before turning to Sheridan. "It's after eleven. What are you doing here?"

"I dropped off my date a few blocks from here and was headed home. I saw your lights and thought I'd stop by." He nudged her aside, stepping in front of her as if staking his claim.

Gerard's fury surged. His gums tingled. It took everything not to bare his fangs. He leaned in—only to get elbowed in the gut.

"The alpha dog routine doesn't impress me," Amber snapped. "And you," she pointed at Sheridan. "Back off. Gerard's a guest."

"He's a murder suspect," Sheridan growled.

"No, he's not. He's helping me with the case."

Sheridan looked as if she'd shot his dog. His face fell. "What!"

Amber shut the door with a sigh. Tension radiated through her shoulders, stiffening her spine. Gerard felt it like static in the air. She turned slowly. "Gerard gave me a lead. Dr. Steve Weldon. Tina Gallagher worked with him at Baldwin Industries."

"So did a lot of people." Sheridan didn't look convinced.

Amber glanced at Gerard, silently asking how much to reveal. He stepped in, sparing her the burden. He told Sheridan about Colonel Timmons—omitting the vampire angle.

"He was supposed to oversee research to enhance soldier endurance," Amber added. "But the military never approved cloning or the other unethical experiments Dr. Weldon was conducting. When they found out, they shut Baldwin down and arrested Timmons for misappropriating funds, but he siphoned most of the money into an offshore account."

Gerard added, "When he was arrested, he gave Weldon access to the account. Amber thinks he's using the money to continue Timmons's research."

Before turning back to Sheridan, Amber gave Gerard a smile that hit him like a bucket of sunshine tossed into the darkness of his soul. His heart thumped.

"Weldon blames Dr. Harper—and by extension, Vincent and Gerard—for shutting down the experiments," she said. "I think the Lifeblood attack targeted them. Tina Gallagher and Richard Baxter were collateral damage."

"How are they responsible for ending the experiments?" Sheridan sneered when he looked at Gerard.

Gerard met his challenging stare. He could use glamour if he wanted, but why bother when facts would suffice? Or at least, the recorded facts. "Megan and Tina left Baldwin when they realized Weldon was performing illegal experiments. When Vincent and I found out, we informed Senator Sherman Jackson. Sherm is head of the Senate Oversight Committee. Lifeblood of America was a major contributor to his re-election campaign. After Timmons' was court-martialed, Weldon took off with the money. He's been on the run ever since."

Sheridan frowned. "If Weldon's a fugitive, he should be in the system." He looked at Amber. "Have you run his plates? Or checked for activity on his credit card? I'm sure the Feds would be interested in exchanging information if they knew Weldon was a murder suspect."

"They'd just take over our case," she said, avoiding eye contact.

Guilt flushed Gerard's skin. Amber wasn't concerned about the FBI taking over her case. She was protecting him. A vampire. At the expense of her own integrity. His chest tightened.

"Weldon's good," he said. "He didn't leave a trail—paper or electronic." If he had, Sonia would have uncovered it.

Sheridan pinned Amber with hurt eyes. "Even if you weren't ready to share your suspicions with Captain Stratford, you should have shared them with me. I'm your partner. You should've kept me in the loop. Besides, none of this explains Axle Travers' disappearance."

"I'm sorry," she whispered. "It's just..." She swallowed hard and took a steadying breath. "I don't have facts. Just theories."

"Then let's put some of those theories to the test. Run 'em by me. Maybe we can figure out how Travers fits into Weldon's plans."

He brushed past Gerard and headed for the living room. Amber gave Gerard an apologetic look and followed. "It's just ideas Gerard and I have been bouncing around since he told me about Weldon," she said.

Sheridan sat in front of her computer and looked at the monitor. A list of links from Amber's search of abandoned US hospitals filled the screen. "You think he's set up a lab in an abandoned hospital?"

"It's a theory," Amber said, settling into a kitchen chair Gerard had brought over. He stood behind her, hands resting on the back.

Sheridan grunted and clicked a link. "You ruled out this one in South Carolina?"

"Yes," Amber said with a sigh. "We think he's still in North Carolina."

"How do you know?" Sheridan turned, meeting her gaze. "What aren't you telling me?"

"I—" She looked helplessly at Gerard. Emotion tightened his throat.

He leaned in, voice low. "Lifeblood's IT specialist, Sonia Dalca, found out Weldon used a man in Raleigh to contact Timmons. It makes sense he's nearby."

Sheridan's eyes narrowed. "Sonia Dalca's your IT specialist? Funny that never came up before." He turned to Amber. "Maybe we should pay Colonel Timmons a visit."

"He's dead," Gerard said, watching Sheridan's shock. "Suicide. About a week ago."

"Well, Timmons was never a suspect," Sheridan muttered, selecting another hospital from the onscreen list. "What about John Umstead Psychiatric in Butner? That's near Raleigh."

Amber leaned forward, reading the caption beneath the picture. "Most of the patients were moved to Central Regional Hospital in 2008, and it looks like they're still using some of the buildings. Weldon would want a facility that's completely abandoned."

Sheridan opened another link. "Old Davis Hospital in Statesville?"

Amber sat up straighter. Gerard felt her excitement. "Scroll down. I need to see the pictures."

Sheridan clicked through the haunting images. A broken skylight illuminated a shadowy stairwell with rusted rails. Crumbling plaster flaked from the walls, and water damage in the lab left mossy green streaks. Vines crept through shattered windows making it appear as if nature was invading to reclaim the property while abandoned lab equipment littered the floor.

"The basement's flooded and there's too much damage." Her voice seemed to fade. Her body swayed.

Sheridan turned to face her. "What about right here in Asheville? There's an abandoned VA hospital and several private sanatoriums that are no longer in use."

"Too close. I'd know if he were nearby." Her eyes drifted shut. Her body jolted.

Gerard leaned in, lips near her ear. "You sense something. Don't you?"

She'd sent out mental feelers and had apparently gotten a psychic "hit" on the clone's location. Sheridan sprang to his feet, glaring down at Amber as if she'd betrayed him. "What the hell's going on?"

"Sit down and pick another hospital," Gerard said, touching Amber's shoulder. A jolt shot up his arm. Brief images flickered in his mind.

Touching Amber while she was in such a trance-like state enabled him to see through his clone's eyes and share the mental images with her. Maintaining the connection was difficult. Speaking took supreme concentration. "Look for abandoned sanatoriums in western North Carolina."

"Western Sanatorium in Black Mountain," Sheridan said between clenched teeth. "Or how about Space Mountain in Disney World?"

Amber's eyes snapped open. Her body trembled. Gerard smoothed his hands down her arms. The shaking stopped.

"Not Black Mountain," she said, voice flat. The connection was broken, but she was still tuned in to the clone's location.

Had his touch increased her abilities as they had his? Had it allowed her to connect with the vampire who shared his DNA? Fear twisted his gut. Was the clone aware of the connection?

"Amber, what do you see?" he asked, keeping his voice steady.

"A basement," she whispered.

"A basement lab?"

"No. A walk-in freezer in a hospital cafeteria."

Sheridan grabbed Amber by the arms and dragged her to her feet. Gerard yanked him off her and sent him flying across the room. Sheridan flipped over the back of the sofa, bounced off the cushions, and landed hard between the couch and the coffee table.

"Stop!" Amber punched Gerard's chest. His heart jolted. Then she darted around the sofa and helped Sheridan to his feet.

Sheridan rubbed his chest. "What the f—"

"He didn't mean it," Amber said quickly. "Gerard sometimes acts before he thinks."

It was more insult than defense, but Gerard's heart still skipped. Dhampir or not, she was trying to shield him. Nurture over nature? Maybe. But Amber made her own choices.

Sheridan shot her a curious look before turning his glare on Gerard. "Somebody better tell me what the hell's going on—now—or I'm calling the station."

"No. Don't. Please," Amber said, leading Sheridan back to the computer as if he were an invalid. She settled him in the kitchen chair and took the more comfortable one, swiveling toward him. "We have a lead in the case, but we need background information before presenting our evidence."

Sheridan wasn't buying it. Amber's excuse was flimsy at best. At worst? Stupide. Real stupid.

"Why the secrecy, Amber? If you had real evidence—or even a solid theory—you'd share it. So what's going on?"

Her gaze slid to the floor. "Trust me, Reid. You don't want to know."

"The hell I don't." He stood again, eyes narrowing on Gerard. "Talk, Delaroche."

Gerard smirked. "Be careful what you ask for."

Amber sprang to her feet, her expression desperate. "Go home, Gerard. Let me talk to Reid alone. You're only making matters worse."

"Damn it, Amber," Sheridan snapped. "What the hell is going on?"

Gerard felt her pain. Her confusion. And he sensed Sheridan's concern. The man might be an ass, but he cared for Amber. And if she insisted on going after Weldon and the clone at noon, she was going to need Sheridan's help.

As much as Gerard didn't want to reveal the truth, he didn't have a choice. Amber's life could very well depend on her partner knowing the facts—all the facts. "You might want to sit back down for this, Sheridan."

Amber paled. "Don't you dare, Gerard. I'll handle this my way."

He met her panic-stricken gaze. "He's your partner. He needs to know. It could very well mean the difference in your living or dying." His safety meant nothing when compared to hers.

"And what about you? Don't put yourself in danger. I won't have it."

He kissed her forehead, then met Sheridan's narrowed gaze over the top of her head. "If you trust him, I trust him."

"I don't trust him not to shoot you with my gun," she grumbled, pulling back to look into his eyes.

Gerard chuckled and then winked. "Well, it wouldn't be the first time I've been shot with that gun."

"Not funny, Frenchie."

Sheridan folded his arms. "Are the two of you drunk?"

"Vampires don't get drunk," Gerard said, flashing a smile. Then he bared his fangs—and watched the color drain from Sheridan's face.

Chapter 18

Amber fanned Reid's face. Sweat beaded his brow, but his cheeks were pale. He shook his head and slumped back into the hard kitchen chair.

"What the hell?" His gaze darted between Amber and Gerard. "I mean, what the holy hell?"

Amber slapped Gerard's arm. "That was mean. You should've let me tell him."

Gerard quirked a brow. "And just how were you planning to tell your partner vampires are real? It was easier to just show him."

"More cruel." She shoved his chest and then dropped into the computer chair, swiveling to face Reid.

Reid blinked, his slack-jawed stare slowly clearing. "This is a joke. Right?"

Amber exhaled, long and low. If only it were. If only Gerard were mortal. If only she could tell Reid everything... "I wish."

Reid stood abruptly and, to Amber's dismay, reached for Gerard's mouth. He lifted Gerard's lip and ran a finger over his teeth. "Those things can't be real."

Gerard jerked back. "Get your damn hand out of my mouth before I bite it off."

"Damn." Reid shook his head and dropped back down to the chair again.

Amber's conscience twisted. She should've found a way to get rid of him before Gerard blabbed. Reid didn't need the stress of wondering whether vampires threatened humanity—or how to protect the innocuous ones from people like Colonel Timmons and Dr. Weldon.

"You're shitting me. Right?" Reid's wide-eyed stare bounced between them. "You can't seriously expect me to believe—"

"That vampires are real?" Gerard offered, earning another glare from Amber.

"Would you please let me handle this?" Turning back to Reid, she took his hands in hers. "If you'll just be patient, I'll explain everything."

Even with Gerard standing there, how could she make Reid understand? Not all vampires were bloodthirsty monsters. Some—like Gerard—deserved peace. Others, like Surratt and the clone, needed to be hunted down and destroyed.

But what if Reid couldn't see the difference?

Maybe it was safer not to tell him anything. Gerard could zap his brain and make him forget everything they'd discussed. Better yet, Gerard could put Reid in a trance and drive him home so he'd never remember stopping by tonight.

The idea was more appealing than she wanted to admit.

She swallowed the temptation along with her guilt and forced herself to trust her partner. He'd never let her down before. Silently praying he wouldn't let her down now, she told him everything. Or almost everything. She didn't tell him she was a dhampir. And she didn't tell him she'd fallen in love with Gerard. That part sounded insane, even to her.

She met Reid's hard stare and braced herself for ridicule.

"No shit?" he said at last, his tone less disbelieving than before. Either she'd explained it well, or he was too numb to argue.

"I shit you not. Vampires are real. Some are good. Some...not so much." She glanced up at Gerard.

He smiled. "I hope you count me among the good guys."

Warmth bloomed in her chest. Her answering smile lit a spark in his eyes. Swallowing the surge of emotion, she turned back to Reid.

His eyes had narrowed, brows drawn tight. Lips pressed into a hard line. He was thinking. Processing. Not defensive. Not in denial. She'd half expected him to look at her like she'd lost her mind. Then again, Gerard had shown him proof.

"Guess I should have taken Carl's offer seriously," Reid said with a shake of his head.

"Huh?" Amber looked at Gerard again. His expression mirrored her confusion.

A logical mind searched for alternate explanations. Reid's response was random. Either he was pretending to believe and changing the subject—or he wasn't as stable as she'd thought.

"What offer was that, Sheridan?" Gerard asked with the same degree of patience cops reserved for the armed and mentally unbalanced.

Reid's mouth quirked upward on one side. "From Carl Matheson. He works for the Department of Homeland Security in the Office of Intelligence Analysis. We went to grade school together. He was a science geek and a bit of a conspiracy theorist, even as a kid."

A chill crept over Amber's skin. She forced herself to speak evenly. "Did he offer you a job?"

"Yes."

Reid was ambitious, and the DHS was a bigger deal than the NYPD. But if the government knew vampires were real—if they understood their psychic abilities—they'd either destroy them or try to control them. Imagine the Intel possibilities. Colonel Timmons had certainly considered the potential threat and benefit of vampires when he hired Steve Weldon to clone them for the military.

She forced a smile. "That's great."

Her gaze sought Gerard's. Apprehension etched his face, but he made no attempt to alter Reid's memory or read his thoughts. Did he refrain because of her? Or did he think he had to prove he wasn't a threat to national security?

Reid's smile looked more like a smirk. "Carl's division of Homeland Security is a Special Access Program requiring Top Secret security clearance. The BBTF—Blue Book Task Force—operates under the Office of Intelligence Analysis."

Amber had never heard of the task force, but Project Blue Book had a familiar ring—a ring that chimed warning bells in her head. Her heart tripped and then beat a little faster. "I'm not familiar with that agency."

Reid glanced at Gerard, who remained silent, lids lowered. He wanted to delve into Reid's thoughts. Amber felt his restraint.

Reid turned back to her. "After Roswell, the Air Force created Project Blue Book to investigate UFOs. In '69, they concluded UFOs weren't alien. By '70, the project shut down. But in 1983, the FBI got a disturbing report—not about UFOs but vampires."

A concussion grenade couldn't have knocked the wind from Amber faster. She gasped on a strangled breath. Her mother had contacted Timmons in 1983. Had she also contacted other government agencies?

Reid might be laughing now, but the threat was real—to mortals and vampires alike. Such an organization could lead to secret trials—witch hunts of suspected vampires. Anyone with a light sensitivity disorder would be suspect. And vampires who only wished to be human again could lose their chance for a semi-normal life. Death would finally greet them.

Fear for Gerard settled like a weight on her chest. Shaking, she raised her chin and met his gaze. He nodded, almost imperceptibly in silent confirmation. A covert government agency knew vampires existed—an agency too secret and too large to control or manipulate—an agency that wouldn't hesitate to destroy all vampires.

A lump rose in her throat. Gerard would be exterminated. And she might be next—unless the Task Force saw value in a half-vampire, half-human detective with a knack for tracking vampires. She'd found Vincent in New York without training, and now she was sensing the clone—even without Gerard's touch to boost her abilities. Even if it meant her own death, she could never serve such an agency. She couldn't bear the burden of deciding which vampires deserved to live and which were merely surviving immortality the best they could.

"What was in the report?" Gerard asked, his voice taut.

"I didn't want the job, so I didn't ask." Reid's voice carried a strange mix of pride and disbelief—cocky, yet disappointed.

Irritation flickered in Gerard's eyes. "What's the agency's purpose?"

"They investigate every crackpot claim, assess the threat to national security, and deny they exist." Reid grunted. "They probably don't."

Gerard's control slipped. His jaw clenched. "Can you be more specific?"

"No," Reid snapped. "I didn't take Carl's offer seriously, and the man he was with gave me the creeps. I made excuses and got the hell out of there."

The warning bells turned to sirens in Amber's brain. "Who was the other man?"

Reid shrugged. "Some guy named Surratt."

Her heart slammed against her ribs. She pressed a fist to her chest, struggling to breathe through the rising panic. Gerard's hand settled on her shoulder—steady, grounding. She looked up.

"Breathe," he said softly.

Her throat opened. Her pulse slowed.

Reid's eyes shone with suspicion. "How do you know Surratt? Who is he?"

Amber swallowed her fear and drew a calming breath. "One of his followers killed my mother. And Andrew. And—" She paused, breath hitching. Confessing put her at risk. Staying silent felt like betrayal. Gerard had revealed his secret so she wouldn't have to lie to her partner. Letting him face the danger alone seemed like desertion.

Gerard's hand remained on her shoulder. She raised hers, entwining their fingers. Strengthened by his touch, she admitted the truth. "Surratt turned my father into a vampire."

Reid's eyes widened. His mouth dropped open and then snapped shut. He smirked. "The guy lives in Florida, and you expect me to believe he's a vampire?"

"I'm not talking about Greg," Amber said, clinging to Gerard's hand like a lifeline. Reid had met Greg—her presumed father—two years ago, when he tried convincing her to move to Florida and bond with her new family. She'd refused. They'd spoken since, but he hadn't returned to Asheville, and she hadn't visited him in Florida—not even for Christmas. She swallowed the lingering heartache and admitted what now seemed like an inarguable truth. "Greg isn't my father."

"But—"

"I thought he was," she said, voice cracking. "But it turns out my real father was a vampire and—"

Reid slapped his forehead. "No wonder that creep was asking so many questions about you."

Amber felt the blood drain from her face. Reid didn't question how she was part vampire. The geek in him probably knew the legends. So did Surratt. Did Surratt also know her memory had returned? Was he assessing her threat level?

Her pulse spiked. Gerard released her hand and circled around to crouch in front of Reid. "The creep. Surratt?"

Reid nodded. "Yeah. Tall. Thin. Pale. Weird accent, and smelled mildewed—like his clothes had hung too long in an old closet with plaster walls."

"He's probably an ancient. Vampires don't age like mortals, but after so many centuries, the skin dries like parchment and odors cling, especially if the vampire follows medieval bathing customs."

Reid leaned forward and sniffed Gerard. "You don't smell musty. In fact, I think I used to have a bottle of that same cologne."

Gerard surged to his feet. "What's with everyone sniffing me lately? Merde! You'd think I smelled."

"Paranoid?" Amber asked, choking down an irrational giggle.

He looked at her and winked. "Maybe."

Warmth flooded her veins. Her world was unraveling, but Gerard's touch, his words, even his damn wink made her feel safe.

Clearing the tightness from her throat, she looked at Reid. "What kind of questions did Surratt ask?"

He leaned back in the chair and met her gaze. "He wanted to know who you were seeing. Who your friends were. How well I knew you outside the department."

"What did you tell him?"

He leaned forward, lip curling. "Really, Amber. You should know me better than that. I didn't tell him a damn thing. I told you. The guy gave me the creeps."

"What was he doing with your buddy, Matheson?" Gerard asked.

"Buddy?" Reid scoffed. "Carl Matheson is a flake. I met him for drinks. He offered me a job. I turned him down. Then his friend showed up and started drilling me about Amber."

None of it made sense. Surratt wanted to protect vampires and keep their existence a secret. He'd protected the monster that killed her mother. When the vampire attacked again in Germany, he made Nicolas erase her memory and keep watch over her so he'd know if the memories returned.

Surratt must know she was a dhampir. Yet, he'd let her live. But what if he knew she was hunting vampires? And why would he associate with a mortal likely searching for proof of their existence?

She looked at Reid. "You said the BBTF investigated unusual claims. Did Matheson give specifics?"

Reid snorted. "The guy's paranoid. Besides requesting a table in a dark corner of the restaurant, he whispered like the place was bugged. He went on and on about Area 51, government conspiracies, and the newest threat to mankind—vampires." He laughed. "Hell, I thought vampires had been around since Vlad the Impaler ruled Wallachia."

"You're not taking any of this seriously. Are you?" she said.

"It's hard to take vampires seriously. But..." He hesitated as Gerard raised a brow. "It's hard to ignore the evidence when it's flashing its fangs in my face."

Gerard's mouth curled into a half smile. "I thought you needed proof."

Reid winced, his expression tight and bitter. "I did." He turned to Amber. "I was mocked for believing in the paranormal as a kid. So I stopped believing in anything I couldn't prove. But now?" He shrugged. "There's enough evidence to confirm vampires exist. Besides Delaroche, we've got Richard Baxter's autopsy report. Right?"

"Right. And now Weldon has Axel," she said quietly. "So either Axel's supplying blood to a vampire—or he's been turned. Either way, we need to save him. If it's not too late."

Reid's gaze drifted. "I wonder if Carl knows about Weldon. Maybe that's why he and Surratt are working together."

Gerard yanked him to his feet. "You said Matheson didn't mention specifics. That sounds pretty damn specific to me."

Reid clawed at Gerard's hands until he released him. Pale-faced and hands trembling, he straightened his collar and snapped, "I'm dealing with vampires, cloning, and secret organizations. Forgive me if I forget a few damn details."

"Withholding vital information could cost Amber her life," Gerard growled. "Is that what you want?"

Color flared in Reid's cheeks. He looked at Amber, his expression raw. "You know I'd protect you with my life. But I'm struggling here."

"Been there," she said with a commiserating sigh. She was still struggling.

Reid raked a hand through his short, dark hair. "I quit believing in anything I couldn't see, touch, or feel when my dad walked out on me and my mom. I was ten. He left us for his secretary—his much younger secretary. Mom had signed a pre-nup so she got nothing. Not even child support. Dad claimed he never wanted kids and swore he'd fight for custody if she demanded support. And he probably would've won, even though he didn't want me."

Amber's heart twisted.

Reid shrugged. "So, I went from rich boy in a private school to poor kid in an inner city school practically overnight. And my space alien, vampire hunter, super hero fantasies didn't exactly win me any new friends."

His childhood explained his initial animosity toward Brit Travers. He'd thought Brit disowned Axle, when nothing could have been farther from the truth.

For the first time, she saw how much she and Reid had in common. His father never wanted him, and the man who raised her—whom she never felt close to—wasn't even her father. She had to give Greg credit, though. He'd tried. He'd raised another man's kid as his own—or at least, his mother had. He just never bonded with her. And that hurt more than she cared to admit.

"What about now?" she asked, her voice soft. Her heart ached for Reid and for the father she never got to know. "You can't deny vampires are real."

Reid smirked. "Sure. But until I meet ET in person, I'm not buying that the government's hiding a spacecraft in Roswell. I'm not a gullible kid anymore. Carl was one of those rich kids from my past. He knew I was a geek. I wanted nothing to do with him."

"You're not a geek, Reid."

"Ça suffit," Gerard said with a groan. "Can we move on to the important stuff—like how Surratt is involved?"

Amber flushed. Avoiding Gerard's annoyed gaze, she turned to Reid. "Do you know why Carl's working with Surratt?"

Reid shrugged. "From what I gathered, Carl's job is to investigate vampires, find proof, and classify them as dangerous or not. The agency then decides which vampires to destroy and which to observe. Supposedly, Surratt was helping him locate rogue vampires who've attacked humans."

Did the government's idea of observation include experimentation?

Amber glanced at Gerard, gauging his reaction. His face was unreadable, but his eyes smoldered.

"The government wouldn't destroy a vampire they could recruit," he said, voice edged with sarcasm. "And since Surratt wants to protect vampires from exposure, it makes sense he'd help Carl locate and eliminate the ones drawing human attention."

Gerard's jaw clenched. Anger simmered beneath his calm. Amber ached for him. His carefully constructed world—a life built on secrecy—was on the verge of collapse. And because she was part vampire and part mortal, she could wind up caught in the middle of two worlds at war.

Anxiety churned in her gut. "Surratt protected the vampire who killed my mother. He erases mortal memories, then converts—or hunts—those whose memories return. Why is he now working with humans to identify and destroy vampires?"

There had to be a trigger—some cataclysmic event that forced the vampire to change his MO.

Tension radiated off Gerard in waves. "Keeping our existence secret is vital. Surratt is sacrificing rogues to protect the species. He can't destroy them alone. If he's as ancient as I believe, he could have hundreds of vampire descendants. If one goes rogue, it endangers the entire clan. If the rogue is from his direct line but several creations removed, the blood link may be too weak for him to control him—but not so weak he can destroy him—or her." He raised a finger, eyes glittering. "Ah, but if he manipulates a government agent into eliminating rogue vampires for him, he gets what he wants without alienating his descendants."

"He's playing both sides of the fence," Reid said.

Gerard nodded solemnly. "And it could spark a war between mortals and immortals."

Amber's fury burned brighter. Her hatred glowed like a beacon in her brain, guiding her emotions. "He's not some philanthropic vampire protecting his kind. He's safeguarding his empire—his followers. He's using Matheson to eliminate threats to his power. He doesn't care about mortals or vampires."

"I don't know," Gerard said with a sigh. "His motives could be sincere."

"Are you frickin' kidding me?" Amber's voice raised two octaves. "He created the monster that killed my mother and Andrew. If Nicolas hadn't destroyed that—creature—he would have killed me too. Surratt did that. He's responsible."

"And you could be biased," Gerard said gently, like a cop coaxing someone off a ledge. "But once Carl's done killing the vampires Surratt marked, he might kill Carl—or convert him. Too many memories to erase. And you?" He looked at Reid with pity. "You'd be just another loose end."

Reid made a disgusted sound in the back of his throat. "Well, doesn't that just bite." He smiled. "If you'll pardon the pun."

"The bastard's got to die," Amber said through clenched teeth. She knew she was biased, but when she looked at Gerard, her fury softened. He was trying so hard to be fair—to protect both mortals and vampires. And for the first time since her mother's death, Amber didn't feel quite so alone.

Chapter 19

Gerard leaned back against the sofa, tapping his foot in a restless rhythm while Amber paced the room. They were waiting on Megan and Vincent's arrival from the airport before making their next move. Upstairs, Sheridan had finally crashed—out cold in the guestroom around three a.m., barely thirty minutes ago.

Wimp.

"Try calling to Nicolas. He knows Surratt. He might know Surratt's next move." Was that move to eliminate the vampire hunter? Amber hadn't fully embraced her nature yet, but she was beginning to tap into her abilities. Would Surratt see that as a threat? Would he come after her again—try to erase her memories? Or worse, destroy her?

Gerard's chest tightened. He'd die before letting Surratt or any of his minions lay a hand on her.

Amber paused mid-stride. "We don't need him."

Stubborn woman.

"I'm not pressuring you," he said, watching her resume her pacing—back and forth between the sofa and the computer desk. "I just think—"

"Yes, you are." She spun, eyes flashing. "You said he should be here. You said he might have vital intel. You said he could protect us if Matheson's goal is to wipe out all vampires, not just the rogues. You said—"

"I know what I said."

"Don't interrupt!" She snapped. "I'm on a roll."

"Then roll on over here." He patted the sofa. "You're working yourself into a frenzy."

Amber raked her fingers through her hair—worn down for once. The wavy strands brushed her shoulders, grazing skin he ached to touch. His body responded instinctively, hardening at the memory of her bare flesh against his. He shifted, trying to mask it. "Come here."

"But we need to find the right hospital," she murmured, eyes flicking back to the computer screen. "We need to find Weldon."

He stood. "We'll find Weldon and G-2 later. Right now, you need to relax."

Amber turned, brow furrowed. "G-2?"

He shrugged, suddenly self-conscious. "Yeah, well... we've got to call him something, and Clone doesn't sit right."

Smiling, she stepped forward and into his arms. They folded around her, absorbing her mortal energy. Her softness. Her—he wouldn't call it love, no matter what he felt from her. Until she said the words, he wouldn't call it anything.

"G-2," she repeated, kissing his cheek. "Definitely not as good as the original."

She nuzzled his neck. Heat surged through him, pooling low and urgent. He pressed his hips against her, voice husky. "Definitely not."

Her lips grazed his throat. His blood sparked. She inhaled softly. "And you smell better too."

Giggling, she slipped from his arms and danced toward the bedroom. At the hallway's edge, she glanced toward the stairs and then struck a playful pose—one finger curled, voice low and teasing. "Speaking of rolls... how about a roll in the hay?"

With a hard-on the size of Texas, he followed her. Every step was a betrayal of the warning voice in his head. Loving Amber put her in danger. Just knowing him did. He was a vampire—trying to live as something he wasn't. Sonia had embraced the darkness. He couldn't. He wanted to be mortal again—or as close as the antivirus allowed.

And he wanted Amber—with every fiber of his immortal being.

Ignoring the voice in his head that warned him to stay away from her for both their sakes, he followed his heart—and another more prominent part of his anatomy—into her bedroom and shut the door. Decorated in browns and turquoise, it was feminine without being frilly—like Amber.

"What took you so long?" Her sultry smile didn't hide the flicker of anxiety in her eyes. She stood beside the brass bed in nothing but that pink lingerie. Her clothes lay in a heap at her feet.

He stepped toward her, silent but sure. His need wasn't just physical—it was soul-deep. He needed Amber's light to chase away the darkness in his soul.

Smiling, she reached for the silver cross necklace she always wore, unclasped it, and let it fall onto the bedside table. "Probably shouldn't wear this when I'm with you, huh?"

"I'd appreciate that," he said, voice low.

Her eyes smoldered with undeniable desire. "Done. Now, how about you tuck me in?"

A horde of vampire slayers couldn't have stopped him from crossing the room and taking her into his arms.

#

Amber melted against him, her pulse quickening as every nerve lit with need. She curled her fingers around the back of his neck and tugged him closer. His immortality no longer mattered. For one night—just one—she would love him and pretend their lives were normal.

Desire, sorrow, and something deeper shimmered in his blue gaze as he lowered his head and claimed her mouth in a brutal kiss. It sealed her fate. She was in love with a vampire.

Her lips met his, bittersweet yearning tempering the lust that surged through her. When his hands found her breasts through the lace of her bra, her nipples hardened to aching points. Heat flushed her skin. Her muscles clenched. Driven by urgency, she fumbled with the hem of his shirt. He broke the kiss long enough to yank it over his head and toss it aside.

Amber's breath caught. His body was sculpted marble—broad shoulders, taut abs, coarse brown hair swirling around his navel and trailing downward in a dark arrow. A path to paradise.

Hoo-ah!

She hooked her fingers into his front belt loops and pulled his hips flush against her middle. His body tensed. His flat male nipples hardened into tight brown pebbles.

Sucking air between his teeth, he lowered his hands to her waist, cupped her hips and pulled her more firmly against his erection. Moisture pooled between her thighs. Her muscles quivered and contracted.

"Je te veux," he said in a thick, husky voice she barely recognized.

"I don't know what you just said, but it sounded sexy as hell."

"I want you," he growled. Pulse racing, she reached behind her back to unclasp her bra. Gerard stayed her hand. "Allow me."

A smile touched her lips as she skimmed her palms over his muscled forearms while he reached behind her. He wasted no time pulling off her bra and tossing it to the floor. Then he cupped her breasts, pressing his palms flat against her heated flesh.

"Je veux te toucher ." His words were barely above a whisper. The husky timber touched off a firestorm in Amber's blood.

"English. Please." Breathless, eager, her head fell back, pushing her breasts more firmly against his palms.

"I want to touch you—all of you." With a passionate groan, his lips descended on hers.

His hot tongue swept inside her mouth, an erotic caress that left her throbbing. Aching. She gripped his hair and nudged him lower, need driving her like a general driving his troops to conquer the enemy. Gerard understood without words exactly what she needed.

Taking one aching nipple into his mouth, he sucked and licked, his caresses hot. Urgent. Then gentle and teasing, dragging responses from her that left her gasping and weak. Need twisted her into white-hot knots. Breathless, mindless, she reached for his pants, fumbling with the metal button and zipper. He reached for her panties, his hands skillfully sliding them down her trembling legs.

Her muscles jumped and quivered. Within minutes, they were both naked, his hard body pressing her into the mattress, her hands sliding down his back to pull him closer. His firm buttocks felt like iron globes beneath her questing palms.

To hell with foreplay. She wanted him. Now. But Gerard was a patient lover. He kissed and caressed, his hands stroking and teasing until she thought she would burst into flames. She very nearly did when his lips pressed against her curls, his tongue darting between her hot folds.

Her body jolted in response, her womb contracting in anticipation of his entrance. Fighting for control, she wriggled out from under him. He slid up her body and kissed her neck. She smelled herself on his breath.

"I'm going to take you slowly this time. When I slide inside you, I'm going to brand you as mine," he whispered, touching more than just her body with those sweet words. He touched her soul.

Unable to speak, she kissed him with a joy and passion she couldn't put into words—a joy dampened by fear—fear of losing him. Gerard was immortal. He wasn't invincible. And Carl Matheson knew all the ways to destroy him. Gasping for breath, she ended the kiss, raising her head to meet his intense gaze. His expressive blue eyes sparkled with desire—and something more.

Her heart clenched. Fear fueled by a desperate need to prevent him from voicing the emotion she saw in his eyes, she pushed him off her chest. Gerard looked as if she'd slapped him.

Ignoring the heartache shining in his eyes, she rolled onto her stomach and reached over the side of the bed for her pants. She unsnapped her handcuffs from her belt and turned to face Gerard. His eyes widened.

She gave him a provocative smile—a smile designed to hide the fear in her heart—fear of the intense feelings he stirred inside her soul. Reaching for his right arm she said, "I know you could easily escape these, but let's pretend for a moment you can't."

Fire danced in his eyes. His Adam's apple bobbled. Without protest, he raised his arms above his head and stuck his hands between the brass bars so Amber could cuff his wrists on either side.

"I'm all yours," he said, his voice raw.

Need speared her. Hot with wanting, she leveled herself up to straddle his hips. Her body yawned above him, pulsing with a soul-deep desire to have him inside her. She lowered her hips, barely brushing the tip of his erection before rising again.

Gerard thrust upward. Amber's thighs quivered as she held herself out of reach, sliding over the length of him without granting him entrance. With a frustrated growl, he sank back to the mattress and relinquished control. Amber felt his restraint—felt him fighting the desire to break free.

"Patience," she whispered from a throat so tight she could barely get the word out. He could snap the cuffs as easily as she could snap a pencil, but he allowed her the illusion of being in control. Taking charge, she bent forward and kissed him deeply.

As she slowly lowered her hips, his hot, throbbing erection filled her. Moaning her pleasure, she took in every inch of him until her thighs rested against his pelvis. He jerked upward with a grunt, his hot breath filling her mouth. Her muscles contracted, contorting her body. He pushed deeper inside her, touching her core. A whimper escaped.

For several heartbeats, she held perfectly still, her forehead resting against his—concentrating on that part of her that so intimately connected to him. Her breathing hitched. Her body pulsed.

Fighting a budding urgency, she forced herself to move slowly—forced herself to prolong the pleasure. Palms pressed to his chest, she raised and lowered her hips, gently rocking against him until the pressure became unbearable. Her body quivered on a sigh. Her muscles tightened around him.

"Bon sang! " He jolted—his body shaking as he fought to control his physical release.

She felt his pleasure as keenly as she felt her own. Throwing her head back as she slammed against his hips, she cried, "Yes." Panting breaths escaped. Her body coiled tighter. She moved faster. "God, yes!"

Gerard surged upward. A growl rumbled through his chest. Amber increased the pace, riding him hard. Racing toward glory.

He bucked beneath her. Her body thrummed—the pressure building until she found her release and shattered above him. Exhausted and replete, her body slick with sweat, she dropped to his chest with a shuddering sigh. Before she settled back to Earth, Gerard snapped the cuffs and clasped her to his chest. Surging upward one last time, he emptied himself inside her with a primal groan.

For several moments, she lay across his chest, her legs draped over his as her breathing slowly returned to normal. Gerard held her, his hands skimming her back, his touch so gentle it made her ache. Raising her head, she met his tender gaze. Emotions she didn't want to feel choked her. Her heart pounded like a steel drum. Her throat constricted.

Forcing a light tone to her words, she said, "I'm going to have a tough time explaining those broken cuffs to the captain."

He smiled. "Afraid he'll find out his best detective has a kinky side."

If she was such a damn good detective, she wouldn't have needed vampire magic to find Weldon. Her gut twisted. Nothing in her life was what it seemed. Her father wasn't her father, and she wasn't a good soldier or a good cop. She was a hybrid freak of nature.

Ignoring the dark cloak of despair settling in her chest, she forced a smile. "I'm not his best detective. But I bet I'm the best sex you ever had."

Even in her befuzzled state she knew what they'd just shared was more than sex—a hell of lot more. She felt as if she'd given up part of her soul to this man.

Afraid to admit she wanted a future with an immortal, she slid off his body, giving him her back. Before she could scramble off the bed, he pulled her against his chest. His arms banded around her waist. His lips brushed the back of her neck.

"Don't you want more?" he whispered.

She stiffened. "Don't get carried away, Frenchie. It was just sex."

Just saying those cold, hard words brought a lump to her throat. She didn't know what she wanted from Gerard, or what was even possible, but she knew she wanted more from him than just a mind-blowing screw.

She wanted...

Happily ever after? Yeah. Right. Forever for Gerard was literal. And she was destined to live and die in the normal human fashion.

"Do you think I betrayed you?" he asked softly, his lips brushing her shoulders.

Her breath hitched in her lungs. "What?"

"This wasn't the result of glamour. I want you to know that," he said in a solemn voice that sounded like a pledge. "Whatever made you want me was real. I didn't instigate it. It's important to me for you to know that."

Her heart melted. Warning bells rang like sirens in her head, cautioning her to tread lightly. She was in grave danger of pledging her undying love to man who could live forever. The very idea was ludicrous. And so incredibly sad.

Turning her head to the side, she rested her cheek against his shoulder. In the stillness of the room, she let her heart feel the love he offered for only a second. Then she slipped from his arms and reached for her clothes.

"Being carefree was fun while it lasted, but we have a lot to do before Vincent and Megan get here. And I need to take a shower."

Gerard stood. Sorrow shadowed his expression. His smile appeared forced. "Go take your shower and slip into some clean clothes. You've had on those same pink undies since yesterday."

Relieved by his light tone, she relaxed her tense shoulders. "Well, you shouldn't have dragged me to New York without letting me pack a bag. I had a shower at Vincent's, but I wasn't about to borrow Megan's underwear."

"You wouldn't have liked her undies," he said with an honest to God twinkle in his eyes. "She wears plain cotton panties."

Amber folded her arms under her breasts, hugging her dirty clothes to her chest. An unexpected stab of jealousy pierced her heart. "How would you know what kind of panties Megan wears?"

He winked. "I'm a vampire. I have my secrets." That damn wink did it for her. It eased her mind and her cares.

Why was she stressing about her relationship with Gerard. It's not like he'd proposed. She didn't need a commitment to enjoy his company or to sleep with him. They could be friends with benefits. No pressure. No illusions about happily ever after. She didn't even have to risk her heart by telling him she loved him. What could be better? She could enjoy his company while it lasted—until she started to get old and wrinkled or he grew bored with his mortal "play thing."

So, why didn't that make her feel better?

Chapter 20

Dressed in shorts and a t-shirt, Amber sat on the sofa with her laptop resting on her thighs. Gerard sat beside her wearing nothing but jeans. Beneath lowered lashes, she stole glances at his chest. He stared openly at her legs, remembering how it felt to have them straddling his hips.

As if aware of his fantasies, she cleared her throat. A flush stained her cheeks when she began another search of Urban Exploration sites for abandoned hospitals in North Carolina. An image appeared on the screen, distracting him from his erotic daydreams. He leaned closer, studying the dark, oppressive photos taken at an abandoned hospital in Banner Elk, North Carolina.

"Cannon Memorial Hospital," he said.

Amber seemed to be concentrating, reaching out with her mind to find his clone. "He's not in Banner Elk. He's further east."

She scrolled down the page to another abandoned facility. When she opened the link, a warren of corridors with peeling green paint and warped doors appeared on the screen. Buckled floor tiles were littered with years of dust and grime. Images he'd seen in his head—images he shared with his clone.

His throat went dry. "Piney Grove Sanatorium."

Most of the windows were broken or bordered up, but the grounds looked freshly mowed and despite an overgrowth of kudzu, the building looked sturdy. Located outside of a small, sparsely populated mountain community northwest of Mount Airy near the Virginia border, it was the perfect location for Weldon's experiments.

Piney Grove was a dying town. Besides the abandoned sanatorium, there was a country store, a church, a bed and breakfast, a gas station, and a handful of scattered houses. The internet pictures were taken by an urban explorer in 2015 who listed the mayor of Piney Grove as the owner of the facility. Although several paranormal investigators had rented the building in the past, the property was still available for sale or lease. Or, it had still been available in 2015.

"Why would anyone build a hospital in the middle of nowhere?" Amber asked as she scrolled through the images. "Even before Interstate 74 diverted traffic away from the town, there wasn't much to it."

"Isolation prevented the spread of consumption." He leaned closer, staring at the haunting images, hoping to get a mental fix on the clone's exact location in the building.

Amber looked at him. "Don't you mean TB?"

"In my day, we called it consumption. Before antibiotics, it was the second leading cause of death in America and the leading cause of death in France. Sanatoriums provided rest, isolation, and fresh air. They also provided a food source for hungry vampires who needed to feed without taking blood from healthy, innocent mortals."

Shame twisted his gut. He wasn't proud of the lives he'd taken. Telling himself his victims were already dying did little to ease his conscience.

"When the sanatoriums closed," he continued, unable to look at Amber and see the condemnation in her eyes, "vampires with a conscience found other food supplies. I stole from blood banks long before Vincent offered me the job at Lifeblood."

The Red Cross was always running short on blood, no matter how much they collected from volunteers. The administrators remained unaware of the real reason for the shortage.

His stomach cramped. He closed his eyes, battling the guilt. The remorse. In France, he'd dined on soldiers mortally wounded in battle. He'd done the same during both world wars. In between wars, he'd found sustenance in sanatoriums and among burn victims after the Chicago fire and other disasters that befell his adopted country. But he had never murdered an innocent. Still...

He opened his eyes and met Amber's compassionate gaze.

"What's wrong?" she asked softly.

"Nothing." He shook his head. She was mortal...a dhampir. Either way, she'd never understand.

Leaning over the laptop, she took his hands in hers. "You never took an innocent life. I know you. Even as a mortal soldier, you wouldn't have shot unless forced."

He smiled, choking back the knot of emotion clogging his throat. "When I was a soldier, I fired a musket, but I did most of my killing with the business end of my bayonet." And he still lived with the memories of every life he'd ever taken.

"You killed in defense of your country. Or to relieve the suffering of someone mortally wounded or terminally ill. You never murdered anyone."

He swallowed thickly. "How can you be so sure?"

"I know you, Gerard. I know your heart, and it has nothing to do with being a dhampir."

"So, you do think I'm one of the good guys." Despite his efforts to sound flippant, his voice cracked. "But according to legend, vampires are evil."

She smiled, dispelling the sadness in her eyes. "Yeah, and dhampirs are supposed to be hideous. I hope that legend isn't true either."

"You're far from hideous," he said, voice catching. "You're beautiful—down to your soul."

Color bloomed across her cheeks. She slipped her hands free and turned back to the computer. "And apparently, there's more to being a dhampir than a desire to hunt and kill vampires."

"No," he murmured. "There's more to you."

The look she gave him sent his heart hammering too fast, even for a vampire. It took sheer will not to pull her into his arms and lose himself in her again. But time was slipping away. And the clone—his clone—G-2 was growing restless.

His stomach twisted. "Scroll through the pictures. See if you feel what I do. Try to pinpoint his location."

Fear flickered in her eyes. "Okay."

She bent over the laptop, scrolling through images: dim hallways, shadow-choked rooms, rusted bed frames buried in decades of debris. By the third photo in a set of nine, Amber gasped. "He's in the cafeteria—in the basement. My earlier impression was right. Weldon keeps him locked in a walk-in freezer when he isn't needed."

Gerard closed his eyes, reaching out to his clone. A sudden craving jolted him. A foreign hunger. He opened his eyes and met Amber's. "He's getting impatient. And hungry."

"There's another vampire," Amber said, fear straining her voice. "I sense him, but I can't get a reading. Is it Axle?"

Amber had never met Axle. Her connection to the clone would only identify him as vampire. But Gerard knew Axle. And if Weldon had used the clone's blood to convert him, Gerard should be able to sense him too.

He closed his eyes again, stretching his mind, searching for a second genetic thread. His body swayed as he stretched his mind further, trying to find a second genetic link. A flash—an image. A body strapped to a morgue slab. Sedated. Still breathing

"Axle." His heart slammed against his ribs. The connection was faint, but real. Axle Travers was a vampire.

"We're too late. Aren't we?" Her voice trembled.

He wanted to deny the truth. He wanted to tell her they could still save him. But she was right. It was too late to save Axle or his soul.

Gerard felt the young man's pain—his fight against the hunger. Had he killed yet? Had he endured the same torment Gerard had suffered in Weldon's lab

Pain tightened his throat. "He's weak. Weldon's using him—testing theories, pushing every vampire legend to its limit. I know what he's going through. I've lived it. A vampire's body heals. The soul doesn't."

"Dear God." Amber's voice was a raspy whisper. "We have to save him before Weldon kills him."

"It may already be too late." Gerard shut his eyes, reliving the agony. He'd never doubted his body would recover. But his mind—his humanity—that had always been at risk.

Amber touched his thigh, grounding him. "Your soul isn't damaged. You've survived horrors without losing your compassion. That makes you heroic—like the soldiers I served with in Iraq."

He met her gaze, seeing more than she meant to reveal. His throat closed. His heart hardened. He'd dragged her into his darkness, and she wasn't resisting anymore. He couldn't let her embrace it—not for her job, and not for him. "I'm no knight in shining armor."

She jerked as if slapped and removed her hand from his leg. "I never said you were. So, don't flatter yourself. I don't need rescuing."

Merde. That was one way to put distance between them—question her strength by suggesting she needed him. Amber hated vulnerability and saw it as a weakness rather than a connection to humanity. Mortals needed one another. Vampires were destined to live alone.

Swallowing the ache in his throat, Gerard focused on the clone. The creature was awake, pacing the freezer like a caged wolf, consumed by hunger. Rage simmered, but he didn't try to escape. Gerard finally understood why their connection had been so faint. The clone wasn't whole.

He turned to Amber, heart pounding. "Weldon made a physical copy. He looks like me, but his instincts are primal. His mind isn't developed."

"He doesn't have a soul." Amber's fingers covered her lips. Her eyes widened. "Weldon cloned a body, but he's not God. He can't replicate a soul. That thing lives to feed. And Weldon's lost control."

Gerard met her gaze, severing her link to the clone. The terror in her eyes slowly faded.

"We have to go in tomorrow—before sunset," she said. "I can't wait to see if the antivirus is going to allow you to awaken sooner or stay up longer. If Weldon unleashes that creature on the world or loses control of him—"

"Don't be a hero, Amber." He grabbed both her hands, knocking the computer off her lap. It slid between her thigh and the arm of the sofa. "Promise you won't do anything stupid. Promise me you—"

The doorbell saved Amber from making any promises she knew she wouldn't keep.

Pulling her hands free from Gerard's she rose and headed for the door. He was hard on her heels, begging her not to go after the clone alone.

"Damn it, Amber. Promise me."

How did he know he could trust her not to break a promise, even if she did make one? How had he gotten to know her so well in such a short amount of time?

Refusing to respond, she opened the door. An airport cab pulled away from the curb. Vincent and Megan stood on her doorstep. Megan had a pocketbook over her shoulder. Vincent held an overnight bag out to his side as if it were a bag of garbage.

"Where do I put this? Megan insisted we pack a bag and stay together tonight—like one big sleep over." He scowled, as if being sociable physically pained him. "I assume you have a guest room."

Amber nearly laughed aloud, the tension of the last few minutes with Gerard draining away, leaving only remnants of her previous fear. "As a matter of fact I have two guest rooms upstairs."

Megan flushed. "I hope we're not imposing." She looked from Gerard to Amber, apparently noticing the tension between them. As if sensing at least part of the reason behind that tension, she added, "I don't trust Vincent not to run off without us either."

Amber put her arm around Megan and dragged her away from Vincent. "They think that because they're vampires, they're invincible."

"They need us if they want to save Axel," Megan agreed.

Vincent slammed the door, getting their attention. Megan and Amber turned together to face two angry vampires with similarly annoyed scowls standing between the front door and the foot of the stairs.

"Ask her who's sleeping in the other guestroom," Gerard said through clenched teeth.

Vincent glared. "I don't think I have to ask."

"What the hell's going on?" Reid stepped off the stair landing and into the foyer. He'd taken the time to dress, but his feet were bare. "I'd say you were making enough noise to wake the dead, but that's kind of obvious since two of you are dead."

Gerard raised his brows, looking somewhat amused. Vincent's scowl deepened. "You weren't supposed to drag other mortals into this Detective Buckley," he said, making her name sound like a threat.

She dropped her arm to her side, stepping away from Megan. "Before you go all vampire on me, perhaps you ought to get your facts straight. Reid shared some vital information that could save all our lives."

Vincent and Gerard made eye contact, communicating without words. Amber hated when they did that.

"Damn." Vincent raked a hand through his dark hair. "That complicates matters significantly."

"What the hell?" Reid looked at Amber. "I didn't say anything."

"Care to share the information with those of us who can't read minds?" Megan asked.

Reid bristled. "They didn't read my thoughts. Did they?"

If the situation hadn't been so dire, the panic-stricken look on Reid's face would have been amusing. But Amber wasn't laughing. "No. Vincent read Gerard's thoughts. It's this thing they do. And it's rude when they do it in front of others."

Neither man looked the least bit apologetic. So, Amber and Reid told Megan about Surratt. "And the government knows we exist," Gerard added.

"Maybe we need to work with Surratt," Vincent said. "If he's made contact with the FBI , then maybe he has a plan."

"You can't work with Surratt." Just the thought of Gerard joining forces with the son-of-a-bitch who created the vampire that killed her mother and Andrew terrified her. How could he trust such a—creature? How could she trust Gerard if he did? Surratt had ordered Nicolas to erase her memories. She was a dhampir—a threat to vampires. Would Gerard see her as a threat if he worked with Surratt?

Sympathy shone in Gerard's eyes when he met her gaze. "We can't decide anything tonight. Let's save Axel first. We'll discuss the future tomorrow night when Vincent and I return from Piney Grove."

"We can talk on the way to Piney Grove," Amber said. "Megan and I won't be staying here."

"Neither will I," Reid said, crossing his arms over his chest.

"Think you can keep up?" Vincent countered.

"You and Megan are mortal. And Amber might be able to travel as fast as we do but she can't travel that fast alone, and Gerard and I aren't going to drag any of you into danger." He turned to Amber, dismissing Reid. "Now show me the guest room so I can get some rest. The higher the sun climbs, the weaker I feel."

"Which is exactly my point," Amber argued. "When you're weak, the clone is weak. And when you feel strong and invincible, so will he. We need to go in at noon, when the sun is highest in the sky."

"And that's something Amber and I can do without any help from vampires," Reid added.

"You're not taking Amber anywhere," Gerard snarled. Then he turned toward Amber, gentling his voice. "You need your rest too, chérie. You've been up all night. Even if you wanted to go to Piney Grove without us, it's a three hour drive. And it's after six now. The sun is up and we all need some rest. Even you, Sheridan."

"I'm good," Reid said. "I'm ready to go if Amber is."

She yawned, feeling as if she hadn't slept in weeks. "I need to rest, Reid. And you look like you could use a bit more sleep yourself."

Gerard stepped forward and put his arm around her. "Let's go to bed. We'll discuss it tonight when we're all fresh and well-rested."

"It make sense," Megan said, the voice of reason.

"We'll devise a plan in the morning—a plan that works for all of us. Tomorrow's Saturday and we have until Monday morning before you have to go back to work. Right?"

"That's true," Amber said, not meeting Reid's gaze or agreeing to anything. She had no intention of waiting until the last minute to go after Axel.

Reid pointed a finger at her. "Don't even think of leaving this house without me. Got it, partner?"

The reprimand sent a guilty flush to her cheeks. "Got it."

With an emphatic nod, Reid turned and headed back up to his room.

After showing Vincent and Megan the other guest room, Megan took the quilt off the end of the bed and draped it over the curtain rod to prevent any random sunbeams from slipping through the blinds when the sun rose higher in the morning sky.

"Don't forget to take your antivirus injection now instead of waiting until you wake up tonight," she reminded Gerard. Before leaving New York last night, Megan had suggested the new dosing schedule. "We're going to need the two of you to remain awake and functional for as long as possible Sunday morning. The liposome sunblock and protective clothing should protect your skin, and if we're lucky, changing the dosing schedule of the antivirus should allow you to stay awake longer during the day."

Gerard nodded. "Yes ma'am."

"Goodnight," Amber said, allowing Gerard to lead her from the room and back down the steps.

After injecting himself with the anti-virus, he crawled under the covers and patted the mattress. "Come to bed , ma bien-aimée. We can argue about it in the evening when we're both awake and fresh."

Injecting himself before falling into the regenerative sleep had worked for Gerard once before, but was it a fluke? Only time would tell. Time they may not have.

"Okay. Fine." Calling a truce, she double-checked the blinds and curtains to make sure they were tightly closed. Satisfied Gerard was safe from spontaneous combustion—or whatever vampires called it when sunlight touched their unprotected skin causing them to burst into flames—she slid under the covers and into his arms.

Chapter 21

Gerard's skin cooled. His fangs extended, brushing his bottom lip. Amber glanced at the clock. It wasn't quite eight a.m. yet. Her eyes felt gritty from lack of sleep, her thoughts sluggish, but she needed to talk to Reid.

She quietly slid out of bed and dressed. Then she slipped from the room and tiptoed down the hall and up the stairs. Feeling like a thief—or a perv who liked to watch people sleep—she let herself into the guest room on the right.

"Reid," she whispered from the door, afraid to step closer for fear of finding out her partner slept naked. "Reid, get up. We need to talk."

He bolted upright. "Yeah. I'm awake."

The covers fell to his waist, revealing a dusting of dark hair over a lean, muscled chest. Reid wasn't as broad or thick as Gerard, but he had a surprisingly well-sculpted chest. Flushing, Amber averted her gaze. "Put some clothes on and join me in the kitchen."

"Okay. Give me a sec."

Amber fled when bare legs emerged from beneath the covers.

In the kitchen, she put on some coffee and waited for enough to drip into the pot before filling her cup. Reid joined her a few minutes later. He grabbed a mug and sat across from her at the table. "We're going without them. Aren't we?"

"That's the plan."

"Shit." He took a gulp, lowered the cup and then raked a hand through his hair, spiking it on top of his head. "You know they're going to be pissed. And they're vampires. Lucky for you, I trust you with my life or I'd be speed-dialing 911 for back up."

"Thanks for the vote of confidence," she said, aiming for sarcasm but feeling humbled.

He smiled. "So, what's your plan, partner?"

"I want to leave for Piney Grove within the hour. If you drive, I can get a little much-needed sleep."

"Like I said earlier. I'm good. Driving will be the least of my problems."

She brushed away the guilt. She hated putting Reid in danger, and she felt as if she were betraying Gerard. But she wasn't breaking a promise. She'd never made one. "Axel's suffered enough. He might be a vampire, but until proven otherwise, he's innocent, and we have to save him if we can. And we don't have time to wait for Gerard and Vincent to wake up. When they're awake, the clone's awake. It's too dangerous."

"You don't have to convince."

"Then we have to go today while they're still asleep. If we reach Piney Grove by noon, we can do what needs doing and keep this situation contained."

Reid eyed her over the rim of his cup. "Do you honestly think you can drive a stake through a man's chest while he's asleep—especially a man who looks like Gerard?"

She swallowed her doubts and fears. "No. But you can. And the clone isn't a man. He's a dangerous vampire without a soul or a conscience. Once he's dead, he should—vaporize into ash or something. That ought to alleviate your guilt."

His brows came together over frowning eyes. He slowly lowered his cup. "Do you honestly believe that?"

Heat crept into her cheeks. "No. But what other choice do we have? He's a proven threat and neither of us have silver handcuffs."

Or silver bullets...

"But we have Megan. She has a sedative. If we bring her, she can shoot 'em up or inject them, or whatever she has to do to make sure Axel and the clone remain asleep until we figure out what to do with them."

Megan didn't trust Vincent not to leave her behind any more than Amber trusted Gerard. But could she trust Megan not to alert Vincent of their plans—either consciously or sub consciously? Vincent seemed acutely aware of Megan's thoughts. "I don't know..."

Before she could say more, Megan entered the kitchen looking as sleep deprived as Amber felt. Her gaze locked on Amber. "I'm going with you. I think you were right about Vincent's blood. I can't read minds like a vampire, but I'm definitely more intuitive. I think I'm some kind of manufactured dhampir." She laughed, self-conscious. "I picked up your non-verbal cues earlier. You didn't say anything, but I knew you weren't waiting for nightfall."

"If you knew Amber," Reid said, "you wouldn't need telepathy. Once she has intel, she formulates a plan and moves forward."

Reid was still in denial, but Amber knew the truth. By injecting herself with Vincent's blood to create the vampire vaccine, Megan had become a dhampir—part mortal, part vampire. Whether the change was permanent was anyone's guess. For now, it was both a gift and a liability.

"Can you mask your thoughts around Vincent?"

"I shouldn't have to," Megan replied. "He's asleep. Even with the anti-virus, he shouldn't awaken before noon—long after we're gone."

"If we're aiming for noon, we need to leave now," Reid said.

Were they really doing this? Going after a mad scientist and his vampire clone without backup?

The truth was—they had no choice.

"I showered last night," Amber said. "Just let me get my gun and my sterling letter opener."

"I need to swing by the apartment for mine," Reid said, rising from his chair. He met her gaze with a nervous smile. "No sterling silver letter opener, but I do have a silver dagger—leftover from my childhood fantasy days."

Megan smiled faintly, though she looked like she might be sick. "All I've got is half a dozen syringes filled with garlic-extract vampire sedative."

"That might be the best weapon in our arsenal," Amber said. But how effective was the sedative? And for how long? What were they supposed to do with two unconscious vampires—stuff them in the trunk?

"Maybe we should take one of the panel vans from Lifeblood," Megan suggested, as if plucking the thought from Amber's mind. "We can keep Axel shielded from sunlight in the back. And if we manage to secure the clone without killing him, he'll be protected too."

"If we don't destroy the clone, how will we contain him?" Amber said, thinking aloud.

"Maybe we should contact whatever police presence they have in Piney Grove—or the Surry County Sheriff's department," Reid suggested.

Amber almost laughed—not because Reid's idea was absurd, but because the whole situation was. "Unless they toss prisoners into forty-foot pits or have sterling silver bars on their cells, I doubt they could hold a rogue vampire."

"But Weldon's human," Reid argued. "And I don't want the case against him getting thrown out of court because we conducted a warrantless search outside of our jurisdiction."

Amber glanced at Megan. Fear flickered in her eyes—a fear Amber shared. Carl Matheson already knew about vampires. If he discovered Vincent and Gerard's true nature...

Amber had never knowingly broken the law. But now, she had no choice. Gerard and Vincent weren't monsters. They didn't deserve to be hunted. She had to protect them. No matter the cost.

"We can't involve anyone else," she said quietly. "We can't get warrants. And we can't follow normal police procedures."

Lines creased Reid's forehead. "And how do you propose we justify storming a facility Weldon's renting to search for evidence without a warrant? Even if we have probable cause that Weldon's holding Axle Travers, Surry County is out of our jurisdiction. How would we explain being there?"

"Vincent, Gerard, and Sonia can create whatever proof or legal documents you need after Weldon's in custody," Megan said.

His brows shot up to his hairline. "You expect me to condone the manufacturing of evidence in a criminal case?"

"Get real," Amber said, feeling as frustrated as her partner. Normal laws didn't apply when dealing with vampires. "We can't get a warrant, and we can't ask for help. We're on our own."

"You really expect me to stake Count Dracula's clone?" He shook his head. "What if I can't? What if that thing wakes up? We need backup."

"No." Breaking the rules didn't sit well with him. Another reason Amber considered asking Gerard to erase his memory.

"What about getting Carl involved?" he suggested.

"He could get a federal warrant. Then, it wouldn't matter what we found. He could take care of the vampires and Weldon. We'd rescue Travers and still get credit for solving the case."

She no longer cared if she got credit for solving the case or not. She knew what had gone down that night at Lifeblood Labs. She just wanted to rescue Axel, destroy the clone, stop Weldon, and protect Gerard from Carl Matheson and any other government agency investigating vampires.

"I don't trust him or his involvement with Surratt. If Surratt finds out my memory has returned and that I know what I am, he might come after me. And I don't want to draw Carl's attention to Gerard or Vincent."

"Amber's right," Megan added. "We can't trust any branch of the government that knows vampires exist. They'd destroy them, contain them, or experiment on them. Probably all three. The government wouldn't consider them human so they'd have no compunctions about the morality of their actions."

Reid shoved his coffee mug aside with a frustrated grunt. "Then what the hell do we do? We can't go in alone, but if we wait for Vincent and Gerard, we risk the clone waking up to snack on our necks or turn us into vampires before they could stop it."

Amber wasn't afraid of becoming a vampire. Vampire blood flowed through her veins. She wanted to save Axle Travers. But if she discovered he'd killed innocent victims to feed his hunger, she'd be forced to destroy him. Time was ticking, and they were burning daylight. She looked at the clock on the wall. It was almost nine. And Piney Grove was three and half hours away.

"We should head to Lifeblood and grab that van, like Megan suggested," Amber said. Megan and I can sleep in the back and you can wake us up when we get there. We don't know what we're walking into, so the only plan is to stay sharp and watch each other's backs. "She turned to Megan. "You can stay in the van. No need to risk your life."

Megan's bleary eyes sparked with defiance. "I'm doing this to protect my husband. I'd do anything to keep him safe. He's suffered enough over the centuries."

Amber's voice softened, but the edge remained. "And you don't think he'd suffer if he lost you?"

Reid stood and placed a steadying hand on Megan's shoulder. "We'll keep you safe," he said, then shot Amber a grin that was just a little too bright. "I wouldn't want to piss off Vincent the Vampire and wind up on the dinner menu."

Killing the clone should leave no evidence, but Weldon wouldn't go down quietly. If she had to shoot, there'd be no clean way to explain it. Even if Gerard and his crew could twist the evidence to clear her name, she'd still be guilty. No matter what happened in the next twenty-four hours, her career was toast.

Megan chewed her lip a second before saying, "Do we need to worry about the police showing up and arresting us for trespassing."

Reid glanced at Amber, daring her to argue. "She's right. We can't just roll into town, flash badges, and break into a private facility without a warrant. Even if your vampire friends can whip up paperwork later, we can't storm in with guns drawn and stakes raised. We'd look insane."

Amber didn't flinch. "It is what it is. Piney Grove doesn't have a police department. The sheriff's office is in Dobson. Mount Airy, Mount Pilot, and Elkin have departments, but Piney Grove? Nothing. Not even a post office anymore. I don't think we're stepping on any official toes.

Why couldn't Reid understand? Working with vampires meant bending the rules—rules she wasn't quite comfortable bending herself. But sometimes, life required doing the wrong thing for the right reason. And to her way of thinking, protecting Gerard was a damn good reason.

"So we're just going to storm Mayberry, kill a few vampires, and rescue Axle Travers without anyone noticing?" Reid scoffed. "Yeah. Sure."

"If all goes according to plan, we're going to go in without anybody knowing we were there."

"What plan?"

Amber's voice was firm. "This we'll defend," she said, invoking the army motto. "We're going to protect peaceful vampires and stop the rogue ones."

Reid looked thoughtful for a moment. "Maybe that's what Carl and Surratt are trying to do."

Hearing Surratt's name sent fire flowing through Amber's veins. "Surratt's idea of protecting vampires puts mortals at risk. He may not have killed my mother, but he created the son-of-a-bitch who did."

"I'm just saying..." Reid's voice trailed off, the words unfinished and ripe with disappointed.

Amber took a deep breath and let it out slowly. Maybe she was overly sensitive where Surratt was concerned, but she couldn't let go of the past, and her future was unpredictable. Hell, everyone's future was unpredictable. And it had nothing to do with vampires. Maybe it was time she stopped living in the past and fearing the future. Maybe she just needed to live in the present and accept whatever pleasures it offered.

It gave her something to ponder as she curled up in the back of the lifeblood van across from Megan and closed her eyes.

Chapter 22

"Wake up," Reid whispered.

Amber opened her eyes to find him squatting before her in the back of the van. He'd opened the sliding panel separating the passenger seats from the cargo section. Sunlight shone through the front window. Sparkling dust motes danced in the wide shaft of light that lit the floor between the blanketed pallets where she and Megan had bedded down for the trip to Piney Grove.

Stifling a yawn, Amber reached for Megan and shook her shoulder. "We're here."

Megan pushed back her covers and sat up, knuckling the sleep from her eyes. "Already?"

"It's almost three o'clock," Reid said, his tone edged with irritation. The detour to pick up weapons, gather supplies, and retrieve the van from Lifeblood had taken longer than expected.

"Crap." Megan yawned. "Vincent could wake up at any time."

Amber had always been a night owl, but she loved the sun too much to surrender it completely. The antivirus allowed Gerard to see the sun rise and set, but he couldn't bask in the warmth of its glow. That one time he'd been awake at noon, he could barely function. Could she live like that? Did she even want to try?

Shoving the thought aside, she strapped on her shoulder harness and glanced at Reid. He wore his harness over a dark blue polo shirt that hung over his belt. There was no sign of his silver blade. "Where's your knife?"

"It's not a knife. It's a dagger," he corrected, mildly offended. He raised his shirt, revealing a utility belt. Then he reached behind his back and pulled the six-inch blade from a sheath strapped to his back. "I'm trying to keep it out of sight. Even if we can get by with wearing our guns in the open, I'd have a hard time explaining a medieval-looking dagger strapped to my leg."

"Good point." Amber shoved her sterling letter opener into her left boot. She wore jeans, army boots, and a fitted camouflage tee shirt. Megan had opted for jeans, sneakers, and a blue striped shirt. "We're at least trying to look like tourists."

"Tourists don't carry guns," Megan reminded her.

A valid point, but their improvised plan made no allowances for weapons. And she wasn't about to hunt vampires without one—or six.

She shrugged. "Reid and I are cops. It'll look worse if we try to conceal them. If you have a better idea, I'm all ears. Otherwise, we'll stick to the script. Reid and I had planned to take a drive along the Blue Ridge Parkway when we got intel that Weldon was in the area. Since he's a person of interest in our case, we decided to come to Piney Grove and talk to him." She looked at Megan. "You were never here."

"Flimsy," Reid said. "But better than nothing."

"If this all goes down the way I fear," Amber added, "we're going to be shit deep in flimsy excuses."

Reid shook his head. "Guess that ends my career."

Being a cop wasn't just a job for him. It was his identity, and he was risking it all for her. Guilt twisted in her gut. "We'll probably both be out of a job after today."

"What are you going to do if you lose your job?" Megan asked.

What could she do? She was a former soldier and a cop. She didn't know how to do anything else. She shrugged. "I don't know. Maybe find a job in private security."

"What do you plan to do about Gerard?" Megan asked. "Just walk away and forget you ever met?"

"I don't know." She couldn't give an answer she didn't have. She looked at Reid. "But maybe you should take that job with Carl Matheson. You'd still be in law enforcement, and you could be the voice of reason if he wants to go on a vampire killing spree."

"You wouldn't object?" He sounded surprised. Hell, it surprised her.

"I trust you with my life, Reid. I'd like to think Gerard can too. If you worked for Carl, you could keep the Project Blue Book Task Force legit—make sure no one abuses that clearance to wipe out vampires—or try to gain their powers. You could also keep an eye on Surratt—make sure he isn't trying to rid the world of mortals who know vampires exist."

"That's a damn tall order," Reid said with a snort. "But it beats working mall security."

"Let's hope we're both alive at the end of the day to work anywhere." Amber touched the grip of her Glock. "Silver bullets would be nice right about now."

Reid grunted. "No shit."

Megan reached for a leather case that resembled a doctor's bag. "I'm so not ready for this," she said, voice trembling.

Amber looked at Reid. "Lock and load."

He winked. "Let's rock."

They climbed out of the van. Reid had parked in a copse of trees a hundred yards from the Piney Grove Sanatorium. The rear doors faced a loading dock. Honeysuckle and freshly mowed grass scented the air. Birds chirped. A mower hummed in the distance. But over the abandoned hospital, a stillness hung—heavy and ominous, like a storm cloud waiting to break.

Kudzu crawled up the rear of the building, its leafy vines snaking around barred windows and slipping through shattered glass like the tentacles of a giant green squid. Grass sprouted through cracks in the crumbling pavement along the drive and parking lot, but near the loading dock, the weeds had been flattened.

A chill slithered over Amber's skin. Shaking it off, she nodded toward the loading dock. "Weldon's getting his deliveries through that door."

"And that's how we get in and get Axel out," Reid said. "Once we secure the facility, Megan can back the van up to the dock. Then you and I can wrap Axel in a sleeping bag and get him inside without exposing him to sunlight."

"I also have the liposome sunblock Vincent uses," Megan said, patting the side of her medical bag. "It'll help protect his skin."

"Sounds like a plan." The hair on the nape of Amber's neck stood on end. Her senses sharpened. It was as if she could hear a pin drop—or hear one being pulled from a grenade. It was just like in Iraq when her unit went out on patrol.

Acutely attuned to her surroundings, she scanned the area.

The facility was old. No surveillance cameras. No guards and no one hiding in the trees. And yet her skin tingled with warning. "Something's off," she whispered, drawing her gun.

Reid instinctively moved in front of Megan, nudging her behind him as he drew his weapon. "What is it?"

"I don't know. But stay sharp and be prepared for anything." Were there hidden cameras or unseen eyes watching from the windows?

She reached out with her mind. Vampires. More than one. Was it Axel and the clone? Or had Weldon built an army?

Nausea churned as they crept forward. The bay door was shut, padlocked. To the right, beside a wire-mesh window, a rusted sign read: "Ring for Service." Amber tried the door. "Locked." No duh. Of course it was locked.

"Should we look for another way in?" Megan whispered.

"No." Amber closed her eyes, recalling what she'd seen through the clone's eyes. "There's a camera at the front and side entrances."

"Why isn't there one here?" Megan asked. "You'd think Weldon would want to keep an eye on the loading dock. Make sure no one absconded with his equipment."

"There was a DPI Security sign on the front lawn," Reid said.

"They probably watch the monitors and alert Weldon if someone tries to get in," Amber said. "But if he's conducting illegal activities, he wouldn't want the people watching the facility watching him. This has to be his private entrance and our best way in." And likely the most dangerous. She wouldn't be surprised if it was booby-trapped—like the houses they'd cleared in Iraq.

"But it's locked," Megan whispered.

"Don't worry." Reid smiled, eyes gleaming with mischief. "There's an app for that." He holstered his gun and pulled a small leather case from his jeans pocket.

"Lock pic tools aren't standard issue," Amber said.

He crouched by the door, casting a glance over his shoulder. "Bought them online. Figured it'd help with my NYPD application. Who knew I'd be committing a little B and E?"

Amber shivered. "What about the alarm? Can you disable it?"

"No," he said, working the picks. "But if it's silent, Weldon's the only one who'll know we're here. And we want to run across him. It's vampires and cops we need to avoid."

The sun was still well above the horizon. Any vampire should be deep in regenerative sleep. And yet... she felt eyes. Watching.

She stepped back, craning her neck to scan the windows above. No faces peered down from the two stories above, but she was too close to see movement beyond the ledges.

Her skin prickled. "Hurry." Something was coming—something dark and dangerous. She turned to Megan. "Get back in the van."

"No. You might need me." Megan shifted her bag into view. "I've got the sedative. You might need it."

Amber didn't want to admit she was right. She wanted to stake the clone, rescue Axel Travers, and find Weldon—without getting caught. But they were diving into the unknown. And she knew she couldn't stake a man—or vampire—with Gerard's face—even if he was a conscienceless killer.

"Then stay behind me and Reid. Vincent will kill me if anything happens to you." And she'd never forgive herself if something happened to a civilian—especially one with no legal reason to be breaking and entering with two detectives operating outside their jurisdiction. "I must be out of my mind," she muttered.

"Or desperate," Reid said, moving the tiny picks inside the lock. "I think you'd do anything to protect Delaroche." He spared her a quick glance. "Anything you want to say about that?"

Denying the truth was pointless. "So, why are you here? Are you so desperate for a job with the Feds that you're willing to step into the unknown and take on a sleeping vampire?"

"No. I'm protecting my partner—and chasing some misguided hero complex I never managed to outgrow." He flushed and turned back to the lock. "The world as we know it no longer exists, Amber. And I just want to make sure that those who think they're in charge don't abuse their power. I'm not exactly a masked avenger, but maybe I can do something to stop the world from tumbling into chaos."

"Be careful what you wish for," Amber said thinking of Gerard.

A soft click shattered the silence. Reid rose and opened the door. Amber tensed. No alarms blared, but she'd bet money Weldon had been alerted. If he was onsite, they were screwed. If he was holed up at the hotel off the interstate, they had twenty minutes. If he was at the Piney Grove B&B or renting nearby... well, they were screwed then too.

"This way," she whispered, veering left down the hallway.

Amber took point, navigating corridors she'd memorized through the clone's eyes. Sweat pooled beneath her bra, trickling down her stomach. Her shirt clung to chilled skin. Her pulse thundered in her ears.

At the elevator, she turned to Reid. He nodded—no words needed. The stairs were safer. No cop wanted to be trapped in a box with one exit.

Reid stepped ahead, leading them into the deep, shadow-soaked stairwell. Amber fell in behind Megan, taking up the rear as they descended into the cold, damp dark. "I can't see a damn thing," Reid whispered.

Amber and Megan exchanged a glance. It was dim, but they could see well enough. Was it better eyesight—or the vampire blood threading through their veins?

"Shit," Reid mumbled as he stumbled off the last step, colliding with the basement door. He shoved the metal bar. The soft click echoed like a gunshot.

Amber flinched, but nothing lunged at them when Reid pushed opened the door and stepped into the dimly lit hall. Only the glowing red exit signs lit the corridor. The power was on, but Amber didn't dare flip the lights. Too risky.

She moved to Reid's side and pointed to the left. "The clone's in a walk in freezer in the cafeteria. We should take care of him first."

Reid nodded and fell into step. Megan stayed close behind. When they entered the cafeteria, sunlight streamed in through the iron bars covering the high windows casting long beams across rust-streaked walls. Moss grew along the baseboards, but one corner of the cafeteria had been scrubbed to a surgical shine, and the stainless steel prep table reflected light like a blade.

Amber shivered. Weldon had used that table. In her mind's eye, she saw him flaying the clone's side, narrating the damage into a headset. Even sedated and chained, the creature—Gerard's mirror—had flinched and moaned.

A thump sounded from inside the freezer. Her mind reached out, searching for the clone's presence behind the metal doors.

"He's awake." How was that possible? The sun was up, and the clone was a vampire. Had the freezer's darkness disrupted his circadian rhythm, keeping him from slipping into regenerative sleep? Or had Weldon perfected the antivirus using Megan's stolen serum?

She swallowed. Hard. Sonia Dalca had scoffed at the antivirus, warning it would weaken

vampires. Was she right? Was the clone now vulnerable? Or more dangerous than ever?

Chapter 23

A thump rattled the freezer door. Amber felt the Clone's rage. He didn't understand what she was, but he recognized the threat she posed. He should've had the telekinetic ability to slide the bolt lock open with his mind, but he lacked the cognitive skills inherent to other vampires.

Another snarl—feral and guttural—rose from the other side as he slammed his body against the door. Metal buckled outward. The door held. Amber stiffened as fear coalesced with an inevitable sense of purpose. She'd found the rogue, vampire clone. Now she had to put him down or die trying.

She glanced at Reid. Fear flickered in his eyes, but his hands were steady. He raised his weapon. Amber already had a round chambered. Whispering a silent prayer, she lifted her Glock as a metal-screeching thump ripped the hinges from the wall. The door burst open and slammed to the ground with an explosive crack that sounded like gunfire.

Before she could shoot—or even blink—the clone appeared on top of the fallen door, fangs flashing and body flexed in a wide stance that resembled the starting position of a pro wrestler. His eyes glowed a fiery red—a predatory wolf with eyes the color of hellfire. Despite a shared resemblance, nothing about the creature reminded her of Gerard.

Filled with fatal determination, Amber took careful aim, knowing she had one shot. If the clone moved, she'd be unable to aim and shoot fast enough to stop him. This was her one and only chance. She had to make it count.

Taking in a slow but shaky breath, she aimed between his glowing red eyes and...the room erupted into chaos. Whether Reid fired and missed or the clone moved too fast to track didn't matter. Hitting a vampire in motion was like catching a bullet with your teeth.

Reid's shot grazed the vampire's shoulder. Amber fired a millisecond later. The shot ricocheted off the freezer, hitting the cinderblock wall to the left—missing the moving vampire by no more than a couple of inches. It might as well have been a mile.

As if by magic, the clone materialized in front of Reid and seized his wrist. Bone snapped mid-shaft. Reid screamed. His gun clattered to the floor.

The clone snarled, fangs flashing like a rabid dog. Amber wanted to blast him to hell and back, but Reid was tangled in the creature's grip like a twisted lover's embrace.

Reid clenched his teeth. His cheeks paled. Sweat beaded his brow. The clone raised Reid's chin, exposing his throat, but Amber didn't have a clear shot. If she fired at the clone's head or chest, she'd likely hit Reid. She fired at the floor next to the clone's feet instead, trying to draw his attention before he bit Reid or ripped off his arm at the shoulder.

The shot echoed, the blast ringing in her ears. Smoke curled upward, the scent of cordite triggering memories of Iraq. Gerard's doppelganger snarled, his head whipping around to glare. Amber fired again. The clone jerked to the left, his head snapping to the side before bullet met bone. Reid was bound to have felt a breeze as the bullet whizzed between his head and the clone's, shattering cinderblock in the wall behind him. He flinched but stayed silent.

As if in slow motion, Reid reached behind his back and drew the silver dagger with his good arm. The clone shook him like a rag doll. Reid's scream pierced Amber's chest. The dagger skittered across the floor. Reid collapsed to his knees and Amber emptied her Glock, striking the clone's arm and shoulder before he shoved Reid aside and dodged her bullets like a fly evading a swatter.

Heart pounding, lungs burning, Amber spun, catching nothing but air as the clone dodged to the right. She spun full circle—and came face to face with him.

One swipe of his arm knocked the gun from her hand and sent her flying. She slammed into the far wall. Her head cracked against the cinderblocks. Stars exploded behind her eyes. Pain shot down her spine, and her muscles spasmed.

Screams echoed in her skull—Megan's? Her own? She couldn't tell. Her vision blurred. The clone's rage-twisted face loomed above her. He opened his mouth. Fangs descended toward her throat. Time slowed—prolonging the inevitable—prolonging her terror.

Her heart slammed against her chest, hard and slow. She counted each painful thump as if ticking down the last seconds of her life. Her breath returned in a gasp, then froze. Gerard's face—not the clone's—hovered before her. His blue eyes urged her to fight. She gulped air into her starving lungs. Gerard's image faded. Her muscles tensed. She refused to let fear paralyze her. Not this time.

She slid her hand down her thigh toward the letter opener in her boot. The clone sniffed her neck like a wolf deciding if the prey was worth eating. A curious light shone in his red eyes—as if he sensed something different about her.

His hand closed over her throat, tilting her head to the side. He sniffed again. Her heart beat faster. Taking advantage of the unexpected delay in her imminent demise, she withdrew the dull silver blade.

She raised her arm and tried driving the letter opener into his side. He grabbed her wrist. His fingers tightened. The letter opener fell harmlessly to the ground. A scream tore from her throat as pain shot up her arm.

"Amber!" Reid's shout sounded a million miles away. A gun exploded. The vampire released her throat with a furious growl. Amber scooted away from him as he turned toward Reid.

Cradling his broken arm, Reid aimed with his left hand. Pain etched his face. Determination shone in his eyes. Not a lefty by any stretch of the imagination, he nonetheless emptied his clip into the creature's flesh. Not a single bullet penetrated his skull or entered his heart.

Snarling with rage, the vampire sprang across the room and knocked the gun from Reid's grasp. Reid fell backward, landing on the freezer door with a painful cry as he hugged his injured arm to his chest and waited for death.

Reid's silver dagger lay inches from Amber. She grabbed it and sprang to her feet. Four steps. One clean swipe.

Blood exploded from the creature's neck, the arterial spray turning to ash as it peppered Reid's face. The clone turned, head flopping sideways held by tendons and muscle. Bone protruded from his neck. His face turned a scalding red and then scorched black before his body exploded in a cloud of ash. The dust settled at Amber's feet.

"Jesus," Reid muttered, wiping his face with his good hand.

Amber dropped to her knees beside him, heart hammering too hard to speak. Ash spiraled upward, dusting her jeans. She gasped for breath. "Are you okay?" she asked, choking on the words.

He raised a brow. "Not really. Arm's broken. Pretty sure I swallowed vampire ash. But I'll live. Thanks for saving my ass."

"Thanks for saving mine." She helped him up, her skin prickling with unease. They weren't safe yet.

"Where's Megan?" Aside from a single scream, Amber hadn't seen or heard her since entering the room. She'd told Megan to stay outside—but Megan never obeyed unless forced. Something was wrong.

"Cowering in the van?" Reid offered, more hopeful than accusatory.

"Not likely." Amber staggered, accidentally jostling his injured arm.

He sucked air between his teeth. "Shit."

"Sorry." She braced him against the wall and gathered their scattered weapons. After reloading both guns, she handed Reid his Sig Sauer. Her head throbbed, but she wasn't nauseous. The room held steady.

"You look a bit wobbly," Reid said, stepping away from the wall to meet her in the center of the room. "How's your head? You got slammed pretty hard."

She should have been knocked unconscious. Touching the lump at her skull's base, she winced. "Hurts like hell." But not as much as it should. No blurred vision. No nausea. Just a headache. Probably not even a real concussion.

A disquieting sense of pride filled her. She felt like an invincible crusader for justice.

"I owe you, Amber. You saved my life," Reid said in a voice so filled with gratitude it made her flush.

Her ego crashed and burned. She wasn't immortal, and she wasn't a hero. "If you hadn't distracted him, I'd be dead. You don't owe me a damn thing. We're even, partner. Now let's move. Megan's in danger."

Reid moved to her side. "How do you know?"

"Dhampir intuition?" She tried to laugh, but fear strangled the sound.

"I don't give a damn what you call it," Reid said, clenching his teeth against the pain. "Just trust your instincts."

Were her instincts more evolved? Was she something more than human?

When the clone had pinned her, hand crushing her throat, she'd been terrified. But even before Reid fired those shots, she'd felt a strange calm—an eerie confidence. Had seeing Gerard's face before her been nothing more than a hopeful hallucination from an oxygen-deprived brain? Or had she actually connected with him on a psychic level?

As they neared the double doors that led into the hall, dread settled in her bones. Something worse than Gerard's clone was waiting. And it wanted her dead.

Chapter 24

Shaking off the fear that had once paralyzed her in Germany, Amber stepped in front of Reid with gun raised. He swayed but stayed upright.

"What is it?" he whispered, struggling to hold his weapon in his left hand while cradling his injured arm.

Amber winced. She should've fashioned a sling or given him a moment to recover—but time was bleeding out. Megan was in danger. She felt it in her bones.

"This way," she said, following the vampire's scent. "I don't know where Weldon is, but Axel's in the morgue. It's the only place Weldon could contain a vampire." The lingering essence in the air didn't belong to the clone.

The morgue lay opposite a cargo elevator at the far end of the hall. Amber moved forward. "Stay sharp. There's another vampire in the building, and I don't think it's Axel."

Reid didn't question her intel. He nodded and fell in beside her. Their footsteps echoed despite their caution, the silence amplifying every sound. If Weldon was nearby, he'd know exactly where they were headed.

They passed a door hanging askew on its hinges. Old files littered the floor. Ceiling tracks ran overhead, wires spilling from a gaping hole in the wall. A faded radiation symbol on the door marked it as an old x-ray room. The darkroom door beyond stood ajar. Despite his injury, Reid detoured inside, sweeping both rooms.

"Clear," he whispered when he rejoined her in the hall.

A small alcove beside the x-ray room had once served as reception. The floor tiles were filthy and buckled, a semicircle of missing ones outlining where a desk had once stood. Rat droppings and dead cockroaches now claimed the space.

Amber shivered and pressed on. The pounding in her skull dulled to an ache. Around the next corner, they hit a dead end. A service elevator was to the right. On the left—just as she'd seen in her mind's eye—was a steel door marked "Morgue."

Reid used the gun he held in his good arm to raise the elevator gate and stepped inside. He glanced up. Nothing lunged.

"Clear," he said again.

Amber nodded and tried the handle on the morgue's door. It wasn't locked. The hair on the nape of her neck stood on end.

"That's not a good sign," Reid said as she eased open the door.

Gun poised, Amber swept low and left. Reid ducked right. No gunfire. No snarling vampires. No surprises. Cabinets with frosted glass fronts lined the wall above a stainless steel autopsy table. A rolling cart held a rib spreader and bone saw. The air reeked of bleach and iron. Despite a recent cleaning, blood still lingered.

Bile rose in Amber's throat as she turned toward the morgue refrigerator—four drawers stacked two by two. Another shiver crawled across her skin.

Piney Grove had been a TB asylum where death claimed lives on a daily basis. During its heyday, there'd probably been a body in every drawer. The unit should've been off, but the mercury thermometer dipped below minus fifteen degrees Celsius. Something—or someone—was in at least one of the drawers.

Reid tucked his gun against his chest, holding it with his broken arm. With his left hand, he reached for the top drawer on the right. Amber steadied her aim. The slides screeched as he slid open the drawer. Empty. He closed it and moved to the next one. Another swing and a miss.

Tension rippled through Amber's shoulders. Her arms trembled as Reid reached for the bottom left drawer and slowly opened it.

A half-naked man lay on the metal surface, clad only in black boxer briefs. His caramel skin had a bluish tint, stretched taut across a sculpted, hairless chest. Ice crystals clung to his military-short hair, brows, lashes, and neatly trimmed goatee. A Celtic cross tattoo covered the curve of his right shoulder. His left shoulder sported an Ankh—the Egyptian symbol of life and immortality—an eerily fitting tattoo for a man who was now immortal.

Reid nodded to the corpse-like figure in the drawer. "He matches Axel Travers's description."

Amber touched the man's cheek. It felt like a block of ice. "Travers is out cold." She gave a weak smile. "Pun not intended, but he's not a threat and for the moment, he's safe. We need to find Megan. She's still in danger."

Reid glanced at the final drawer. "You don't think she's in there? Do you?"

Amber shivered. "No. Weldon has her."

"Yes he does," said a voice from the doorway.

Amber crouched and spun, weapon drawn. Megan stood in the frame, an arm locked around her throat, another around her waist. A man no taller than she held her against his chest, using her as a human shield.

"I'm sorry," Megan whispered. Terror shone in her eyes, but she didn't cry. She held herself stiffly in Steve Weldon's grip.

"Police!" Amber said with forced bravado. "You're under arrest for the kidnapping of Axle Travers and the murders of Tina Gallagher and Richard Baxter. Now, raise your hands and step away from Dr. Harper."

Weldon's brown eyes narrowed. He peeked around Megan's head and smiled. "No. Drop your weapon or I'll snap her neck like a twig."

Reid and Amber exchanged a glance. Weldon's arm tightened around Megan's neck, but he didn't have a weapon.

"We can't do that, Dr. Weldon," Reid supplied before Amber had a chance to respond. "Now, release Dr. Harper, and I won't be forced to shoot."

"You couldn't fire a water pistol. Your arm is broken." A wicked smile stretched the corners of his mouth when he swung his gaze back to Amber. "And do you really think you can kill me?" He shook Megan. "Tell them, Megs, tell them what your blood has created."

Fear slammed into Amber's chest. "No."

"Oh yes," he said, voice laced with glee. "I'm a new breed of vampire—a day walker. As long as I avoid direct sunlight, I can stay up all day and night. Just need a nap when I'm low. Usually noon does the trick. And I owe it all to my dear friend and former colleague, Dr. Harper."

"Jesus! You turned yourself into a vampire?" The incredulity in Reid's voice told Amber exactly what he thought of immortals.

"Not intentionally," Weldon snorted. "After creating the clone, I tried duplicating the antivirus using my own blood—in the lab of course. I didn't want to risk becoming a vampire by injecting myself with vampire blood. I created a vaccine from the serum and then injected the clone. To test whether he was still a vampire, I exposed a small section of his skin to a sunlamp. It nearly burned his arm off. While scraping away the charred flesh so the regenerative sleep could heal him faster, he moved and the scalpel slipped. It sliced my arm, mixing his blood with mine. I didn't know I was infected until I woke up in my make shift lab drenched in sweat and craving warm blood. I then treated myself with the vaccine created from Megan's blood. It worked—to a point, but I still craved blood. So I broke into Lifeblood."

He shook Megan again, rattling her teeth. She whimpered like a frightened puppy.

"Sadly," Weldon said with a smile, "my little friend here wasn't there. So, I helped myself to the serum samples. The clone took out the first security guard before I could stop him. He's not very bright, but since I created him, he follows my commands. So, I instructed him to capture the younger one."

"Who killed Tina Gallagher?" Amber asked—for Gerard. If she lived long enough, she wanted to give him closure.

From the corner of her eye, she saw Reid inching toward Axel Travers' cold body. Weldon didn't seem to notice. His attention was locked on her.

"I did. I needed sustenance but couldn't bring myself to bite into her warm flesh." He shivered, repulsed. "Still can't. I slit my victims' throats, draw the blood with a catheter-tipped syringe, and drink from a glass. Wouldn't want the authorities catching on. And drinking from a glass is much more civilized. Don't you think?"

Weldon was bat shit crazy. He was also lethally dangerous.

"You can't get blood from a blood bank like other vampires?" Amber kept her tone steady, her eyes locked on him. She needed him focused on her, not Reid. Whatever Reid was planning, she had to buy him time. "Gerard doesn't kill to feed. So why do you?" Not that it mattered. Weldon's crimes went far beyond murder. There was nothing in the penal code about cloning and torturing vampires.

"Warm, fresh blood strengthens a vampire," Weldon said. "The antivirus weakens us just a bit. To counteract the side effects of the vaccine, I drink fresh blood. Not much—just enough. The vaccine lets me eat some food, but only fresh blood will do. That's why so much of Tina's was wasted." He laughed, low and cruel. "I know you think I was trying to stage the crime scene, but the truth is I didn't need that much. I also didn't need her alive."

Amber's fear dissolved into rage, hot and pure. She clung to it and fed it, awaking her dhampiric instincts. Her senses sharpened. The headache vanished. She stepped closer to the maniac.

"Let Megan go," she said, voice like steel.

"Not a chance." Weldon barked a laugh. "Her blood holds the key to the antivirus. For the vaccine to work, the donor must carry the mutated gene for xeroderma pigmentosum. That's why Megan matters. With her blood and the Liposome sunblock, I can create an army of vampires impervious to sunlight."

"I can't let you do that," Amber said. Then she moved, faster than mortally possible.

She dove behind Weldon, landing in a squat before rolling to the side and springing up behind him with gun drawn. He yelped and shoved Megan into her path. The two women crashed to the floor in a tangle of limbs.

Reid shoved the drawer holding Axel Travers' body closed with his hip, protecting the sleeping vampire from harm. Then he awkwardly fired eight rounds from his Sig Sauer P-220. Weldon took hits to the arm, neck, and shoulder, slowing him down but not stopping him.

Roaring, Weldon pounced, striking Reid with bone-shattering force. He flew backward, barely missing the autopsy table before smashing into the cabinets. Glass exploded, pelting Reid's scalp and forehead. Blood streamed down his face, pooling in the corner of his left eye as he slumped unconscious to the floor.

Amber shoved Megan aside and scrambled to her feet. Weldon spun toward her, lightning-fast. She barely dodged the blow, but it still caught him off guard. He paused, not winded, but wary. Amber's breath came in rapid bursts. She was close to hyperventilating.

"Well, well. You're more than you seem, aren't you, detective?" He leaned forward, sniffing the air. "You're not a vampire. What are you?

"Your worst frickin' nightmare." She pulled the letter opener from her waistband and lunged.

He sidestepped easily, grabbed her from behind, and pinned her arms to her sides. "Drop your weapon. Now." His grip tightened, elbows crushing into her ribs until he thought they'd break and puncture her lungs.

"No," she ground out between clenched teeth, refusing to let go.

"Then I have no choice," Weldon said, voice thick with distaste. He lowered his head, mouth opening.

Amber felt his warm breath on her neck seconds before his teeth grazed her skin. Struggling to pull away, she screamed loud enough to wake the dead.

Chapter 25

Gerard couldn't explain what had awakened him from regenerative slumber shortly before three in the afternoon—earlier than usual. Had the new dosing schedule granted him that extra half hour of daylight? If he continued taking the injections in the morning, would he wake even earlier in the afternoon? Would he be able to stay up longer?

He ran his tongue over his teeth. His fangs descended. Still a vampire. But no longer strictly bound to the day sleep. He was wide-awake. Alert. And the sun was shining. A miracle.

So why the anxiety clawing at his chest?

The bed beside him was empty. Not surprising. Amber was mortal—for the most part. Despite staying up most of the night, she'd never sleep through the day.

A sense of doom pressed down on him. His stomach knotted. He dressed quickly and stepped into the hall, nearly colliding with Vincent.

"Something's wrong," Vincent said, voice taut with worry.

"I feel it too." Amber was afraid. Gerard sensed danger surrounding her—more acutely than when G-2 attacked and Nicolas intervened.

They rushed to the kitchen. The coffee in the cups on the table had grown cold. "They have a head start," Vincent muttered, curling his fingers around a mug until it shattered. Coffee spilled over his hand and onto the floor. He flung the shards aside and spun on Gerard, eyes blazing. "Amber went after Weldon. She took Megan. If anything happens to her, I'll rip—"

Gerard struck palms to Vincent's chest, knocking the wind out of him. "You're not going to touch her, Vin. Not while I draw breath."

"She's putting my wife in danger!"

"You don't think Megan chose this?" Gerard's voice sharpened. "She's not a shrinking violet. If she thought she could end Weldon's experiments, she would've insisted on going. Amber would have had to put her in handcuffs to stop her and you know it."

Vincent raked a hand through his dark hair, growling. "Damn it. Don't you think I know that? Megan never does what she's told. I can't control her."

"Then stop trying, mon ami."

Fear ravaged Vincent's face. "You don't understand. It's my fault she's in danger. If I'd erased her mind instead of marrying her, she could've lived in blissful ignorance. Instead, I selfishly kept her. And now I may have forfeited her life." A tear slipped down his cheek. "I can't live without her."

A lump rose in Gerard's throat. He swallowed against it, understanding too well. "L'espoir fait vivre—Where there's life, there's hope. Let's not give up just yet. We can save them. Maybe even keep them too."

"We'll burn. Megan has the sunblock."

Gerard wasn't giving up. "Amber's car is in the garage. How fast can you drive?"

They covered every inch of skin, grabbed comforters from the beds, and vanished from the house in a vampiric blur.

#

Amber opened her eyes against the pain. Her vision shimmered, hospital lights stabbing through the haze. She tried to raise her arms to shield her face but couldn't move. Her wrists were strapped down. So were her legs.

She inhaled slowly, fighting the rising panic. Cold metal pressed against her back, leeching through her shirt. Weldon had strapped her to the prep table in the kitchen. But where were Reid and Megan?

Turning her head, she caught a glimpse of the refrigerator. The busted door had been propped back into place, a twisted metal rod looped around the hinges to hold it shut. Had Weldon locked her partner and Megan inside?

"Reid? Megan?" Her voice came out strained, barely audible.

"It's about time you woke up." Weldon stepped into view. "Your friends are safe—for now. The seal's broken, so they won't freeze. But they'll be damn cold when they wake up."

"What did you do to them?" Amber asked, straining against the straps binding her to the table.

"Nothing." He shrugged. "Mortals are fragile. The other cop was out cold. I gave Megan a tap—just enough to knock her out. I'd never hurt her. She's far too important to my research. Don't you see?"

Amber glared, silent. Her mind raced, searching for escape.

"I saw you snooping around Lifeblood after the murders. My vampire tried to capture you when he went after Megan. But she was gone—and another vampire saved you. Who is he?"

Amber held her tongue. She'd learn more keeping silent than by antagonizing him. And anything she had to say would most likely piss him off.

"You are a quiet one. Aren't you, detective?" He smiled. "Yes, I know who you are. I know all about you and your partner. But I don't know who that vampire was."

If her arms were free, she'd have folded them across her chest. Instead, she turned her head toward the freezer.

Weldon's bony fingers pinched her chin, jerking her face toward him. "Who is he? Why would he save a mortal?"

She imagined a brick wall, blocking his attempt to read her mind.

"How are you doing that?" He leaned in and sniffed. "You don't smell mortal. You didn't taste mortal." A flicker of fear crossed his eyes. "What are you?"

She bared her teeth—normal, human teeth. He hadn't converted her. Thank God. "I told you. I'm your worst nightmare." An impotent boast. She was no threat to anyone at the moment, especially a vampire.

A demonic light flared behind his eyes, turning brown to blood-red. "Then I'll experiment on you and find out."

Amber swallowed hard, terror clawing at her throat. She twisted against the straps, sweat slicking her wrists. Miraculously, one hand slipped free. She cast a frantic glance over her shoulder. Weldon was gone.

Had he gone to retrieve his tools? A bone saw? Rib spreader?

The rusted buckles were ancient, relics of the sanatorium. Once her left arm was free, she sat up, frantically working the straps loose from her ankles. Before she could free her left leg, Weldon returned.

Metal clattered to the floor. Glass shattered. Then his fingers clamped down on her shoulders, forcing her back. "You bitch."

"Let go." She tried twisting free, but his grip was too powerful. It felt as if he were crushing her bones.

He pulled a strap up from the table leg and looped it around her neck—then stopped. The pressure eased, and a roar filled her ears, primal and deafening.

Gerard!

Amber sat up, heart pounding. Gerard had Weldon in a chokehold, dragging him away. Gerard's face was a mask of fury. His eyes blazed blue before flaring red. Weldon snarled and broke free. Gerard lunged, fists raised. Weldon dodged.

Where was Vincent?

Before she'd completed the thought, the freezer door sailed across the room.

"Megan!" Vincent stormed inside, rushing to his wife.

Amber freed her legs and jumped down. Megan's medical bag lay on the floor, the bone saw beside it. She hovered over the saw—useless without power. The shattered remains of a vial with a purple stopper lay nearby, along with a twenty-two gauge needle and an empty syringe.

Weldon had planned to draw her blood. And then what—amputate a limb to see if it regrew like a starfish? Oh, hell no. His experimenting days were over.

Rage surged through her, burning away fear. She reached into the medical bag and pulled out a pre-filled syringe. She lightly depressed the plunger, releasing a single drop of garlic-scented yellow fluid. Vampire sedative.

She rose, armed and ready. Gerard and Weldon circled like mismatched fighters—a welterweight against a heavyweight. Weldon was faster, dodging Gerard's inhuman strikes. But was he stronger? It didn't matter. Amber wouldn't let Weldon hurt Gerard again. She'd knock his ass out first.

She stepped forward, syringe raised, waiting for her moment, hoping Vincent would come out of the freezer and assist. But Vincent was still with Megan, oblivious to the fight.

Weldon whirled out of Gerard's reach again. Amber stepped closer, syringe raised. A hand seized her wrist, yanking her back. The musty stench of mildew filled her nose as strong, bony fingers held her wrist in a vice-like grip.

She turned. Her heart sank. "Surratt."

Chapter 26

Amber stared into the eyes of the vampire who'd created her mother's killer. She waited for him to flash his fangs or snarl like the monster he was. Instead, sympathy flickered in his gaze, shadowed by resignation.

"Let go!" She twisted in his iron grip. He didn't release her.

"You mustn't interfere," he said in an accented, almost reverent voice as deep and smooth as honey.

Tension drained from her body. Her fears abated. Though she knew she was under his control, indignation refused to rise. Detached, she watched Gerard and Weldon clash.

The air stirred and Nicolas materialized, his blurred form rushing in from the hall. Amber barely registered his arrival before Gerard seized Weldon's arm and spun him around. Nicolas stepped in behind, cutting off Weldon's escape but didn't otherwise intervene.

Gerard's fist crashed into Weldon's face. His head snapped back—hard enough to break a mortal's spine. He shook his head as if he'd bumped it. Blood sprayed from his mouth and nose, painting the walls. Nicolas leapt aside, avoiding the splatter.

Weldon couldn't dodge the next blow. Or the next. Gerard hammered him until his face was a pulpy mass of blood and bone. Choking, gurgling, Weldon collapsed in a boneless heap. His exposed brain matter hissed—and then his body fizzled red hot before erupting into a puff of ash and smoke.

Gerard wiped his knuckles against his palm, smearing blood. Then he turned. His gaze locked on Amber. His eyes widened, the red draining away.

"Don't hurt her," he said to Surratt, his voice tight with fear.

Surratt nodded once and let go. Released from his grip, Amber's thoughts and feelings returned, relief the dominant emotion.

"Gerard!" She threw herself into his arms, clinging to him, kissing his bruised face.

He kissed her back. Deeply. Thoroughly. Then he pulled away, his face raw with emotion. His already healing knuckles grazed her cheek. "Are you all right?"

She nodded, unable to speak. He tucked her under his arm, eyes shifting from Surratt to Nicolas. "I don't know whether to thank you for blocking Weldon's escape or beat the shit out of you for leading him to Amber." He gestured toward Surratt.

Nicolas arched his brows and looked at Amber. His gaze was so intense, she couldn't hold it. "Amber's my daughter. I wouldn't let Surratt within a mile of her if I thought he posed a threat."

Blood roared in her ears. Greg Buckley wasn't her father. She raised her chin, meeting Nicolas' warm brown gaze. "Did you rape my mother?" she asked, knowing the answer before he gave it.

"No." His voice held no heat, no defensiveness—just quiet understanding. "I loved her. She was my wife."

The world tilted. Amber's knees buckled. Gerard caught her. "Wife?"

How could her mother have hidden something so monumental? She'd never seen a photo of her with another man—only that one picture of Greg, her supposed father, standing beside the soldier she now knew was Nicolas.

"We eloped right after graduation," he said with love in his eyes. "I joined the army, and we moved to Germany. I was stationed at Grafenwöhr. We lived in Eschenbach. Everything was perfect—until an explosion during a training exercise tore me open. By the time I reached Landstuhl, I was dying. I begged to see my wife, my Helen, one last time. Surratt granted me that wish on the condition that I erase her memory afterward. Neither of us knew until later that I'd gotten her pregnant."

"He turned you into a vampire." Amber's voice was sharp as glass. She glared at the musty old man who resembled a gaunt version of Christopher Lee's Dracula. "He created the blood-sucking bastard who killed my mother—your wife."

The hurled accusations didn't faze Surratt. He merely inclined his head as if in agreement. "Klaus was a mistake. A descendant of sorts. I thought he'd serve the cause, but he became what we were trying to fight. An uncontrollable monster and he killed your mother. I'm sorry."

Fury tangled with grief, choking Amber's voice. Gerard had no such restraint. "I don't know how the two of you found her or why you're following her, but she doesn't pose a threat to vampires. At least not to those who don't pose a threat to humans."

Surratt dipped his gaunt chin. "Precisely why I'm here."

Gerard's fangs descended. His eyes flared crimson. "What the hell does that mean?"

Surratt smiled. "I had to see for myself that she isn't a threat to our kind. It's my job."

"Your job?" Amber asked, her voice so tight it hurt to speak. "Who the hell hired you? And exactly what is your job?"

"I'm leader of the Shedu, a benevolent breed of what Mesopotamian folklore call the Utukku. Europeans call us Vampire."

Amber's pulse jumped. "How damn long have you been around?"

"Since 4000 B.C."

The answer staggered her. Her knees buckled. Nicolas stepped forward, but Gerard drew her close. She felt caught between two immortals—drawn to both. "Jesus," she whispered.

"Long before him," Surratt said with a wan smile. "But not as long ago as some believe. Neither Lilith nor Cain was a vampire. Yet fear of Cain's wrath has kept many murderous vampires in line."

"Is that your job too? To keep vampires in line or destroy them?" She pulled away from Gerard, stepping in front of him as if she could protect him from the ancient vampire.

Gerard pulled her back, placing her beside him—not behind him. Her heart softened as their minds briefly touched. They were equal partners in the tenuous relationship they'd formed.

"Surratt protects mortals from the Ekimmu," Nicolas said. "He's been watching over you since you were born."

Amber's gaze darted between them. "But I'm not mortal. And he knows it."

She didn't know what an Ekimmu was, and she didn't care. Surratt was the enemy. But what about Nicolas? If Surratt wanted to destroy her, would he stand in the way? Or stand aside?

"I am not your enemy," Surratt said. "I am a benevolent Utukku known as the Shedu. I lead the Brotherhood."

Gerard stepped away from her like an earthbound spirit drawn to the light. "You have the answers I've been seeking for two centuries," he said in a voice filled with awe.

Amber wanted to grab his arm and call him back, but her feet wouldn't obey. She couldn't move, and she couldn't speak. It was if her voice had frozen in her throat.

Surratt nodded as if granting Gerard permission to speak.

"Is there a cure for what I am? Am I damned?"

"I am not God," Surratt said. "I can neither redeem nor condemn. But since you have chosen the path of the Shedu, you are in no immediate danger of eternal damnation."

"I don't know the Shedu," Gerard said, his voice as desperate as his desire for redemption. "But I need to know if I'm cursed. Or if this is a disease, like Megan says."

Surratt nodded again, his voice that of a sage. "It is no curse, though many believe it so. It is an ancient disease—born in Mesopotamia."

He continued, weaving myth and truth. "The Sumerians ruled Mesopotamia, birthing cities, civilization, and religion. But war and disease ravaged them. Young men died suddenly—on battlefields or from plagues. Legends claimed their spirits, unwilling to die, awakened in the grave. They rose, seeking blood to sustain their existence.

"In truth, a virus born of death, killed the body but spared the soul. The afflicted suffered a wasting disease. Only blood could halt the decay. They became known as the Utukku—a spirit that could be either benevolent or evil. They were still men—men afflicted with a disease. Like all men, some were good. Some were evil.

"To hide their affliction, they emerged only at night. The sun drained them. Blood restored them. At first, they took only small amounts—from sleeping loved ones—leaving behind peace and pleasant dreams. But soon, they learned killing enemies was more efficient. Some didn't stop there."

"That sounds pretty damn evil to me," Amber said. She'd found her voice, but her feet remained rooted, shackled by invisible chains.

Gerard's wounded gaze pierced her. He had to know she didn't count him among the damned. Didn't he realize she loved him regardless of what he was?

The chasm between them widened—a breach too wide to cross.

Surratt looked at her with pity. "As the Utukku regained life and vitality, they tried to rejoin the living, but the sun scorched their skin and they still needed blood. So, they adapted to darkness and living in the shadows. For a time, they were content, but loneliness crept in. Some deliberately infected old friends and loved ones, and the thirst became insatiable. The only way to appease it was to drain a body completely. The divide among the Utukku deepened—much like the one you feel now."

Amber wanted to scream. He was in her head. But she couldn't move. Couldn't speak. Trapped between Surratt and the man she'd loved—and hurt. Even Nicolas had stepped back, as if abandoning her. A tear slid down her cheek. Her throat tightened.

"Choices must always be made," Surratt said, and she heard the weight behind the words.

She had a choice to make. Did she want to defend vampires or destroy them? She could never hurt Gerard, but would destroying vampires destroy the friendship they'd formed. Could she choose to leave vampires in peace, knowing what they were capable of?

Surratt met her gaze, understanding her dilemma. "Some Utukku resisted killing innocents, and the hunger faded. They learned control. They learned to live in harmony with mortals. Those unable to resist doomed their souls to eternal thirst. And soon, a new faction emerged. They called themselves The Seven Demons. Samarian and Mesopotamian mythology referred to them as Ekimmu. They inspired vampire legends and gave the Utukku a bad name."

"I don't need a history lesson!" Her head ached, confusion making her and defensive.

Gerard flinched, as if she'd driven a stake into his heart. "But I do."

They stood no more than three feet apart. It might as well have been a continental divide.

"And so you shall have it," Surratt said. "For a thousand years the Ekimmu were feared by the Mesopotamian Empire. They were angry spirits, denied peace, yet growing stronger with every life they stole. The original seven became many. They lured more Utukku to the demonic side of their nature and taught them how to deliberately infect mortals. Their powers increased.

"But they began to fear the wrath of the gods. Even the carved images of Sumerian deities and the temples that housed them became unbearable.

Churches and temples became holy ground they could not enter. Eventually they came to fear their on reflection and soon, they cast none—or at least none anyone could see.

"Those who resisted the darkness and refused to kill became known as the Shedu." He straightened, pride flickering in his eyes. "And I am their leader."

Amber's voice was brittle. "Is that why you recruited Nicolas? Are you still fighting a war that started four thousand years before Christ?" How much hatred does it take to sustain a war that ancient?

Infinity, whispered a voice inside her. The battle between good and evil was never ending.

"Surratt didn't recruit me," Nicolas said. "I was already dying when an Ekimmu came to my hospital room to feast on what remained of my blood. Surratt arrived, and he fled. Then Surratt offered me a choice between a painless death and a chance to see your mother once more. I chose her and willingly joined the Brotherhood."

He sighed, and pain etched his face. "The Shedu take vows," he continued. "We don't kill mortals. We don't kill Ekimmu. But I broke that vow when I killed Klaus."

Surratt released his mental hold on her. She could move as easily as she could speak, but her feet remained rooted to the floor. "But you didn't stop Klaus from killing my mother," she said in a voice so raw she could barely speak.

Nicolas flinched as if struck. His eyes dropped. "I was too late. I'm sorry."

"But you let Klaus get away with murder. And he killed Andrew. Andrew didn't have to die too," she said, tears streaming down her face.

Gerard stepped forward but stopped when she raised a trembling hand. If he touched her now, she'd collapse in a weeping hot mess from which she might never recover. She needed the truth. Every painful detail.

"I was trying to honor my vows to the Brotherhood," Nicolas said, his voice as raw as Amber's felt.

"Choices," Surratt said, in his sage-like voice. "We must all make them."

"The Shedu are only able to protect mortals from the Ekimmu because they remain hidden. If mortals knew Utukku—vampires existed, they wouldn't consider if we were Shedu or Ekimmu," Nicolas said. "They would destroy us out of fear. And if an Ekimmu finds a lone vampire—one without a clan or abandoned by their creator—they seduce him to the demonic side."

"Sonja protects Vincent. Vincent protects me," Gerard said, as if someone had flipped a switch inside him.

Amber still wasn't ready to drink the Kool-Aid. "Why don't the Shedu destroy the Ekimmu?"

"Violence begets violence," Surratt said. "It is why we must honor our vows not to kill. Your father is still Utukku, but he killed Klaus, so he can no longer be a member of the Shedu Brotherhood."

"And I would kill again," Nicolas said. "To protect my daughter."

Amber's voice cracked. "Am I the reason my mother is dead?" Guilt pressed so heavily on her shoulders she didn't resist when Gerard stepped forward and wrapped her in his arms.

"Klaus is responsible for your mother's death," Surratt said. "Not you. She was protecting you. She knew what you were as did your father. Because Klaus and Nicolas shared my blood, Klaus knew. But he had been seduced by his Ekimmu lover, and there is nothing an Ekimmu fears more than a dhampir.

"The Shedu watch over them. Since we have taken vows not to kill, we protect dhampirs so they might one day rid the world of the Ekimmu. The Ekimmu hunt them."

Chapter 27

Gerard held Amber in a protective embrace, silently vowing never to let her go—vowing to shield her from the Ekimmu with his final breath. But before he could speak the words aloud, she pulled away. Her eyes widened in horror, stealing the breath from his lungs.

"Reid! And Megan!" She broke free and sprinted toward the freezer.

Vincent had torn away the busted door and flung it across the room. Amber rushed inside and dropped to her knees beside her unconscious partner. Reid's broken arm was secured in a crude splint, lashed tightly to his chest.

"Reid?" She touched his throat, feeling for a pulse. She looked up at Gerard who'd followed her inside the freezer. "Where's Megan? And who splinted Reid's arm?"

"Vincent took Megan back to the house in New York. He came back to tend to your partner."

"How do you know?" Confusion clouded her storm gray eyes. "You've been out there." She pointed behind him. "With me."

Gerard raised a brow. "We share a mental connection. Remember?"

"But why did he leave Reid? Why not take him to a hospital?"

"Mortals can't travel at vampire speed," Nicolas said, stepping into the freezer.

Amber's gaze darted to him. "Then how did Vincent get Megan out?"

"You were right about her," Gerard said, pride threading through his voice. Amber wasn't just beautiful—she was brave, brilliant. "Infecting herself with Vincent's blood gave her vampire-like abilities. When she created the vampire vaccine, she turned herself into a dhampir."

"A secret no mortal can ever learn," Surratt said, his tone grave, stepping behind Nicolas. "A secret The Brotherhood of the Shedu will protect with our lives."

"Or the lives of others?" Amber challenged, though her voice lacked heat.

"If need be. Special Agent Matheson and his team serve many uses. He's on his way to collect your friend now and assist with the cleanup of this mess with Dr. Weldon."

"Carl Matheson? The vampire hunter?" Amber looked at Gerard, her eyes wild with fear. "Oh hell no." She rose to her feet. "He's not getting within a hundred feet of Gerard."

"I agree," Surratt said. "I need Carl. He can kill the Ekimmu. I cannot. But I'm not naïve enough to think he trusts me or any other vampire." He looked at Gerard. "You may not be Shedu but you are no Ekimmu either. Live as you have, and you'll remain safe. But if you ever need us, someone from The Brotherhood will be watching—both you and Nicolas's daughter."

A sense of peace settled over Gerard. The constant ache in his chest he'd felt since the day he woke up infected with the vampire virus seemed to fade. He no longer feared eternal damnation. And the vampire vaccine gave him hope—hope that one day, he'd be completely human. Then there was Amber. He looked at her, heart tight in his chest. "I'll keep Amber safe."

"Not alone, you won't," Nicolas said. "She's my daughter."

"I can take care of myself," Amber muttered, turning back to Reid.

"You and Nicolas get her out of here," Surratt said to Gerard. "Take her home, get whatever personal items she wishes to keep and then get her out of Asheville. She's no longer safe."

Amber rose, locking eyes with Surratt as if daring him to challenge her. That fire—her defiance—was what had drawn Gerard to her. But it could just as easily get her killed.

"I can't just move. I have a job," she said. "I'm a cop. Even if I resign, I have to give notice."

"You died here today," Surratt said. "It will go in Carl's report. A body will be produced, and everyone will see your face when they look at it. You are no longer safe."

Amber's voice cracked. "What about my father? And Reid?"

Gerard's heart twisted. It didn't matter if she loved Reid—if she always would. He only wanted her happy.

"Nicolas is your father," Surratt said.

"But he didn't raise me." Her voice trembled with pain, and Gerard felt it like a blade to the chest. He'd do anything for her—move mountains if he could, change Surratt's mind if he had too.

"There has to be another way," he said.

Surratt nodded. "Very well. I'll see what can be done. In the meantime, do not let her out of your sight."

If Gerard had his way, he'd never let her out of his life. Amber was his for as long as she would have him. Unless she chose Reid—or chose no one—then he would protect her from afar—for as long as she lived.

Epilogue

"It's done," Amber said, placing the five-year service plaque from the Asheville Police Department into her suitcase and snapping it shut.

After the Lifeblood murders and their work with the FBI, she and Reid were ready to move on. Or so the records claimed. In truth, Amber still wasn't sure what had happened. Reality and illusion had blurred until she couldn't tell fact from vampire glamour. According to Surratt, perception was the only reality that mattered.

Surratt had twisted so many minds, it was a wonder he remembered what truth looked like. According to police files, Amber and Reid had solved the Lifeblood Murders by linking Dr. Steve Weldon to the crime. Since he'd used stolen government funds to set up a lab to continue the cloning research he'd started for Colonel Timmons, they'd contacted The FBI.

FBI records showed that Amber and Reid had assisted Carl Matheson and his agents locate Dr. Weldon and rescue Axel Travers. Reid and Axel Travers were injured. Dr. Weldon was killed. But the truth was more complicated.

After his rescue, Axel had been taken to the hospital by EMTs working for the BBTF. Carl ensured that any blood drawn by ER or lab personnel vanished before it could be tested. With Megan's help, Vincent falsified Axel's medical records to show normal labs. Had anyone actually tested his blood, who knew what they'd have found? But Axle refused testing by anyone, even Megan. At her urging, he left the hospital AMA and went to his father's house, where Brit Travers guarded his son's privacy like a mother honey badger. No one got access.

Amber remained curious about Axel's abilities. Weldon had used vampire blood cloned from Gerard to turn him. Megan, who carried the XP gene, had combined her own blood with her husband's to create an mRNA vaccine that cured Axel of the virus's negative effects. He was now part of the new breed Weldon had once bragged about—only better. How much better? That was anyone's guess.

The vaccine hadn't worked as well on Vincent and Gerard, but it was still a miracle in Gerard's eyes. A siesta from noon to three was the only sleep he needed. Amber had adopted his schedule and didn't feel the worse for wear.

It wasn't exactly warm acceptance, but she'd embraced her dhampir side. That meant saying goodbye to her former life and leaving the Asheville PD for good.

"You almost packed?" Gerard asked from the doorway.

Amber glanced around. There were few things she couldn't replace. She picked up the suitcase and turned. Gerard took it from her hands.

"This thing weighs a ton." Not that he'd notice. He could pick up a refrigerator and barely break a sweat.

"Yeah. Right," she said with a smile. "It's mostly pictures, jewelry, nic nacs—things with sentimental value that can't be replaced."

"Ready?" His voice was hesitant. He still wasn't sure if she was just leaving Asheville or moving with him to another country.

Her father, whom she now knew was Nicolas Dalton, wasn't even Nicolas Dalton anymore. Since the Weldon incident, his real identity had begun to attract attention, especially since he looked closer to thirty than his true age of sixty-five. So, in true vampire fashion, he'd reinvented himself—in Austria.

"I'm not going," she said. Then, seeing Gerard's face fall, added, "Not just yet."

"But Nicolas is expecting us."

Nicolas had sold his house in Germany and the cabin in Cedar Plank. Following Surratt's advice, he was relocating to Austria under a new identity as Nicolas Reinhardt, a millionaire playboy killed by the Ekimmu in 2009 alongside his parents.

After the murders, the Reinhardt's luxury ski resort, Hotel Almhof Reinhardt, had gone into probate, and Reinhardt Village emptied almost overnight. With Sonia Dalca's help, Nicolas erased all evidence of Nicolas Reinhardt's death and returned as the missing heir to "claim his inheritance" and reopen the resort. He wanted Gerard and Amber to join him. Gerard had agreed. Amber was undecided, but that didn't stop Gerard from assuming.

"You can't stay here. Klaus is dead, but you don't know if you're safe. Some other vampire might be working for the Ekimmu."

"I'm not leaving without saying goodbye to Greg. Blood or not, he's still my father."

"Fine. We'll go to Florida, say goodbye, and over the years we can send him cards from the tropics or Timbuktu. But he can't know you're going to Austria as Nicolas's half-sister."

She planted her hands on her hips, trying to look tough. Inside, she was shaking. "What makes you think we can make this work?"

"Because I love you," he said, melting her heart. "Marry me."

"No!" She backed up until her thighs hit the bed. She dropped to the mattress. Her heart rose into her throat. "I can't marry you. Connecting your name to mine will endanger your life. Any Ekimmu who knows what I am could come after you."

He smiled. "So, you do care."

"My feelings are irrelevant." She closed her eyes against the hope she saw in his loving gaze. "Reid's going to work with Carl Matheson at Project Blue Book. He can help keep the government from killing good vampires—Shedu, Utukku—but what if he can't protect you? Linking your name to mine could be dangerous."

"Then don't link them." He sat beside her, taking her hands in his. "You can just take my name or we can live in sin. I don't care. I just want to spend eternity—or however long dhampirs live—with you."

"But—"

"You'll have papers. We'll change your name. You can be Nicolas' older sister from an illicit relationship before Lukas Reinhardt married Lena Gangloff. Or you can be my wife and use my name since my identity hasn't changed since my birth."

"Gerard Delaroche is your real name?" How was that possible? His birth predated the American Revolution.

He smiled. "Vincent and I have always used our real names. Before computers, it was easy to forge documents. Now, Sonia takes care of the information in digital databases. According to public records, Vincent was born in New York to second-generation Bosnian parents, and I legally came to this country when I was ten." He shrugged. "Explains the French accent."

Could she do this? Could she have a relationship with both Gerard and her birth father? If she told Greg she was getting married and moving to Austria, could she maintain their distant but meaningful connection?

She met his steady gaze, swallowing the golf-ball size lump in her throat. She wanted to say yes, but there were so many obstacles, and the danger was still very real.

"What if it doesn't work? What if you grow tired of me? What if—"

He placed a finger over her lips, silencing her. "À cœur vaillant rien d'impossible—Nothing is impossible with a willing heart, Amber."

Was her heart willing? Damn skippy!

She wrapped her arms around his neck and kissed him with all the love in her willing heart.

Please enjoy this sneak peak of Edge Of Darkness, Book Three in The Darkness Series:

"Ms. Connors?"

Haley jumped. Then looked up—and froze when she saw Axle for the first time in fifteen years. His eyes weren't a weird color as Gordon had described them. They were two amber-brown jewels set in a caramel face, and a trim goatee framed full lips, any woman—and some men—would die to kiss.

His hair was buzzed short now, the wild curls and high fade gone, and he was no longer lean and lanky. He was as tall as she remembered, but he'd bulked up. Considerably. His shoulders were wide, his chest deep, and his designer suit was tailored to perfection.

Her breath caught, and she nearly dropped her phone. "Yes?" The word was more of a squeak than an actual reply. Flushing, she rose to her feet, and her heart did a familiar flip-flop she hadn't felt in years.

Axle stepped closer and held out his hand. "Hi. I'm Axle Travers."

His smooth baritone sent a jolt straight to her solar plexus. His fingers curled around hers, and a long-buried, helpless desire surged through her.

Great. Ab-so-freaking-lutely great. Once again she was crushing on Axle, and he didn't even remember her.

"Hello Axle."

He frowned and released her hand. "Have we met? You look familiar."

A word about the author...

Lilly Gayle is the mother of two grown daughters and Gigi to four grandchildren. She lost her husband of nearly 42 years in 2022 and still resides in their North Carolina home with her maltipoo, Thor. When not working full time as a radiologic technologist and mammographer, she's writing, hanging out at the beach with Thor, or spending time with her family. **Embrace the Darkness** is the sequel to **Out of the Darkness**.

Lilly writes historical and paranormal romance, including western romances and a time travel romance. Besides being Indy published, she is also published with The Wild Rose Press, Inc.

Thank you for purchasing this publication. For other wonderful stories by Lilly Gayle, please visit her at: http://lillygayle.com. Her books are available at Amazon and most major retailers. If you've enjoyed any of Lilly's books, please leave an online review.

Don't miss out!

Visit the website below and you can sign up to receive emails whenever Lilly Gayle publishes a new book. There's no charge and no obligation.

https://books2read.com/r/B-A-GCGG-YQYWG

BOOKS 2 READ

Connecting independent readers to independent writers.

Also by Lilly Gayle

Darkness Series
Out of the Darkness
Embrace the Darkness

Standalone
Winds of Time

Watch for more at https://www.lillygayle.com.

About the Author

Lilly Gayle is a widow, mother, grandmother, dog mom, and breast cancer survivor. She writes part time while still working full time as a mammographer. She hopes to retire in the next few years and make writing a full time career.

Lilly writes paranormal and historical romance. She is both self published and traditionally published with a small publisher, The Wild Rose Press.

Read more at www.lillygayle.com.

About the Publisher

www.ingramcontent.com/pod-product-compliance
Lightning Source LLC
Chambersburg PA
CBHW070729280626
47159CB00023B/2950